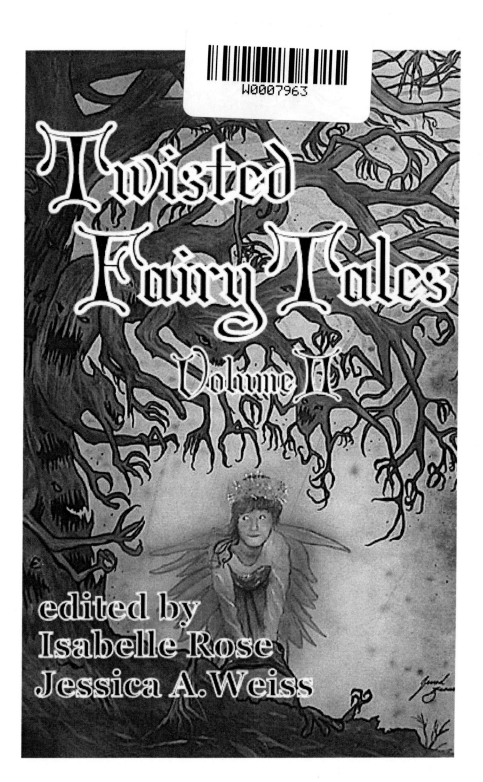

Twisted Fairy Tales

Volume II

edited by
Isabelle Rose
Jessica A. Weiss

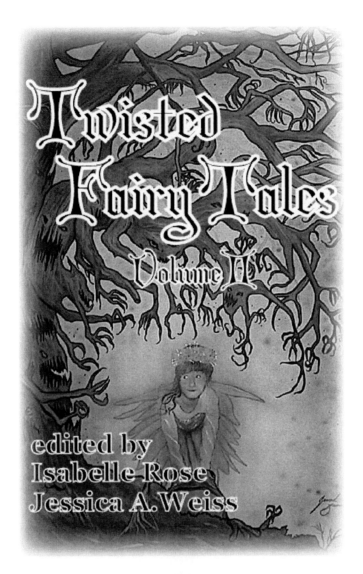

Twisted Fairy Tales

Volume II

edited by
Isabelle Rose
Jessica A. Weiss

To Anne
from

I just wanted to take this opportunity to thank Jessica Weiss for giving me the chance to put this anthology together. It was a huge leap of faith on her behalf and I will be forever grateful. I also want to thank all of the writers that submitted their work for their incredible amount of patience. It has been a long...long journey. So thank you from the bottom of my heart.
~Isabelle Rose

Table of Contents

6-30-16

Medications

LIPITOR - 10 mg 1X
ASPIRIN - 81 mg 1X
VITAMIN D3 - 2000 I.U. 1X
CALCIUM - 1500 mg 1X
TAMOXIFEN - 20 mg 1X

Ms. Anne Bangs
308 Windsor Ave
Brightwaters NY 11718-1403
631-666-4617

Hope and Apple Seeds
Jocelyn Adams

Halloween had always been one of Jack's favorite days of the year, and it had come at last. After climbing off the school bus, he bounded along the walkway to his house. Gold and crimson leaves scurried across the cement in his wake, spiraling up in the cool, autumn air.

His heart pitter-pattered as he twisted the silver knob of the front door and ran inside. Silence greeted him as usual. With a grin, he shed his holey green windbreaker and stepped around packing boxes that littered the living room carpet from the move-in a month earlier. Before Jack made it to his room, the bitter scent of whiskey wrinkled his nose. His heart plummeted into his tattered sneakers. Stalling, he stooped and untied his shoes instead of kicking them off the way he normally did.

"Dad?" Fear knotted Jack's stomach as he searched the usual places with a frown, the couch in the den, the hallway floor, the chair closest to the window in the kitchen, the big bedroom. His chin quivered, but it steadied as his fingers pushed open the bathroom door. The stench of sickness drifted out.

Dad raised his shaggy head from a pool of vomit and held a large hand up to the light spilling over him from the hallway. "Shut that damn door...middle of the freakin' night." With a groan, the large man rolled toward the tub and curled into a ball.

Eyes downcast, Jack shut the door and waited until his Dads breathing hit that deep, steady stroke of sleep.

Shoulders slumped, tears stung Jack's eyes as he trudged to his bedroom. Once inside with the door closed, he snatched the picture of Mom from the nightstand and flopped onto the bed amongst the jumbled mess of covers. Jack closed his eyes and held her to his chest.

Teenagers racing their cars had lost control and mounted the sidewalk where Mom had been enjoying her evening stroll. She died before the ambulance got her to the hospital. Her image lingered in his memory, but the picture gave him comfort that he would never forget her warm smile. The blanket stored in a bag in his closet still carried her sweet scent, fresh like a spring rain.

"I miss you, Mom." The familiar words drifted out in a whisper.

After kissing the picture, he smiled and sat up straight again. His eyes followed the path of his hands as Jack replaced the frame on his nightstand. With renewed enthusiasm, his thoughts turned to his costume. If Dad couldn't take him trick-or-treating, he'd go by himself. At eleven years old, he wasn't a kid anymore.

From the far reaches of his closet, Jack withdrew the Yoda mask he'd found at a garage sale the week before. It had cost a whole dollar, but he considered the awesome rubber mask worth every penny.

The cream-colored shirt belonged to Dad, not that Jack thought he'd remember lending it. From the bottom drawer of his dresser, he pulled out a brown pair of cords, and the last component lay across the back of his chair. Jack had begged the next-door neighbor, Mrs. Higgins, for the burlap sack she kept over one of her plants.

Sack in hand, Jack sped down the hallway to the kitchen, withdrew the scissors from the overflowing junk drawer and set to work cutting a vest out of the burlap. Two armholes and a big circle for his neck to poke through completed the task. Perfect.

A peanut butter sandwich cured the rumble in his belly as he waited for darkness to fall. Other than the mostly empty jar of *Skippy*, the cupboards were empty. Jack would have to raid Dad's wallet and go grocery shopping the following Saturday. The weekends used to be his favorite time of the week, but not anymore.

At seven o'clock, Dad still hadn't emerged from the bathroom. With the door open a crack, Jack listened for breathing. Satisfied Dad would be okay for a while; Jack pulled on his costume, retrieved the spare pillowcase from the chest at the end of his bed and rushed out the front entrance.

Cool, damp air swirled around him and ghostly clouds danced across the silver moon—a perfect night for Halloween. House after house, Jack knocked on the door and held out his sack for the treats that poured in by the handful. By the time he made it to the end of Raven Street, his arms ached from carrying his heavy load, and sweat pearled along his forehead under the mask.

In the distance, a group of boys from his school crouched together and peered over a cedar hedge.

Curious, Jack plodded over to them. "What are you doing?"

The closest boy, red-haired and willowy, cranked his head to the side. "Shut up, would ya?" In the eerie light of the moon, shadows fell over the boy's eyes and highlighted a pizza's worth of pimples on his cheeks.

Jack squatted beside him. "What's in there?" He parted the bushes a little, but found only a dark yard beyond.

Pizza Face cupped a hand over his mouth. "This is Mrs. Flynn's place. The guys dared me to go up and knock on her front door." His eyes met Jack's, and through their shadows, fear shone out.

"What's wrong with Mrs. Flynn?" Jack pushed up his mask and scratched his head.

Another boy leaned toward Jack, his black hair falling over his eyes. "She's a witch, moron. What are ya, new?" The three boys snickered and shoved one another.

"I uh—I just moved in last month." Jack's face warmed as he pointed his thumb over his shoulder.

The black haired boy whispered to Pizza Face.

Laughter rose up from the three of them, causing spiders to crawl up Jack's spine. He jumped to his feet and turned to leave.

"We dare you to go," the black haired one said to Jack. "Bet you're chicken."

"I'm not chicken!" Jack peered over his shoulder at them, swallowing the lump in his throat.

Pizza Face gestured toward the black house. "Go on, then. Prove it."

Heart thundering in his ears, Jack pulled down his mask and stared at the crooked, iron gate that stood between him and Mrs. Flynn's walkway.

"Bock, bock, bock," chanted the three boys, flapping their arms.

Jack raised his chin and shoved the gate open, wincing when it gave a mournful screech. His eyes swept the path as he walked through. So many trees overhung the property, that only a few dots of moonlight made it through to the gloomy landscape. After a few seconds, his eyes adjusted to the lower light. Gnarled bushes formed a winding corridor to the slanted stairs of her porch. A chilled wind ruffled the downy hairs on the back of his neck, and his breath hitched.

Each step forward took effort. A glance over his shoulder revealed three sets of wide eyes watching him over the hedge. Only a few more paces and he'd reach the stairs.

Come on. You can do this. She's just a lady.

The mantra repeated in his head. His feet shuffled forward another inch.

"Good evening, young one." The gravelly voice came from behind him.

Jack squealed and turned to face the monster his imagination conjured. His bag of candy dropped to the ground and spilled its payload into the grass beside him.

An old woman in a long white dress stood a few feet away on the stone walk. Her wiry gray hair hung down to her waist, the top pushed back from her wrinkled face with a red hair band. "You must be new to Crossroads. Most fear me."

Jack's fingers fidgeted with a scratchy thread from his burlap vest. "Wh-why, ma'am?"

"Because I'm a witch, haven't you heard?" She threw her head back and cackled, a sound like glass breaking.

The moisture evaporated from Jack's mouth. He backed up. "I don't believe in witches, ma'am. I mean..." his eyes darted left and right for paths of escape, "you're not really a witch. Right?" He glanced around the woman for the boys, but they'd disappeared.

"My name is Mona." She took a step closer, cocked her head and reached a hand out as if caressing Jack's cheek from afar. "You've lost something precious. You wear it like a scar upon your soul."

Jack pulled off his mask and averted his eyes. A twinge of pain tugged on his heart.

"You're in luck, young one, for I'm feeling generous on this beautiful Samhain."

Jack's brow wrinkled. "What's Samhain?"

Mona stared down at him as if he'd just shed his skin. "Why, it's the magical night when the veil separating the world of the living, and the realm of the dead, is thinnest."

"You mean...the dead are...out there somewhere? Like, we can talk to them?" Jack leaned forward, as if the action would somehow make her words true. Dad had told him that once the corpse rots away in the grave, that was it—people didn't exist anywhere, not in heaven and not in hell. He said all that religious mumbo-jumbo was nonsense.

Mona dismissed him with a flick of her fingers. "No time to explain. Wait here. I have a gift for you."

With a nod and a tiny smile, Mona passed by Jack with such fluid grace he wondered for a moment if her feet touched the ground under that long dress of hers. Up the stairs, she went, the swishing of her dress the only sound breaking the silence, and disappeared through her front door.

Jack edged toward the iron gate, but the tiny bit of hope she'd planted in him had already started to grow. Did Mona know how to find Mom? Could he really see her again just the way she looked before? He paced three steps one way, three steps back, his Yoda mask still crumpled in his fingers.

A few minutes passed before Mona returned and thrust her hand out to him. The shiniest, reddest apple Jack had ever seen sat in her palm. "Eat the flesh of this fruit and plant the seeds in a place rich with moonlight. You'll find what you've lost."

Wide eyed, Jack reached a tentative hand toward the beautiful apple, but she pulled it back.

"Hear me, now, young one. The path will only appear when the sacred light falls upon your chosen place, and my gift will not last forever. Knowing this, do you still want it?"

Daring to hope for the impossible, Jack nodded, dropped his mask and took the offered fruit. He cradled the cool apple against his chest as if even the movement of air could shatter its fragility.

Mona picked his candy out of the grass and replaced it in the pillowcase, along with his mask. With a tender smile, she handed it to him. "Be well, young one. Go with my blessings."

Jack ran through the open gate without stopping to see if the boys were still waiting for him. Breathless by the time he made it back to his house, he heaved the door open, dropped his candy and locked himself in his room.

He didn't believe in fairy tales, but he had lost so much he wanted to believe Mona's gift could give his Mom back to him. After staring at the apple and turning it around in his hands, his eyes closed and he bit into the ruby skin, praying to whatever spirits may have been listening. Sweet juice exploded into his mouth. As if starving, he devoured every speck of bright white flesh and licked his fingers afterward.

Sated and calm, Jack went out the back door into the yard. From the garden shed, he retrieved a small shovel and chose an open piece of grass where the largest patch of moonlight painted a circle. Arms tense, he dug a hole, planted the core, and covered it with a generous helping of dirt.

Uncertain what to do, Jack sat down cross-legged on the damp grass and waited. A few minutes passed, and then an hour as the moon climbed higher in the sky. When nothing happened by the time the grandfather clock in the house struck midnight, tears wet his cheeks. Was Mona playing a prank on him? Maybe she was just a crazy old lady.

Despite the crushing weight on his chest, Jack could hardly bear to walk away from the only promise of happiness he'd had in two years, but cold seeped into his flesh. He debated for only a moment before trooping to his room, where he pulled the blanket from his bed, and returned to the back yard. After arranging the blue fleece near the hole, he laid down on it. Cuddled in his quilt, Jack eventually drifted off to sleep.

***

Jack woke shivering under a coating of dew. The half moon still shone through gray puffs of cloud.

"Jack?" The mellow voice sounded hollow and distant. "Where are you, sweetheart?"

"Mom?" Jack leapt onto all fours and gaped.

In the place where he'd planted the apple core, a twisted framework of tree roots had formed a ladder down into a narrow hole in the earth. Only the top rung showed above the grass, and bright emerald moss grew around the opening as if it had been there for years.

With his breaths coming short, Jack peered inside. Through the darkness, a tiny, flickering light shone. "Is anybody down there?" His words echoed.

Mom's faint voice came again from the depths. "There you are. I can't come up, so you'll have to come down. Be brave, Jack. There's nothing to be afraid of."

With shaking hands and Jell-o legs, Jack mounted the ladder and started down. The shaft didn't smell of mud pies like he expected; only the scent of wood met his nose. After a few minutes climb, a shadow moved behind the ladder. Jack froze and squinted in the dim light. A black spider the size of his thumb scurried upwards along the grainy surface. The walls looked funny, as if they were lined with wood. No, not lined, a tree-trunk surrounded him. Had the apple core really grown into a mammoth underground tree in a few hours?

The further he went, the harder his heart pounded against his ribs. He climbed hand over hand, foot over foot for what seemed like a mile. Legs and arms aching, he stopped and shifted his body to look down. The light below had grown larger, brighter. "Coming, Mom."

Energy burned in his legs as he neared the bottom. Jack descended faster, his mind whirling with hopes. Amber light and warmth engulfed him as he stepped onto a huge rug. What would he say to her? Would she want to know about the 'A' he got on his science project? Would she still look the same? After what Dad had said, he wondered if she'd be nothing but a skeleton. After a few deep breaths, his growing courage allowed him to turn around.

Before his eyes, lay his old room in Benton Hills. A familiar star-lit sky twinkled beyond the big window. His old bedspread, with a giant picture of *Buzz Lightyear* on the front, decorated his single bed.

Beyond that, Mom stood with her hands clasped in front of her looking just as he remembered. His breath came out all at once at her rosy appearance. She wore the same pretty, white dress they had buried her in, with long sleeves and sparkly beads along the cuffs. Her dark brown wavy hair tumbled around her shoulders. Deep blue eyes stared back at him, and her unique scent perfumed the air.

It's really her.

She walked around the bed and held out a hand. "Take your time, sweetheart. It's all right." A weird bluish light surrounded her, and a bright smile spread across her lips. "You've gotten so big."

After staring at her for a while, Jack pinched himself a few times to be sure he wasn't dreaming. When it hurt, his heart sang. He ran to Mom, wrapped his arms around her waist, and sank into the comfort in the safest place he'd ever known. A sense of rightness settled over him, one he'd almost forgotten.

"We don't have much time, Jack. What should we do?"

Questions clogged his thoughts, but he didn't want to waste a single moment with her. A glance at his old bookshelf gave him an answer. "Can we read in bed the way we used to?"

With a smile, she nodded, turned and pulled back the covers. "Hop in. I'll pick out one of your favorites."

Side-by-side, they leaned back against the blue head-board. Jack's shoulder pressed against Mom's as he listened to the sound of her voice reading from the first Harry Potter book. Sleep tugged at his eyelids, but he resisted.

The touch of her cool hand on his arm broke his trance. "You need to go now, Jack."

Panic wrapped around his chest like an iron fist. "But why?" He sat up, grasped her hand and begged her with his eyes. "Why can't I stay here with you?"

"Because this is a magic place—where neither of us belongs. Find me again when the moon is high." Mom kissed his forehead, climbed out of bed and disappeared through the door.

Jack leapt from the bed to follow, but the exit she'd used vanished, replaced with a solid wall. "No! Come back. Please?"

Scrubbing at his frustrated tears, he pounded a fist against the fire truck wallpaper. He took a few moments to gather himself before returning to the ladder and climbing up. *I'll come back tomorrow night. I promise.*

Jack's feet dragged as he trudged into the house through the kitchen.

Dad sat at the table with a mug of steaming coffee cradled in his hands. "Where the hell'v you been?"

"I...uh..." Jack shot a glance to the door, and back to Dad. He'd never believe the truth. "It was a nice night, and I kinda fell asleep."

Dad raked fingers through his salt and pepper hair and stood. He sniffed at Jack as he came closer. "You been sleeping in that blanket of hers again?" His words came out stiff and jagged, like barbed hooks. "You smell like her."

"No, I-I haven't touched it since you told me not to."

"Where is it?" Dad launched past Jack and went into his bedroom. Clothes and books flew everywhere as he searched.

Jack's chest heaved as he watched from the doorway.

The growling man withdrew the bag from Jack's closet and pulled the blanket from it. The muscles of his arms bulged under his shirt as he tore the white cloth into strips.

Tears trickled down Jack's cheeks. "Stop it. Please! I saw her. She's in the ground. Come with me, and I'll show you!"

With a creased brow, Dad stopped and stared at the mess of cloth at his feet. "You just had a dream, kid. Told you before, she's dead and gone. Now forget her, like I have. You'll be better off." He stormed out of the room and left Jack with the torn pieces of Mom's blanket and an empty heart.

"I'll never forget her." Jack's whisper fell on silence.

***

Jack fidgeted in his seat at school all the next day. Worry about the cloud cover hiding that night's moon kept his mind away from the math problems on the board. When the teacher threatened to call Dad, Jack tore his mind away from the apple-tree ladder and pretended to pay attention.

As he feared, no moon shone that night, hindered by dark, slate clouds and heavy rain. With a painful heart, tears wet his pillow until he fell asleep.

The next few weeks of clear weather allowed Jack free access to the ladder, and to Mom. They laughed and sang; played board games, taking turns rolling the dice. Jack played the robber and Mom, the cop, as she chased him around the room and over the bed. Sometimes they sat in happy silence, their fingers entwined. She never allowed him to stay very long so his sleep wouldn't suffer, something he argued about at first, but soon accepted. A smile arched his lips all day long, except when under the scrutiny of Dad.

Each time Jack returned to the house, he snuck along the hallway on tiptoes. Air freshener he'd stashed in the garden shed took the scent from his clothes just in case the booze didn't keep Dad unconscious.

When winter fell over Crossroads, few opportunities arose for the moon to open the path for Jack. Alone in his room most nights, books helped him pass the time until he could see her again.

On Christmas Eve, Jack found a clear, twinkling sky and a full moon beyond his window. His heart swelled along with his excitement. Dad wouldn't take him to get a Christmas tree, but he didn't mind—the only present Jack ever wanted was in his back yard.

Once Dad's snoring drowned out the TV in the den, Jack tip-toed to the kitchen and pulled on his jacket beside the back door. A tug to free his boots from the pile of shoes sent the brooms in the corner sliding along the wall. They crashed into the pots lining the counter, clanging to the white tile below.

As footsteps pounded the floor, Jack scrambled to get out of his jacket, but didn't make it in time.

"Where the hell d'you think you're going?" Dad's gruff voice came from behind him, thick with sleep and slurred by alcohol.

"Anywhere but here." Jack winced the instant the words passed his lips.

Dad's hand grabbed Jack by the collar and whipped him around until they were face to face. "That's a lousy thing to say!"

Jack's eyes narrowed and anger swelled in his stomach. "You're always drunk and you yell all the time." He took a deep breath and stared into the emptiness of Dad's gray eyes. "I hate you, and I miss Mom."

Dad's hand released him, and swung wide before smacking him across the face.

Jack cried out and he stumbled sideways, raising fingers to his aching cheek. Pain burned across the bridge of his nose and down his neck.

Dad stared at his hands as if they'd become snarling beasts.

Holding fingers against his throbbing nose, Jack rushed out the door. Tears and cold stung his eyes as they landed on the ladder that once again rose out of the frozen, snow-covered earth. Chest heaving from his sobbing, Jack plowed through the frozen crystals in his sock-covered feet and climbed down faster than he ever had.

At the bottom, Mom gathered him into her arms, sat him on the side of the bed and rocked him until he quieted.

"I've been selfish," she said after a long silence. "I see, now, that coming here isn't good for you."

Jack wriggled out of her embrace. "Don't say that. Please!"

She smiled, wiped the tears from his cheek with her soft fingertips. "This time with you has made me so happy, but we both knew this wouldn't last forever." She placed a gentle kiss on Jack's forehead. "Your place is with the living. Dad needs you, and you need him. I won't stand in your way anymore." A tear sparkled on her dark lashes. "We'll see each other again, someday, I promise. You have to let me go, now."

"No!" Jack wailed, jumped up from the bed and pressed his hands to his ears. "I hate him. I'm not going back there. I'm staying here." He fell to his knees and wrapped arms around Mom's legs.

She stood. "I know it's a lot to ask because you're so young, but you've always been strong, and right now he isn't. Reach out to him." She stroked his hair and pried his arms away before moving away. "Goodbye, Jack. I love you."

Jack blinked. Mom disappeared along with his old bedroom, replaced by a frigid blanket of white and a blustery wind. "No! No, no, no!" Shivering, he dropped to the ground and dug into the snow with his bare hands. Sobs wracked his body as he scoured the yard until his arms shook too badly to continue.

Chilled down to the bone, Jack collapsed into the hole he'd made. Numbness travelled from his fingertips up his arms. His legs below the knees seemed to be missing. With a terrible pain in his heart, Jack closed his eyes and let the relentless shivers rattle his body.

"Jack?" Dad's voice came from the distance. "Damn it, son. Where are you?"

Jack didn't move. He wasn't sure if he could, even if he'd wanted to. "Goodbye, Mom." His eyes closed and darkness descended.

Blips of light and a blaring sound reached Jack in a moment of consciousness. Warmth; a large hand wrapped around his. Something sharp in his arm followed by cold liquid rushing inside him.

Darkness, again.

***

A steady beeping drew Jack from the depths of sleep. He blinked at an unfamiliar white ceiling. Sunlight painted a golden strip along the wall to his left.

"You're awake."

Jack turned his head toward the deep tone. "Dad?" His voice cracked.

The bulky man nodded, and pulled his chair closer to the bed. His eyes, though wet and rimmed in red, didn't have the distinctive gloss booze usually gave them. "I'm so sorry." He shook his head and gripped Jack's hand.

"I don't want to forget her." Jack licked his dry lips. "I won't. And you shouldn't either."

Dad rested his forehead on the bed, silent sobs heaving his shoulders. Jack had never seen him cry, not even on the day the police came to tell them she'd been killed. Not even at her funeral.

After a few minutes, Dad looked up. "I will never—never raise my hand to you again. I promise you that."

"It's okay, D—"

"No, it's not okay. First thing when we get home, the whiskey goes down the drain. You've been the man of the house for far too long. Time for me to step up." He straightened and gave Jack a warm, steady stare. "I've set up a grief counselor for the two of us."

Jack leaned toward Dad and squeezed his hand. "She's happy, you know. We'll see her again, I know it." *She promised.*

"I sure hope so." Dad smiled, returning his face to the way it used to look. Jack had missed him with his entire soul.

A small sound drew Jack's gaze to the doorway. Mona stood there with a subtle grin. "I didn't want to interrupt."

Dad nodded a greeting to her. "This kind lady's the one who found you." He stood. "I can't thank you enough."

Jack's eyes flew wide. "You found me in the snow?"

"I did, young one, and not a bit too soon, either." She swept into the room in a light blue dress. Her eyes sparkled as she sat on the edge of the bed and placed her hand on his cheek. She glanced at Dad for a moment before locking eyes with Jack.

"I see you have found what you've lost."

Author Bio:

Jocelyn Adams lives in Muskoka Ontario with her husband and young daughter. She's an author of fantasy and romance short stories, novellas and novels. Her debut novel, The Glass Man, will be released in October and four of her short stories will be published this year, in Roar and Thunder Magazine, the Hall Brothers Villainy anthology, Midwest Literary Review's Winter Canons anthology, and The Red Penny Papers.

The Seven
Shannon Connor Winward

There once was a king who had seven sons, though all he truly wanted was a daughter. When finally his wife gave him a girl, he was filled with joy. However, the child was sickly and they feared she would soon die.

To save her, the sons were sent to fetch water from a holy well. Each wanted to be the first to dip out the water, such was their eagerness to heal their sister—or was it to please the King? In their struggle, the bucket fell into the well, and the seven were left empty-handed. There they stood, not knowing what to do, and not one of them dared to go home.

Great was the king's rage when they did not quickly return. "They have forgotten what they were sent for," he cried. "Damn those idle, spoiled boys. I wish that they would turn into ravens and fly away—I would trade all of them for this one beautiful girl."

Hardly had the King spoken these words, when there came a great fluttering sound, and seven ravens took to the sky.

For it happened that the well was watched by a witch, jealous and cruel. She used the king's wish to weave a spell, condemning the seven to a life as birds. They were sent to live in a castle on a glass mountain beyond the sun and the moon, beyond the stars.

Or so the story goes.

***

She came to the sun, but it was too hot and terrible, and ate little children.

She found him alone, resting, at a table in a great hall. Or perhaps we should say she found *them*; for when he opened his eyes it was clear that there was more than one mind looking back at her.

The doctors had told her there were three, at least. Perhaps as many as five.

In fact, there were seven. The Six were meant to keep the One locked away.

"Do you know who I am?" she asked.

The First regarded her with lust that blazed like fire.

She was not daunted. "Do you remember me?"

His hands had been laid, hooked and rigid, like kindling in his lap, but as she spoke one unfolded and reached for her.

The orderly in the doorway flinched, but she did not.

The First twirled a strand of her hair on his finger. It was fine, and long, and blacker than a blackbird's wing. Black as an eclipse, the same as his.

"My name is Ute," she said. "I am your sister."

The First leaned towards her. His breath was hot on her cheek. It smelled of meat. "When the dinner bell rings, I will spread you out upon this table." He licked his lips. "I will eat you from the inside out."

"They say you did things to me before they took you away," she whispered. "They say you tried to drown me, but I do not believe them."

The First leaned closer, still, until their brows were touching. "I will suck the marrow from your bones, little bird."

The orderly took a step into the room, but Ute waived him back. She smiled at the First and said, *"I am not afraid of you."*

She came to the moon, but it was cold and also wicked.

His hand fell away, and the First withdrew. The Second looked down from eyes like hers, a blue as pale as moonlight in a well.

"Do you remember?" asked the Second. "I held you under the water. I held you down and watched your eyes roll back into your head. I held you down while she screamed and pounded on the door."

His voice was different than the First; passionless, remote—and yet—it pulled at her. She had not known when she came here, not for sure, but now, suddenly, she could remember. Now she could see him, a smear of pale skin over the bathtub's rim.

He was the sky above her, floating just out of reach. She could have tickled his face, had she been inclined to lift her hand.

"There were no ripples," he said.

"I trusted you."

"You were too young to struggle."

"I knew what you were doing."

"Fantasy," said the Second. "You imagine."

"No," she said. "Don't you see? *I remember you.*"

She came to the stars, and they were good to her, each one sitting on its own little chair.

He was the sky above her, and a million points of light, each one bursting in the darkness as she sank deeper under the water. Then he was gone, and her mother replaced him, flooding the stars and pulling breath into her body.

After that, they became her world—Mother, Father, sun and moon. They tried to make her forget that he had ever even been. They tried to make her think she was alone.

"When Mother found out that she was sick, she drew up papers. Papers that let me manage her affairs." Ute spoke loudly now, so that all of them could hear: the orderly in the doorway, the doctor trying to hide behind him, and the Thirds, who were watching now. The Thirds looked not with malice, but kindness and—she thought—with glimmers of hope.

Encouraged, she reached for her bag and withdrew a document. It was stained and bent from handling. She flattened it on her knees and showed it to the Thirds.

"See; 'M.P.' *Manu propria*. It means "in my own hand". I asked a lawyer, and he said it's all there. This lets me speak for Mother now."

The Thirds said nothing.

"It lets me speak for you, now, too," she told them. "So… you can come home, if you want. You can come home with me."

Still the Thirds said nothing. Ute slipped the document back into her bag and waited.

Finally, the Thirds shook their heads. "Not us," they said, in whispers like embers turned to ash on the wind. "There is no home to us. You seek the one that is within."

"Within where? How can I find him?"

"Within, within. Look within."

Ute looked, but the Thirds squeezed their eyes shut. "Not yet!" they hissed. "You mustn't go yet! You cannot go within without the key. *Come sit with us, and we will give it to you.*"

So Ute climbed upon their lap. The Thirds guided her hand. They fastened it around the key.

The men stirred in the doorway—frightened and fast, they entered the room, but by then the Fourth had Ute by the wrist.

The stars told her, "You cannot open the glass mountain without it."

On her hand she wore a silver ring—a man's ring with a garnet in it that could leave canyons in a young boy's skin.

The Fourth rose from the chair, and Ute went with him, stunned and fragile in his hands. He was bigger, much bigger, than she had guessed.

"That's enough," said the doctor. The orderly shouted,

"Put her down!" But Ute was beyond their reach.

The window had bars on it. She could feel them digging into her back, but she saw only him. His eyes were white with rage, his knuckles white, and his fingers white around her throat.

"Wait...!"

She could say nothing more, for the Fourth had begun to squeeze. Her body slumped against him, not fighting, crushed between the Fourth and the iron bars. She could not breathe.

She touched the twisted root of his nose, an old break improperly set. She touched the garnet-sized scar on his cheekbone, the deep fissures on his knuckles. He had stolen her voice, and so she looked into his eyes, willing him to understand.

Then she was free. He set her down gently and cupped her ring hand in his own.

"He's gone now," she told him. "He died, soon after you left us. He can't hurt you anymore."

The orderlies were on him, then. Three of them—more—they had swarmed from doorways, peeled like paint from the walls. They covered him, they took him from her. Ute shouted. "Stop! Let him be!" But they did not listen. The Fourth went down.

The Fourth writhed and bellowed, and the world trembled beneath her feet. She could not stand, so she slipped to the ground, and she searched through the tangle of heads and limbs until she could see him.

Through the forest of men, she met his gaze.

"Come home with me," she said. "And no one will hurt you again."

They had pushed up his sweater. They pulled down his slacks. Bones, chicken bones by dozens fell loose from his clothes. They lay scattered on the floor around him, snapped and broken beneath the knees of the men.

"That's enough," the doctor said again.

They had exposed a mound of pale, scarred skin. The

needle went in, and soon he did not look so large after all. He looked quite, quite small.

A little dwarf came up to her and said, "My child, what are you looking for?"

He did not know her when he woke.

He was huddled in the bedclothes. He blinked at her, confused and wary.

"Are you hungry?" she asked.

The Fifth sniffed.

"You slept through dinner." Ute held out her hand. They had taken the bones away, but she had crackers in her purse.

The Fifth snatched the snacks. Up, up, up into his mouth they went, until they were gone, and then he licked the wrappers. He scavenged every bit of salt and crumb.

He tried to shove the wrappers into his pockets when he was done, but they had left him wearing only a gown. He tucked the wrappers up under his mattress, instead. Only then did the Fifth address her.

"Why are you here?"

"I'm looking for my brother," Ute told him. "I've come to take him home."

"Well he isn't here," said the Fifth, "but you can wait for him, if you want. Here with me. Have you got any more food?"

"No, I haven't," she said. "And I can't stay much longer. They're going to make me leave."

At this the Fifth sat up in the bed. He looked very, very concerned.

"I can bring you something next time," she said. "Whatever you like."

Urgently, the Fifth shook his head. "If you're going to find him, you must do it tonight. They won't let you make it this far again."

"What can I do, then?" she asked. "Can you bring him to me?"

The eyes of the Fifth darted around the room. He thought, furiously. He watched the open door. There were always spies on him. Especially here.

"The ceiling panel," he said, pointing above the bed. She knew it hurt him to tell her, to share this with her. "The last one. Quickly, look there."

Ute climbed onto the bed beside him and raised her hands to the ceiling panel in the corner. At first it stuck, but on the third try she knocked it loose.

She slid the tile aside and reached into the crevice. Her hand closed around a shape and she brought it into the light. It was a clear plastic drinking bottle—meant for water, but containing an inch of a sluggish red liquid. Ute glanced down at the Fifth, who looked as if he were about to cry.

"Not that one, no, the last one!" urged the Fifth. "Back, back, the very last one."

So, she dug with her hands, touching bottle after bottle, each one with some liquid in it, all of different colors and different measures. Finally her fingers graced a surface unlike the rest—a red plastic thermos, heavy with a liquid she could not see.

"Drink it, drink it all," he said, "and then put it down. He will know that you've been here then. Then he will come."

The Fifth clung to the edge of the bed. He did not have the strength to leave it, from the drugs they had given him, but he shook so badly she feared he would tumble off it. She could not tell if he truly wanted her to drink what was in the thermos, or if he was afraid she might.

She did.

The last raven said, "Who has been drinking from my cup? It was a human mouth."

The liquid that flooded her mouth was tasteless, odorless, ageless. She drank it all, and wiped the last bit from her lips.

Water.

She put the thermos on the ground and waited.

The Sixth came then.

"I took such pains to get it," he said, looking at the empty thermos. "They would not let me leave the house, do you remember? But I snuck out, when the moon was full. I left it under the moon, in the grove at the end of the property. I used to walk with you there, when you were very small."

"Is it you, then, brother?"

"No. And you are not *sister*." The Sixth wrinkled his nose and would not look at her. "You reek of him," he said. "I smell his sweat in the folds of you. Would that she had let me finish what I started. Then I might have washed the sin from your body, and made you clean again."

"But I drank the water, just now. I have passed all your tests. Am I not cleansed?"

"You have drunk, but you are not clean. You have been bathed by her hand, all these years. The Witch. The Spoiler. She would scrub, she would burn, trying to hide the stains, but she only made them deeper. You bear the touch of both of them. You cannot be redeemed."

The Sixth glanced at her, briefly. "God grant that our sister might be here; then we would be set free."

When she heard this, Ute came to kneel before the Sixth. "God grant that I could wash it away," she told him. "God knows that I have tried. But perhaps I can be redeemed, after all."

With that, she reached into her bag.

The ravens were restored to their human forms. They hugged and kissed one another, and went home happily.

She laid the item in the lap of the Sixth—a bundle of

cloth, carefully wrapped. He unwound it slowly, and with every twist of cloth, his eyes began to brighten. Innocence and wonder transformed his face. By the time her gift was revealed, it was the Seventh that received it, and the Seventh was he—the boy, the One—that she had been searching for. Embracing over the gift, the siblings cried out in joy.

"Do you see now, brother?" sang Ute—though in whispers, so the men would not come and find the severed hand that she had brought him. "I punished them—both of them. *Manu propri*—by my own hand. The power is mine now. We may not be clean, but we are avenged."

Ute smiled, and gently kissed her brother's face. "You can come home, Bertram. We can be together again."

The boy began to weep, and in his lap, the hand of his mother caught his tears.

Author Bio:

Shannon Connor Winward is a Delaware writer of speculative poetry and fiction. Her work has appeared or is forthcoming in such venues as: *Pedestal Magazine, Flash Fiction Online, This Modern Writer [Pank Magazine], Vestal Review, Witches & Pagans Magazine, Ideomancer, NewMyths.com, Silver Blade Magazine, Illumen, The Magazine of Speculative Poetry,* and *Dreamstreets,* and the upcoming anthology Jack-O'-Spec: Tales of Halloween and Fantasy (Raven Electrik Ink). To read her accounts of writing, witchery, mommyhood, and general sassiness, stop by her blog at http://ladytairngire.livejournal.com.

Daughter of Plant and Woman
Michael Andre-Driussi

As the wife sat fanning herself by the window, a wondrous, delicious aroma came to her from the herb woman's garden below. It quickened her blood and gave her powerful cravings. She awakened her husband and pointed out the desired plants, which happened to be the newest hybrids in the garden.

"I want to eat a few of those," she told him.

"Wait until after nightfall," he said, and he went back to his Italian siesta.

When it was dark midnight, the husband crept over the wall, quickly stole a handful of the greens, and returned home. His wife ate the plunder and declared it delicious, but instead of quelling her appetite, the salad inflamed her desire to eat more.

So, the next night the husband again slipped over the wall and took two handfuls, thinking that this amount would satisfy his wife's cravings. Unfortunately it did not, and she became rapacious—she wanted more of those greens, and refused to eat anything else.

On the third night the husband again went over the wall, and this time he took four handfuls—all that remained. Just then the herb woman caught him.

"Who is this flying goat that is eating my fodder every night?" she said, and when she opened her lantern, she recognized him. He stood rapt, as if held by a net she had cast over him. "You! Rapscallion, why do you plunder my garden by night while others come to my front door by day?"

"These greens, good woman Gothel," he said. "I can find them nowhere else, but my wife refuses to eat anything else." He told her the whole shameful story, and as he did so her anger faded, replaced by interest in the curious details.

Gothel had intended that the new simple would be used as a curative for horses—specifically she was hoping to aid her neighbor the stable master. But, the simple itself was now revealing its nature, and it seemed more powerful than any she had ever grown. The spirit of the simple was trying to speak in its own silent way, focusing on a wife by singing a song of scent. The woman had already come under its spell—but to what end?

Gothel said to the husband, "Tell me of your wife. What is her heart's desire, beyond these greens?"

The husband hemmed and hawed before blurting, "She wants to have a baby. We have tried these five long years, but still we have no child."

Gothel began thinking in the old language. "The plant is part turnip, which is *rapum*," she thought. "The woman has become *rapax,* snatching and greedy. The plants are plunder, which is *rapina*." So when the husband told about his wife's deepest desire, the pieces of the puzzle strangely came together for a moment.

"Take this *rapina,* this loot, back to your wife," said the herb woman. "Let her eat it, then plant your turnip and get her with child. If this is done her craving will be cured."

The husband did what she had told him to do, and the next day his wife was cured. When spring came, the wife gave birth to a baby girl. The husband came to Gothel's front door and told her the good news.

"Glad tidings upon your house," said Gothel, glad to see a happy end to such a bad beginning. "But be careful, rapscallion—now her womb is unlocked. Find your bliss but do not plant the turnip in the garden for a few years yet."

"Yes, yes, mother, thank you," said the husband. "We are so grateful, we named our daughter after your magic plant."

"How can that be?" said Gothel. "The mischievous simple has no name yet."

"But you told it to me, that night," said the husband. "You called it 'rapina' and that is our girl's name."

Gothel knew at once that this was a terrible name, with all sorts of bad magic about it. The spirits would hear that name spoken and they would be inspired to make cruel mischief upon the poor girl.

Scarcely ten months later, the husband's wife gave birth to twins, and the little family was in dire trouble that winter. Bad luck seemed to be following them and they blamed it upon Rapina, who had been a colicky infant. The root of their increasing misfortune was that name, since every time they said "Rapina" they attracted more bad spirits, so that by the time the twins were born there was a horde of unseen creatures surrounding the family and subjecting them to cruel jests. The husband had a wild look about him, as if he were planning to abandon the child.

This troubled Gothel. The infant was fey, since the plant was as much a parent as her mother and father. In her, the spirit of the plant had achieved human form and now it called out to the spirit world as it had once called to one woman. Gothel could see this much, and she feared for the young woman whom the infant would become. The spirits and the men they sometimes rode would take her by force, would violate her repeatedly, since that was what her name meant to them. Even worse than this was the likelihood that the offspring of such ravishment would be a terrible new race of fairy, a plague set loose upon the world.

At last Gothel came up with a plan to save the girl. She closed up her house and made ready to leave the city for another place far away, and then she offered to take Rapina with her, raising her as her own daughter. The wife wept tears of regret mixed with gratitude and finally gave the baby over.

As soon as they were away, Gothel put her face close to the baby and said, "You are Parsley. My daughter Parsley."

They went to a city in the south of France, where Gothel again practiced her trade and Parsley grew into her new name.

Parsley's hair was blond and her eyes were green. She was a plain-looking child, at first, and they lived for several years in quiet happiness; but by the time she was five years old she was a pretty girl, and a few times Parsley heard a whisper when nobody was around. It surprised her, so she asked Gothel, "Mother, I heard a whispered word—what is 'Ray'?"

"It is a bad thing," said Gothel.

They moved from the city to a town. They lived there in relative comfort, but Parsley's appearance continued to improve, and by the time she was nine, she was beautiful. The whispering came again to Parsley, in moments of quiet twilight or silent night.

"Mother, I hear whispering like when I was a child," said Parsley. Gothel's eyes grew wide. "What is 'Ray-Pee'?"

"It is a very bad thing," said Gothel.

They moved again, this time to a village where they lived in poverty. Still Parsley's beauty blossomed, and when she was twelve, she was no longer simply beautiful: she was the most beautiful girl under the sun.

The mischief stormed around them. Parsley saw that Gothel now had a wild look at times. There was an evening when Parsley was tending the garden and a passing farmer stopped to say something strange to her. She looked up at him, a man she had known for years, and was frightened by his glowing eyes.

She ran crying to Gothel, who comforted her and listened to the story until Parsley asked, "Mo-mother, what is 'Ray-Pee-N --'?"

"Don't say it," cried Gothel, interrupting her. "It is a terrible thing, never to be spoken!"

The next day Gothel took Parsley into the forest to gather wild simples. In the middle of the forest they came upon a tower that had neither stairs nor doors, only a big window eighty feet above the ground.

"Child," said Gothel, "this is our new home."

They lived at the tower for years. By day, they gathered simples from garden and forest, and prepared compounds. At night, they slept in the tower. On market days, Gothel took bundles of simples and compounds to town to sell them, and during those times, Parsley was alone.

To enter and leave they used a rope ladder. As time passed, one part or another would wear. They repaired it by twisting some of Parsley's hair into the rope.

Parsley was very excited one day when Gothel came back from the market town. "Mother," she said. "A man was down there!"

"A man?" said Gothel, so surprised that she nearly fell off the ladder. "A hunter, was it?"

"He said he was a troubadour," said Parsley.

Gothel muttered at that, and then she asked, "Did he ask you to let down the ladder?"

"Yes," said Parsley.

"And did you?" asked Gothel.

"Oh, no, Mother!"

"Good girl," said Gothel, and she began climbing again.

Once Gothel was inside, Parsley told more:

"He played the lute and sang a beautiful song about a knight who met a shepherdess—'The other day I went wandering'—that's how it began."

"What happened to her, in the song?" asked Gothel, knowing that nine times out of ten *pastorelas* she was violated.

"She refused his advances," said Parsley with a laugh. "She hit him on the head with her crook! Then he went away, saying he hoped she would favor him one day."

The troubadour came again a few days later. Marveling at their rope ladder, he asked, "How did you manage to get up there the first time?"

"There was a string that went up around yon beam and down again," said Gothel. "We tied a rope to the string and drew it up and over the beam."

The troubadour said, "But how did you get the string up there?"

"We had a little help," said Gothel.

At first Gothel was very suspicious of him, but he answered her questions directly. He was a troubadour, well versed in the arts of courtly love.

Gothel spoke to him of the *Cathar* ideals as well as the erotic arts they were rumored to practice. She told him of "mining black earth"; she showed him the symbol of Pisces, the two fish swimming head to tail, and had him explain its significance in this context; they discussed Sodom and Gomorrah and agreed that the true sin had not been what the men did for carnal pleasure with themselves but their violation of others. She started an immoral story made immortal by Boccaccio, and he finished it. She asked whether he knew male continence; he said he did, and she believed him.

Gothel envisioned a solution to all their problems. The young couple separated from the world, with herself to help and nurture them -- it would be an earthly paradise, Eden regained. There would be amorous delight but no offspring, and thus the bad seed of the mischievous simple would come to an end. After Parsley was past her childbearing years, once age had ravaged her terrible beauty, then she could safely go out into the world as a crone and be a great herb woman, or she could live out her remaining days in the forest.

Gothel spoke to him. "As you can see, we are living here in imitation of the *stylites*, above and away from the world. Perhaps you can stay with us and we could live in the purity of the *Cathars*. Failing that lofty ideal, you and she could practice the earthy arts of the *Bogomils*. I offer you my only daughter and an earthly paradise, with only one rule—there must be no offspring. Just like the *Cathars*. Can you swear with good conscience to such a bargain?"

As he considered, she looked about his head and shoulders for signs of possession past or present, and then she looked deep into his eyes. She saw that he was human and pure of heart.

"Yes," he said. "I swear it."

The first season was a very happy time. Just knowing that Parsley was not alone while Gothel was away, made the herb woman feel more at ease on her visits to the market town. They sang *tensos*, the cerebral debate songs of love and ethics; they sang *sirventeses*, the visceral partisan songs shining with praise or oozing with vitriol. But the best was when they would sing a sweet *pastorela*, with him singing as the knight and Parsley singing as the shepherdess, followed by an alba, song of lovers in the night: "Ah God, ah God, the dawn it comes too soon..."

Seeing the young couple together was a delight to Gothel, and hearing them sing so sweetly together brought tears of joy to her eyes.

After spring came summer, and Gothel's heart was so full of happiness she thought it might burst. Then one morning at the end of summer, as Parsley was struggling to put on her clothes, she said, "Mother, why are my clothes getting smaller?"

Gothel glanced over at her and, as if the scales had fallen from her eyes, she could see that Parsley was with child.

"Oh, you wicked creature," cried Gothel. "You carry another life inside you; you have broken the one rule!"

"No, no," wailed Parsley. "That is impossible! The safe days, the sign of the Pisces, the vinegar sponge, the arts *bougre*—Mother, sweet Mother, we followed the law you set down. I cannot be pregnant!"

"Alas, you are," said Gothel. She took up her knife with grim determination and said, "I should save the world by killing you now. Come here."

Trembling with fear at this dreadful change in Gothel, Parsley knelt at her feet. Gothel reached down and sliced off her long braid, which made Parsley sob.

"My Oath to Hippocrates has spared your life," said Gothel. She forced her daughter to climb down from the tower and then drove her into the wilderness.

"You were cursed before your birth," Gothel raged at Parsley as they hiked along their pathless way. "I have spent seventeen years trying to change your fate, and all for nothing. Your name will be more known than fabled Lilith or Pandora, of this I am certain, but I fear you will be remembered as mother to demons."

After many hours they came to a clearing with a few ruinous cottages used by swineherds. Gothel pointed them out and then spoke her final words to the young woman: "You walk alone henceforth. Cast yourself upon their mercy! I have no daughter, and your name is not Parsley."

As the twilight deepened toward night, the troubadour arrived at the base of the tower and whistled. The rope ladder was lowered and up he climbed, expecting to find his beloved Parsley alone. Instead, he found Gothel, sitting at the table with only a guttering candle-stub for light.

"Mother Gothel!" he said. "I thought you gone to town."

"No, not yet," she said. "But soon." Her voice was old and tired.

"But Mother Gothel, it is night now!" he said, surprised at her words.

"Yes," said Gothel, staring into her cup.

"Where is Parsley?" he asked, growing uneasy.

"She is gone," said Gothel. "She has been cast out for being with child. I trusted you, and you betrayed my trust."

"Wait—wait!" squeaked the troubadour in fright. "Isn't there a compound to remedy her condition?"

She glared at him with a baneful eye. "Yes, there is such a compound, and she knows it, too. She is an herb woman. I wash my hands of it, and you both." With that, she stood up, drank the cup, and spit its fluid into his face. He screamed as the poison blinded him. His limbs felt heavy as stone, making him fall over. He tried to rise but could not. He fainted as she worked her terrible revenge upon him, and then she left the tower forever, leaving a tribe of spirits the charge of tormenting him.

***

Parsley found a swineherd's wife who was willing to add her to the household in exchange for helping with chores and practicing her medicine. When Parsley's time came the wife helped her give birth to twins, a colicky girl with pointed ears and a quiet boy.

One night the swineherd's wife suddenly spoke in a different voice: "*Rapina.*"

Parsley saw the eerie gleam in her eye. "Who are you?"

"We watch your *troubadour* wander the forest like a wild man," said the eerie voice. "He has gone in circles for two years."

"He is still alive?" said Parsley, weeping with hope.

"Barely," was the answer. "He will die soon."

"Please bring him to me," cried Parsley.

"Would you still have him? He is blind and unmanned."

"Please!"

"We will trade him for your twins."

"What?" Her blood ran cold. "What are you saying?"

"We will give him to you if you give us your children."

"You are monsters!"

"Yes," said the voice. "And we claim the children are our own."

"No. Not my babies. No!"

"Your man will die before sunrise."

"No! This is too much."

Parsley trembled as she grappled with the horrific offer. *It is impossible,* she thought, *a devil's bargain—there is no way to win, either way.*

"Not both—" she said, the thought coming out before she could halt it. She groaned, bending over.

"Just one child?"

"I—I can't make the choice," said Parsley.

"To bargain or not?"

"No!" hissed Parsley. "Which—which child..."

"You know and we know which child. The girl."

Parsley began panting.

"This is your final offer," said the voice. "Take your daughter to the stream and sing as though your heart were breaking. Go now."

The glow faded from the wife's eyes and she started as if suddenly awakened. "What was I...?"

Her befuddlement changed into concern as she saw Parsley's face.

"You look like you've seen a ghost! Where are you going?"

Parsley took up her sleeping daughter and ran out into the night. At the stream's side she sang a lament; she sang a *sirventes* against the cruel oppressors; she sang an alba, but at the first "Ah God, ah God, the dawn it comes too soon" she broke down in sobs.

As soon as she could breathe again, she bravely began their sweet *pastorela*: "The other day I went wandering..."

After a time she heard a shout and a crashing through the bushes on the other side. Then the ragged troubadour appeared there in the moonlight, and he sang his part of the song.

Parsley's heart leapt at the sight of him. He waded out into the stream. She started to go but hesitated. He stumbled as if shoved and she saw dark hands pushing his head down toward the water.

She stepped into the water and waded out to the middle. The dark hands released him and reached out for the baby.

She gave up her daughter and regained her lover.

The couple wept in their embrace. The troubadour's long

beard, tangled with twigs, was wet from his near drowning.

"Parsley, forgive me," he said. "Forgive me for making you with child." He wept fresh tears of regret.

"My love, I forgive you," she said. "I have given you a son!" And then she cried her own tears of regret.

Author Bio:
Michael Andre-Driussi lives in the San Francisco Bay Area. His stories have been published in such places as the *ParaSpheres* anthology, *M-Brane SF*, and *Interzone*. A scholar on the works of Gene Wolfe, he wrote the reference books *Lexicon Urthus* and *The Wizard Knight Companion*, with a third title, *Gate of Horn, Book of Silk*, on the way.

Soul of the Ocean
Rachel Ayers

My father was the ruler of Eldim, a small coastal kingdom, a little cove between two large and powerful lands. I, sixth daughter, grew up in the full knowledge of my duty to marry and secure an alliance—of wealth or power or protection. Although our kingdom was small, it was beautiful, and although we hadn't a great wealth of gold or jewels, our palace was decorated with the most amazing flowers, fountains, and gardens. Colored glass was fitted into every window, and generations of women had woven tapestries for every wall. I grew up convinced that no home could be more lovely.

My sisters and I were each a year apart, and though we were kept in our palace, on our fifteenth birthday, Father took us, one at a time, on a sailing voyage. From fourteen miles out, we were told that we could see the entire length of the kingdom, from the mountain range on the north to the mouth of the river at the far southern border of our kingdom and Oasha.

I remember when my eldest sister returned from her voyage, sunburned and smelling of fresh wind and salt. Her excitement was contagious as she spoke of the vastness of the sky and the endless reach of the sea. We all wanted to go after that, but each must wait her turn.

When our second sister came back, she spoke of looking down over the edge of the boat at the strange and wondrous world she'd seen there, full of fish more brilliantly colored than any she'd seen in our ornamental ponds, and wavering plants that seemed to reach up to the sky, as though with longing arms.

My third sister pleaded with Father, that she might have a nighttime celebration, and have a great many fireworks set off from the ship. After consulting with the captain, Father agreed, and my third sister returned to us early in the morning, her quiet thoughtfulness broken only to tell us that the stars were far superior to any display of man-made sparks.

I was suffering from great impatience by the time my fourth sister went on her voyage. I longed to see such a distant view, to experience the freedom and exhilaration that had captivated my sisters so. My fourth sister came back and spoke of the clouds rushing overhead, racing the ship back to land and then leaving it far behind as they continued inland and out of sight.

When my fifth sister turned fifteen, I felt it my duty to point out the vast unfairness of having to wait so long just to take a little journey out to sea. My nurse, Amalthea, scolded me, "It is an occasion of great importance, and you will better appreciate it when you've waited."

Our fifth sister had asked to sail out and then down to the southern river. She came back to tell us of the place where the water poured out to sea, and trade vessels congregated like a great flock of geese, just as noisy, calling to one another in many languages.

On my fifteenth birthday, my Father called me to him.

"You are grown, now, my dear, and it is time for you to sail out with me, to see our kingdom. Have you any request to make of me at this time?"

I lowered my eyes but trembled with the excitement. "Father, I have longed for this day since my eldest sister came back and told us of her trip. My only wish is to sail out on a ship and see the ocean and feel the sway of the waves beneath me."

My Father laughed, not unkindly. "You are so young, my lovely daughter. Yet perhaps it is best if I speak to you on the sea, otherwise you will be entirely taken up with your impatience."

The great vessel was prepared in anticipation of our venture. Father and I left after breakfast, riding down to the coast in an open carriage. He called out to many of the fishermen and tradesmen that he knew. I tried to look regal and not to squirm indecorously as we went.

I couldn't keep a skip out of my step as we mounted the gangway. Father pointed out all the trappings and rigging, telling me names that went out of my head as soon as he said them. He laughed again, at my delight, and told me I would do better to be attentive to him than the seagulls that flitted around the ship.

We were underway in short order, and I raced to the bow and put my face in the breeze. The wind rushed into my face. I took deep, gasping breaths with each wave we crested. The sun shone down and clouds flitted across the sky. I watched the ocean floor drop away as we moved out of the harbor and far below I could see the ship's shadow, passing over sand and seaweed and sea creatures that dashed out of the way as the sun was blocked out.

Father waited until I was calmer, and then joined me in the bow of the ship. "Did you know," he asked with seeming casualness, "that Prince Alan of Oasha has just turned fifteen as well? You are very near in age."

"I did not know, Father," I said, although I'd been vaguely aware that the prince of Oasha was young, of an age to be marriageable to myself or one of my sisters.

"I have corresponded with his father, and we would like to make an arrangement." His hand dropped onto my shoulder, and he turned me gently to face him. "Lorelei, I would not ask this of you if I did not think you capable. Would you help me to form this alliance? Would you marry Prince Alan, for the sake of our kingdom?"

I looked at his familiar face as if from a great distance. He took his hand away, stepped back. "I do not ask you to answer immediately, my dear. Shall we go farther out to sea, or would you like to head back?"

"Farther out," I said, though now my thoughts were divided.

We rode the sea out until late afternoon. I looked back, and the land had disappeared. There was only ocean, endless ocean, as far as I could see. "Where did it go, Father?" I asked.

"Over the horizon. It's out of sight, but it's still there."

I thought about my beautiful, beloved kingdom. I thought of the way Father knew almost all the sailors and captains, shipwrights and tradesmen, who came to our port, and how they all knew and respected him. My father was a careful, kind king, and I knew he would not ask me to do anything that he did not believe would be good for me, as well as the kingdom. My decision was simple enough.

"Yes, Father," I told him as the captain yelled orders to turn the vessel around. "I will marry Prince Alan, if he will have me."

He smiled down upon me, and we sat together peacefully. When the evening air turned cool, he wrapped his tremendous fur cloak around my shoulders, and we talked about my sisters and cousins, and some of the courtiers, and a dozen other insignificant things, watching the stars come out slowly as the sky darkened.

***

The preparations for my new life began in the morning, before I'd even awakened. My sisters rustled into my room with lengths of cloth and ribbons and beads, and began an excited chatter about my future wardrobe and future husband.

My old nurse Amalthea was pleased with the arrangement as well. Oasha was wealthy and powerful, and would make a strong ally, but I think she was more interested in accompanying me to a place that was reported to have most excellent pastries. She found me in the garden, where I'd gone for a few minutes peace from my sisters. We wandered the pathways, curving through blossoming vines and around glittering ponds.

I stopped and watched the fish flash through the water. My nurse chatted on about the customs and traditions of Oasha.

"Are they so different from us?" I asked her.

"Well, their ways are more formal than ours. We follow old traditions, old ways of thinking about the world. Old magic. And of course they speak a different language," she told me. "Not to worry, my lovely, your father is sending you to Saint Adjutor's Abbey as soon as we can make ready. It lies by the mountains at our northern border, and the Abbess there will school you. She is from Oasha, and by your wedding night, you'll be as graceful in their ways as you are in ours."

My departure, then, would be more immediate than I'd realized. My sisters went into a frenzy of sewing and packing, preparing for me an entirely new set of gowns, dainty slippers, delicate undergarments, and every accessory I could dream of. Not a month had passed when I was again on a ship, this time sailing north to the Saint Adjutor's, my sisters and nurse accompanying me on this journey.

Saint Adjutor's was by a little bay, surrounded by high blue mountains, still snow-capped at this time of year, even though our kingdom was a warm one. Fruit trees grew around the building, and palm trees bordered the front door. The sand of the beach was as fine and white as any I'd seen. I dawdled, searching for shells, as my trunks were unloaded and my sisters scurried around and my nurse headed purposefully toward the convent.

They settled me in and were departing long before I was ready to see them go. The next morning my eldest sister held me tight against her, whispering into my ear, "I love you, darling Lorelei. Be good, be smart, we'll see you again in a few months."

I hugged her back and then, to be brave, let her go and stepped back. However, I watched until the ship was out of sight down the coastline. Then the Abbess took me in and we began on my language lessons.

In only a few weeks I had settled to a regular routine, most of it spent learning the customs and languages of Oasha, a large portion also spent on devotions and prayer. My old nurse, Amalthea, was there, too, so although our lessons became more clandestine, she continued to teach me the old ways. Every night she told me a tale of the folk under the hills or the spirits of the air or the mermaids—my favorite.

"The mermaids have voices far more beautiful than any human voice," she would tell me. "Sailors and superstitions folk," (she did not count herself among this number) "believe that mermaids lure sailors to their doom, but they simply sing to drowning men. They don't understand that men cannot live beneath the sea, so they sing to welcome them to their enchanting underwater land. Mermaids live many years longer than mankind, and don't understand or mourn death the way we do."

One night, a few weeks after I'd been there, a crack of thunder startled me out of sleep. Moments later, more lightning flashed, and I watched the bizarre shadows thrown on the wall through my window. Then the rain came crashing down, and I listened for long hours through the morning as the storm rolled through.

The sky was lighter when the rain slackened, and only an occasional crack of thunder could be heard. Knowing that I would have to get up for morning devotions soon, rolled off my little bed. I gathered a heavy robe around my shoulders and went out into the misty morning.

Birds sang, assuring each other that they were still alive. I stepped through the fog, out through the little garden tended by the sisters of the abbey, and onto the soft wet sand of the beach.

I thought that I must be seeing shapes in the mist, or even still dreaming. I watched a struggling form push its way out of the water; I could not make out what it was. Curiosity had me three steps forward before it occurred to me that it could be something dangerous.

The shape separated for a moment, and I realized I was looking at two bodies, although the fog still made them strange to my eyes. One of them seemed to be tending to the other. Could they be shipwrecked sailors, dragged onto shore with the incoming tide? I hardly thought anyone could have stayed afloat after the fury of the morning storm.

I took a step closer, hoping to offer aid, or at least to clarify the vision before me. The bells rang for Matins, and one of the shapes slid back into the water. It was not long before the Sisters filed into the garden. They were quickly about their business, and did not see the shape on the beach.

Was it a body? I could not leave it there. I hurried across the sand to find out.

It was a boy—no, a man, but a young one. I knelt at his side, looking out to sea for his companion.

There was nothing but the waves, rippling up and down the shoreline. I turned my attention to the man—by his garb, a sailor. I reached out to touch his face, hesitated, and then put my hand upon his forehead. His skin was cool, but not as cold as I thought it would be, were he dead.

He coughed, then, his eyes fluttering beneath their lids. I moved my hand to his cheek, and decided that he was a very well shaped man—strong jaw line, smooth skin, dark, curling hair.

He opened his eyes, and I was looking into the perfect blue of the calm sea. My breath caught. My fingers, seemingly of their own accord, traced down his cheekbone and smoothed back the hair behind his ears.

He reached up and touched my face. A faint smile slipped across his lips, then faded away as his eyes closed again. His hand dropped into my lap, and I held it there, feeling the warmth seep back into his fingers.

"Help!" I turned and called back toward the Saint Adjutor's, not leaving his side. "Help! Please, Sisters, a sailor, washed up on shore!"

They turned, then came running as I spared a hand to wave and call to them again.

***

He was placed in a small chamber, with a Sister constantly watching over him. I went by his room whenever I had a spare moment—which I quickly had less of, as the Sisters and Abbess seemed to find it necessary that I have endless extra things to occupy my time. Still, I stopped by when I could to see if he had awakened again.

It was thus that I happened to be there when he did, at last, open his eyes again. I can only put it down to the spirits of fortune that Sister Margaret had gone to fetch herself some tea, with a guilty look at me and an admonition to mind myself.

He looked at me, and I was transported across the room with no knowledge of how I came to be at his side. I smiled. "You're awake," I said. "How are you feeling?"

"Hello," he said in Oashian. His smile was sleepy.

"Hello," I said in the same language. "How..." if only I'd studied more! "You?"

He grinned. He spoke slowly, but I didn't catch very much of it. Something about feeling better, I thought.

"Good." I reached out and touched his hand, surprised at my own boldness. He caught my fingers in his, and now his skin was warm, his grip strong.

"Oh, my," I said faintly in my own language. He seemed to understand; he eased himself up into a sitting position and looked at me intently, his eyes going back and forth from my face to our hands.

I sat cautiously next to him on the edge of the bed. "From Oasha?" I asked.

"Yes. You?"

43

"Eldim. Here. Find you..." I pointed out the window, in the general direction of the beach.

"You found me," he said, and I understood him well enough.

I nodded, and freed one of my hands to point at myself. "Lorelei."

He smiled again, and I leaned closer to him, drawn to his eyes. "Pretty, Lorelei."

I wasn't sure if he meant the name, or me, but either way I was quite content.

Sister Margaret interrupted us then, *tsking* over my impropriety. She shooed me out, speaking rapid Oashian that I could follow no more than the cries of the birds. The door was shut firmly in my face, the patient back in the care of the sisters.

***

A ship came and took him away in the early dawn, while I was at prayers. I did not see him again, but I dreamed of him.

My studies continued, and I felt a little more warmth toward my future home. A little more eagerness. At least if that one wonderful man was from there—perhaps the rest of them would be a bit wonderful, too.

I started taking long walks before the sun had quite risen—as though I thought he might wash up on shore again. The beach was beautiful in the morning mists, stretching out endlessly, and its craggy dead ends hidden by the gray fog.

That is how I saw her—though it was some time before I knew if she was a hazy, early morning dream, or real.

She was like a reflection of myself, out on the water in the cloudy vapor. Long, dark hair shifting in the lazy breezes, milk-pale skin like a final glow of moonlight. She stared across the waves at me, as startled as I was.

Then a skim of mist blew between us, she was gone, and I

was left blinking, wondering if I had even truly seen her.

The next morning she was there again, and this time I was a little surer of her. I began to watch for her, and although I did not see her every day, I spotted her most mornings, gazing up at the beach as if she'd left her soul there.

Until several mornings passed, and I did not see her, and then several more, and then I never saw her there again. I dreamed that she had been looking for my castaway sailor— perhaps she had brought him to shore and wanted to reclaim him for the sea. As the next months passed, my thoughts of her faded and I thought surely I must have imagined her, or perhaps seen only my own reflection in the misty morning light and dreamed up a story of her.

***

Before I scarcely felt ready, it was time to pack my things again, to return to my old home for a week of festivities crowned by my marriage.

The town was already in full regalia when we arrived; word quickly traveled to us that Prince Alan had arrived the day before. Chapel bells rang as we docked, banners floated above us, every decoration and adornment of the city on display. There was a carriage waiting for me at the dock, and I was bustled up to the palace amid a city's worth of fanfare.

I felt my hands shaking, my heart trembling. I had expected some time at home before the arrival of the prince; now I had only moments before meeting him.

I was hurried to my old rooms first, where my sisters rushed around me, changing my gown and brushing my hair. My eldest sister held my hands tight in hers and told me, "Do not worry, little sister. We will be with you." She smiled at me, reading the anxiety in my eyes, and then kissed my cheek.

Soon they deemed me presentable, and then there was

nothing between me and meeting my intended husband.

I was led, in the gaggle of my sister-princesses, to the throne room. I saw my father standing before his throne, talking to a young man. Around them were a retinue, several servants, an older woman with regal bearing and elegant attire, and a young maiden. Their backs were to me, for the most part, though my father nodded at me as I entered the room, I had a moment to observe them before they turned.

The little maiden was very attentive to the prince, and I wondered if she were his younger sister, though she did not resemble him much. The older lady regarded this young maiden with a mixture of sympathy and amusement.

Then the prince turned, and I felt for a moment as though my heart were dancing.

I knew him.

My lost sailor, after all these months, stood before me in fine regalia. Prince Alan looked at me, stunned disbelief marking his features. I am sure my own face wore the same expression.

Then he threw himself down before me and grabbed my hands. "It was you," he said, "who saved my life when I lay dead on the beach!"

This caused instant exclamations from everyone in the room, and in the midst of the cry he got up and went to the little maiden. I heard him say, above the other babbling, "I am too happy. My fondest hopes are all fulfilled. You will rejoice at my happiness, for your devotion to me is great and sincere."

She said nothing in return. I wondered at this strange relationship and manner between them. But then thoughts of it were lost amid the joyful outcry. The prince related to everyone in the room that which had happened, that he had been cast up upon a beach, all but drowned, and that there I had found him, and had called until help came, and he had looked at me and known that I was the only woman he could love.

At this I blushed, heart racing, but I could not say I had

not felt the same when I had seen him.

When he told of the time I had come to him as he was recovering, there was some amused tittering from my sisters and nurse. Then he spoke of his heartbreak, at thinking that I was a novice of the order, that I had given my life to the church, and his unspoken vow never to love again. I saw my father exchange a delighted look with the older woman, who was a moment later introduced to me as the prince's mother, Dowager Queen Candace.

"I am delighted to meet you, my dear," she said, kissing me upon the cheek, "and even more so that my son is delighted to meet you, again."

Prince Alan returned to my side, pulling with him the mysterious maiden in his retinue. "This," he said, "is my foundling. I call her Muirne, for she loves the sea more than any sailor I have ever known."

Muirne regarded me with soft, expressive eyes. She had a sadness about her, but her devotion to the prince was clear. She nodded at me and took one of my hands, giving a little half bow above it. It seemed more a forfeit than a mark of servility, but still she did not speak.

"Muirne, I am pleased to meet you," I said. "I am Princess Lorelei."

She nodded as the prince spoke for her. "She has no voice. I have never heard her utter a sound. We found her wandering on the beach near my home, and she's been a constant companion to me ever since."

It was clear to me from the girl's expression that she would have liked to be more than a Constant Companion. Her eyes seemed to call out to him, but his gaze was turned to...me.

Then my thoughts turned only to him and our ability at last to speak to one other. We managed to slip away from time to time over the next few days, in the whirl of wedding preparations, and to talk and gently touch. Slowly thoughts of everyone else fell away, and my heart was full.

***

My happiness was tempered by dreams of drowning, every night after I met the prince. After four days I told Amalthea. She looked into my eyes, at my throat, and regarded my palms. She swirled tea leaves and stayed up late that night to gaze at the stars and their reflection in the shallow pool in the palace gardens.

"There is a threat to you, my dear," she said the next morning, her eyes troubled and distant. "I cannot read it, it is very vague, and may pass you by without any action on your part. I don't like it, though." She shook her head, as though to clear a daze, and then looked at me and tutted. "No matter, my lovie, go about your wedding business and leave this to me. Think no more upon it."

Easier said than done.

Still, over the next week, I managed to turn my mind to thoughts of appetizers, flowers, and cake decorations; the exact trim of the lace of my wedding dress and the particular string of pearls for my hair.

More than that, I spent time getting to know Alan. He told me of his home as I showed him mine. We shared bits about our childhoods, and talked through long hours as the wedding bustle went on around us—less important to me than the fact that I was marrying this wonderful man.

Muirne was sweet, and did not interfere with our quick courtship. She was often with us, listening with rapt attention as he spoke. She seemed to feel some affection for me as well, but I would occasionally catch the sad looks she would cast upon him, and I would wonder about her again until Alan engrossed me again with a story or conversation.

The morning of my marriage, my nurse shook me awake

long before dawn, whispering my name frantically.

"Come with me, child," she said when she saw I had roused. "We've work to be done this morning, and very little time to do it." She hurried me into a long silk robe and dragged me out of my room and down the abandoned back corridors that the servants used; dodging with ease the single guard we passed.

"Where are we going?" I asked when we were outside.

"Down to the water." She rushed me down the sea path, a series of stone switchbacks which were rarely employed since the main road had been built; although it was a quicker way, there was an element of vertigo that most people chose to avoid.

We reached the lapping waves and she pulled me down to kneel beside her. She stared into the water long enough that I began to fidget at her side, wondering for a moment if she had finally cracked like my eldest sister said.

"There," she said at last, and as I watched, though the sky grew lighter, the water grew darker, until it was an almost inky blue in front of us. Then it surged and twisted, as though the very ocean were in pain, or contained some secret poison that it would heave up.

A head rose from the water. A woman, and a beautiful one, although with sinister aspects, that I was afraid to meet her eyes. I felt her powerful curiosity ripple across my skin and I shivered. She spoke to my nurse in a language I didn't know, in a voice so lovely I wanted to weep.

Strangely, as she spoke, I understood her intent, though I could not now repeat a word that she had spoken. My fiancé's fey companion was a child of the sea, who had given up her home and her voice and her long life to be with him, hoping for a husband, love, and an immortal soul. Now she was watching it slip away, but the creature before us had offered her an alternative—if the prince was to die before sunset, the child could return to her home and family.

The sea woman reached toward me, a calm, cruel smile

on her face. She offered us a trade; she would do away with the changeling in exchange for—my nurse cut her off.

"Be gone, Sea Witch!" Amalthea said, her voice a ringing challenge I had never before heard from her. "That is no bargain."

The creature gave her a long, studied look. Then she slipped away beneath the waves, and moments later the sunrise on the water cleared away all trace of the duskiness that had surrounded her.

My nurse gripped my arm, pulling me to my feet. "Come, dearie. There is another path open to us."

I followed her back up the hill, bewildered by what had happened, and soon gasping out of breath as she charged up the path with more energy than I would have thought possible. She led me back to our gardens, sat me down clasping the stitch in my side on a bench beside the pool. She took some powder from a little pouch at her side and tossed it into the water.

Nothing seemed to happen for a long moment, until I saw that the air above the water was shimmering.

That was all; no form took shape, no woman or creature appeared, sinister or wrong. Only a shine in the air, dust in a sunbeam.

"Give us another way," my nurse commanded. "The sea witch will only offer death or pain to those who bargain with her. I believe you know another way."

I heard a sighing, a sound like the wind through the leaves at night. Voices whispered out of the air, not in full words or even a language, yet once again, I felt understanding from deep in my heart.

The child wishes for a soul...We have none to share...

"Share?" I asked sharply. "What does it mean, share?"

My nurse looked uneasy. "I have heard of such magic. It is old, and those ways are lost to us."

The air rustled around us again, then sharpened, and it seems that I very nearly heard the words as I came to understand them.

She wishes to share a soul with her husband. She wishes for the eternal life after her mortal death. A bond such as marriage would tie them together—he would share her soul. But that way is nearly closed to her now. The sea witch offers her back her old life in return for the death of the prince. Her sisters have encouraged this. Otherwise she will end.

"There must be another way!" I cried, for in spite of my initial hesitation, I had grown fond of Muirne, impressed by her silent dedication and love toward the man I loved. "Is...is that the only way to share a soul?" I asked the air around me.

My nurse hissed in a breath, but did not interrupt.

Anyone may share a soul with love.

The sun came fully into the garden at that moment, and the heavy shimmer of the air dissipated, leaving us alone.

"How?" I asked my nurse.

She shook her head. "I do not know the way of it."

My sisters found us then, and I was caught up in the final wedding day festivities.

***

Muirne was at the ceremony. I saw her as we gathered, watching her prince with hopeless intensity. She made no disruption, and when Alan caught my hand in his, I saw only his ocean blue eyes, which regarded me with a depth of love that took my breath away.

Surely we had love enough to share? I pondered it even as I repeated the vows, as the rings were exchanged and the blessing bestowed.

We held a grand reception, with nobles from both our lands in attendance. There was a feast laid out in the great hall, and the ballroom was flooded with candlelight, every surface gleaming and rich. An orchestra played and alone in the middle of the room, Muirne danced for us. She was truly the most graceful being I had ever seen. She smiled upon us, but I thought her eyes shone with tears, not joy. Alan clapped and laughed, looking back and forth between us. I wished I could share his pure happiness, but the shadow of worry clouded my heart. Would Muirne try to return to her family? I couldn't believe she could kill; everything I had ever seen of her was gentle and sweet.

"I am worried about Muirne," I confided to Alan when I was sure no one could overhear us.

He looked surprised. "Why? She seems happy enough."

I gave him my complete exasperated attention. "Alan...I think she loves you."

He laughed. "Of course she does. She is my most devoted friend."

How could a man be so thickheaded? "I do not mean as a friend, or even a sister. I am afraid we may have broken her heart today."

"But that—but she—" He stopped, thinking it over, and then turned to watch her where she stood quietly at the side of the ballroom. He looked at me again, now stricken. "Have I been a cruel man all this time?" He grabbed my hands, held them tightly in his, and moved to speak urgently in my ear. "Lorelei, if I had known all that I do now, I could not change a thing, for I am happiest when I am with you, and I could not give you up. But I fear I have hurt my dearest friend, and I do not know what to do."

It struck me forcefully how little I knew him yet.

"I shall speak to her," I said slowly. "Perhaps if she knows that you do care for her...it will be enough."

He raised my fingers to his lips. "I am so lucky," he said, and shut his eyes.

***

"Muirne, may I speak with you?" I said when I found her later, out on the balcony. She was watching the ocean, a wistful look on her face. She turned to me and nodded. "Muirne, I think it's fair of me to say that you care very much for Alan."

She nodded again, her face calm—yet I could see a deep sorrow behind her eyes.

"I think you care for him more than he ever knew."

Once more, that sad little tilt of the head.

I reached out, touched her arm. Her skin was soft as rose petals, and she smiled at me, so beautifully, and for that brief moment I would have traded my own future for her dream, if I'd known how.

***

It was not full dark when Alan and I retreated to one of his father's tall-ships, *Aerie*, where bridal quarters had been made up in the captain's cabin. Alone at last, Alan watched me remove my veil and take my hair down, and then he moved toward me to help me with my buttons and lace and layers.

***

I awoke to a strange creak. The cabin had been swaying in the waves, and though a ship is made of a thousand wooden groans, this one called me up from slumber. I lay with my eyes shut, listening.

"Lorelei..." Alan murmured, and I felt his arm tighten around me.

"Hmmm?" I said, but he only breathed a sigh into my hair; he'd been talking in his sleep. The realization left me with a warm tingle, and I smiled and opened my eyes.

She was there, standing above us. There was a glint of moonlight through the window, and it flashed along the edge of the knife she was holding, a strange blade of shell and gold. She watched him with tears streaming down her face; I do not think she even knew that I was awake.

Then...she was there one moment, and the next, fading away into air and mist. The knife clattered to the floor.

"Wait," I whispered, sitting up and holding a hand out to where she'd been. But there was nothing there.

I slid carefully out of the feather bed, not wanting to wake Alan. I walked around the tiny cabin, wondering if I'd imagined it in a sleepy daze—and at once it came back to me, the dream woman I'd seen at Saint Adjutor's, on my morning walks out on the beach. I'd thought I'd just imagined her.

Then I thought farther back, and remembered the apparition I'd seen after the storm, which had turned out to be Alan. Now it came back to me: at first I had believed there were two bodies. She had brought him to shore. She had saved his life as much as I had.

There, at the foot of the bed was a bizarrely worked knife, still seeming to shine with its own light.

I bent and picked it up.

In the whitely lit night, I walked out of the cabin and to the rail at the side of the ship. The moon's reflection danced up at me from the rippling water.

"Please," I implored the air, the sea, the sky. "Please. There must be another way. One such as she does not deserve this ending. Not for falling in love."

The wind sighed through the sails. I held the knife out above the water, flat across both palms.

"If there is another way...if it can be done—I love her, as I love my sisters. For saving my husband and for seeking a soul in this world." I fell silent, unsure how to end my plea. "If a husband could share his soul with her, surely she can share mine."

I went to drop the knife, and it twisted in my hands,

nicking my fingertip as it fell. A drop of my blood went with it and I stuck my finger in my mouth. Perhaps it was only my fancy, but it seemed the wind kicked up a bit at that moment. I thought I heard, in that echoing airy voice I'd heard so briefly that morning, *"She will be offered a chance..."*

Now, with the breeze blowing across my skin, I shivered. I went back into our cabin and warmed myself beside my husband.

***

In the morning, there was no trace of Muirne. Alan had the ship searched, and then the city. He was disconsolate for a time, and at last I told him what I had seen and discovered. I do not know if he believed me at first, but I watched him think over her strange appearance, her sweet manner, and all the things he did know about her.

That might have been the end of it; we began our lives together, and soon had our time occupied between court and children. We had, at the end of five years, two girls and a boy, and Alan was a devoted father. We named our eldest daughter Muirne.

We thought of my husband's silent companion often. I remembered her dark, expressive eyes when I saw my son watching his sisters' games, and I thought of her gentle manner when our youngest daughter played in the garden, tending flowers but never picking them.

One rare evening when we were alone, I saw him staring into the fire and asked if he was thinking about her.

He nodded. "I am. But dearest, do not think that I am not happy. I just wonder what I could have done—if I did something wrong."

I knelt at his side and looked up at him. "I do not think so. I believe a false marriage would have been no better for her."

"And my heart was already given elsewhere," he said,

touching my cheek and smiling.

"But I think..." I hesitated. "I feel her sometimes. Her quiet, watchful ways. Sometimes when our babies are being good as gold—"

"The rare occasion!"

I laughed. "I think at those times I feel a happiness above my own. And...it feels like her."

I thought he would shrug it away or laugh, but he nodded slowly. "I know this feeling. I believe she will watch over us, and our children, if she can."

We sat together, regarding the flames and thinking of the sea.

Author Bio:

Rachel Ayers lives and writes in Kansas, from whence she hopes to hitch a tornadic ride to adventure in another world. In the meantime, she reads, daydreams, and moderates a fairy tale discussion forum on LiveJournal. She has a Creative Writing degree from Pittsburg State University. Her novelette "Sister and Serpent" won Honorable Mention in the L. Ron Hubbard Writers of the Future Contest, and her story "Job Hunting" won First Prize in the 2010 HarperCollins Radiant Prose contest. Her work has appeared or is forthcoming in: Isabelle Rose's Twisted Fairy Tale Anthology volumes 1 and 2 (Wicked East Press), A Thousand Faces, Puffin Circus, and Death Rattle.

The Queen's Huntsman
Shiloh Carroll

The wolves trotted through the forest, noses to the rain-soaked ground or testing the air, paws silent on the wet leaves. The Huntsman followed, his well-worn boots as noiseless as the wolves. He held his crossbow low in front of him, ready to raise it and fire if any prey made itself available.

One of the wolves paused, sniffing at the air. The Huntsman waited, watching the forest around him for a sign of what the wolf smelled. The others caught the scent, as well. With low whines, they led the Huntsman off the game trail and into an area of the forest thick with undergrowth. They slunk through the brush, the Huntsman close behind them, until they reached another game trail.

The wolves hunkered low on their bellies just off the trail, waiting. The Huntsman took a knee and watched the trail. It didn't take long; a lone buck wandered up the trail toward them, browsing at the damp leaves to the side of the path. The Huntsman raised his bow, and the wolves gathered themselves to spring.

The deer flung his head up, reared and swiveled on his back legs, and dashed back down the trail. The wolves were after him in a flash, white bodies low to the ground, powerful legs thrusting them forward. The deer bounded off the trail and through the woods, zigzagging among the trees. The Huntsman ran after, long training permitting him to keep up, if only just.

The pack ran the deer to exhaustion, then pounced. One latched onto the deer's back leg, crippling him. Another sank her fangs into his throat, dragging him to the forest floor. The buck kicked, catching a wolf on the side. Her yelp rose above the growls of the other wolves and the squall of the dying buck.

The Huntsman raised his bow and released a bolt into the buck's eye, killing him. The wolves released their various grips on the deer and moved away from the carcass, waiting for the Huntsman. He dropped to one knee beside the buck, drawing his skinning knife.

"We thank the forest for this bounty," he murmured as he drew the knife up the deer's belly. "May we prove worthy of her sacrifice."

When the deer was cleaned, the wolves fell on the innards, only the occasional squabble over a choice bit breaking the silence of the forest. When the wolves had eaten their fill, the Huntsman wrapped the deer in an oiled cloth to keep the blood from his clothes and hefted the carcass over his shoulders. Together, he and the wolves headed out of the forest, back toward the castle.

The Queen would have her venison tonight.

***

The Queen was enthusiastically grateful for the Huntsman's efforts, not even waiting for the Huntsman to clean up before accosting him in the hall outside his room. Her gratitude left him drained, panting, and dripping with sweat in a way the hunt never did. He didn't know why she chose to grace him with her attentions—perhaps she was lonely—but he didn't question them.

One did not question the Queen's wishes, after all.

She was a vision, tall and willowy, blonde hair that reached her knees when unbound, and piercing blue eyes. She was insatiable, often appearing in the Huntsman's bed in the middle of the night, or summoning him to her bower, or pinning him to the wall in a hallway. She didn't seem to worry that the servants might gossip, but then, whom would they tell? The King was dead, her stepdaughter the Princess not yet ten years old, and there were no Princes or Kings in neighboring kingdoms of age to court the Queen. She was free to do as she wished, and she did.

When the Huntsman had cleaned the sweat and blood from his skin and clothing, he went to tend to his wolves. They were sprawled in the courtyard, white lumps of fur on the hard-packed dirt. The Princess sat in the middle of them, a wolf's head in her lap as she stroked the wolf's fur.

"She's hurt," the Princess said.

The Huntsman crouched next to the Princess and ran a hand along the wolf's side. "She was kicked by the deer," he said. "A cracked rib, I think."

The Princess imitated his movement, her small hand feeling for the rib. "She'll be better soon," she said.

"Ribs take some time healing," the Huntsman said. "A few weeks, at least."

The Princess shook her head. "She's fine now."

Humoring her, the Huntsman checked the rib again. It had mended, and the wolf got her feet under her, standing without a hint of pain. The Huntsman stared at the Princess. She had always loved animals, but this was new. He knew better than to ask her about it; the Princess was like a deer herself, beautiful and fragile and easily spooked. It was no wonder, with both her parents dead, no one in the castle her age to play with, and a beauty that was growing to challenge her stepmother's, a woman who did not take challenge lightly.

Instead, the Huntsman stroked the Princess' raven hair and went to check the rest of the wolves.

"Tell me again why you hunt with wolves," the Princess said, following him. "The last Huntsman used dogs."

"Because," the Huntsman said, crouching to pet one of them, "wolves are smart and independent. They stay with me because I raised them and trained them, but they do not depend on me. A dog, when faced with a problem, will come find me to solve it. A wolf will find a way to solve it herself."

"How did you get them?" the Princess asked.

It was a story she had heard many times, one in which she herself had played a major role, but she never tired of stories, and she hardly remembered the incident, having been very young at the time. The Huntsman suspected that she was lonely, like the Queen, but without the outlet the Queen had. She did have more prospects for the future, though; there were several Princes nearby between the ages of ten and fourteen who could seek the Princess' hand when she got older. With her jet-black hair, milk-white skin that the sun never darkened, deep green eyes, and full, red lips, she would have no lack of suitors when she came of age.

"When you were only four years old," the Huntsman said, "you wandered into the woods. Your father was quite worried, and sent his Huntsman to find you. I went along to help, and found you in a clearing, surrounded by wolf cubs. You had no idea of the danger you were in, and refused to come home without them."

"I am in no danger in the woods," the Princess said softly, scratching a wolf behind her ears.

"Let us hope we never again have to test that statement," the Huntsman said. "At your insistence, I brought the cubs home and trained them. After your father died and his Huntsman retired, the Queen passed the title to me."

"Because you're the best huntsman in the kingdom," the Princess said proudly.

"Partly thanks to you, Your Highness," the Huntsman replied. "Now, if I'm not mistaken, it is time for your lessons."

The Princess went back into the castle without a protest, though the Huntsman knew she would much rather be playing with the wolves, or the birds she could coax to her hand, or the stable cats, or any other animal she could find. But her disposition was too sweet to allow her to complain about her lessons, and she bore them with good humor.

Movement at a window caught the Huntsman's eye, and he saw the Queen looking down into the courtyard. Not at him, but at the Princess. And her look was anything but friendly. Perhaps she didn't like the Princess spending so much time outdoors, the Huntsman mused. Perhaps he should send her inside earlier. But she loved the wolves so much, and they her, that it felt cruel to deprive them of each other's presence.

Deciding to put it out of his mind unless the Queen said something to him about it, the Huntsman went back to his wolves.

***

But, the Queen never did mention it, and as the years passed, the Princess grew more beautiful. By the time she was twelve, she had several suitors. When she was fifteen, the Queen received eight requests for the Princess' hand in marriage. The Queen sought the Huntsman out more and more often, though she enjoyed his company less, it seemed. Rather than taking her pleasure in him, she paced and ranted, her hair swirling around her like a cape when she turned. The Huntsman wasn't sure what her rants were about; he could never seem to remember what she had said after she left the room. The lapse occasionally bothered him, but he put it from his mind. Perhaps the Queen was upset because the Princess had suitors while the Queen had no chance to remarry. The King had died only a year after they had married, after all. Having no wife of his own, the Huntsman knew how lonely it could be. He allowed the Queen her space; let her continue to set the tone and direction of their relationship, if it could be called such.

On the Princess' sixteenth birthday, the Queen called the Huntsman to her bower. She was naked, standing before her mirror, her eyes flashing with anger.

"Do you find me beautiful?" she asked.

"Of course, Your Majesty," the Huntsman said.

"More beautiful than the Princess?"

The Huntsman hesitated. He rarely thought of the Princess' physical charms; she was like a daughter or niece to him. But when he compared her slender form, the contrast between ebony hair, white skin, red lips, and emerald green eyes, he realized that she was, indeed, beautiful. Easily comparable to the Queen. Thinking of the Princess in this way made him quite uncomfortable, and he filled his eyes with the Queen's beauty in order to stop such thoughts.

"Of course not," he said.

The Queen frowned. "Then explain this." She stared deeply into the mirror. "Mirror, mirror, on the wall," she intoned, "who is the fairest of them all?"

A white face swam up out of the reflection and spoke. "My lady's form is fair, it's true," the face said. "But the Princess is fairer, far, than you."

The Huntsman stared in horror at the mirror. Rumor had long held that the Queen was a sorceress, that she had enchanted the King and then had him killed, that she intended to use the Princess for some nefarious purpose. The Huntsman had believed none of the rumors—until now.

The Queen whirled to face the Huntsman, her fists clenched at her sides. He prayed his fear did not show in his face. "Is she more beautiful than I?" she demanded.

"Not to my eyes, Your Majesty," the Huntsman replied.

"That answer may well have saved your life," the Queen said with a feral growl. The Huntsman took an involuntary step back. "Now. Take the Princess into the woods and kill her. Bring me her heart to prove that you have done this deed."

The Huntsman stared at the Queen, unable to believe his ears. When she showed no sign of changing her mind, he bowed. "It shall be done," he said.

As he searched the castle for the Princess, his fear of the

Queen warred against his love of the Princess. He had no desire to choose between them, and his mind raced, seeking a way to make no choice at all.

He found the Princess in her dayroom, perched on the windowsill, patiently picking out misplaced embroidery stitches. The sun pouring through the window made her skin glow, and the blackness of her hair deepen. She looked up at his approach, surprised to see him, but not alarmed.

"Come with me, Princess," he said. "There is something in the woods you must see."

She followed him trustingly, pausing only to change her shoes and toss a cloak over her shoulders. He whistled for the wolves as he left the castle, and together they went into the woods.

"It's beginning to rain," the Princess observed. "What is it you need me to see?"

"Just a little farther, Your Highness," the Huntsman replied.

The trees were dense, keeping underbrush low, and the wolves ranged out to either side of the Huntsman and the Princess. As they traveled, the trees drew closer together, their trunks darkening from dampness, their branches seeming to reach for the pair. The Princess stumbled on roots several times, and the Huntsman had trouble keeping his feet as well, though he suspected it was more from guilt than the ground.

When the Huntsman judged they were far enough from the castle, he stopped, grabbing the Princess' arm and pushing her up against a tree.

"What are you doing?" she asked, still unafraid, trusting him.

"Your stepmother has ordered your death," he said. "I'm sorry."

She stared at him in disbelief, and then fell to the ground at his feet. "Please," she begged. "Don't kill me. I've done nothing!"

"I am the Queen's Huntsman," he said, tears streaming down his face. "I must do what she requires of me."

Gritting his teeth, he drew his knife from his belt and would have plunged it into her breast, but a wolf grabbed his hand between her teeth. She didn't break his skin, but he dropped the knife in surprise. The wolves had never turned tooth or claw on him before. Another wolf imposed her body between him and the Princess. The rest circled him and growled.

The Huntsman clutched his bitten hand to his chest and considered the wolves for a long moment. They were truly *her* creatures, not his. He had forgotten her affinity for wildlife, and that the wolves were his only to be near the Princess. The Huntsman frowned, but knew he could not obey the Queen, whatever the consequences may be.

"Your life has been spared, not by my will, but by the wolves'," he said. "Run, now, Princess. And may fortune smile on you."

The Princess scrambled to her feet and ran, disappearing into the woods as the skies opened and rain poured down.

"We need a faun," the Huntsman told the wolves. "One with a heart of a similar size to the Princess'."

The hunt was swift and fruitful, and the Huntsman returned to the Queen with the faun's heart. He did not wait to see what she did with it.

***

The castle was darker without the Princess. Fewer birds graced the gardens with their songs. The stable cats grew suspicious and feral, and the Huntsman's wolves left him, disappearing back into the forest. The Huntsman continued to try to do his duty, but his heart was no longer in it. He lived in fear that the Queen might discover his lie, and he missed his wolves. After his tenth unsuccessful hunt without them, the

Huntsman went to the Queen.

"I must resign as your Huntsman," he said. "I can no longer do my duty without my wolves."

"Can you not train hounds to do the same job?" the Queen asked. She sat in front of the magic mirror, brushing out her long hair.

"I could, your Majesty, but there are other huntsmen who already have trained hounds. It will take me too long to obtain and train my own. If you desire fresh meat, one of them would better serve you."

"Very well. You are dismissed," the Queen said, and turned away from him.

The Huntsman retired to a small cabin deep in the woods, where he spent his days learning the finer points of trapping. He had not realized how oppressive the castle had become without the Princess until now when he was again surrounded by nature. Away from the Queen's influence, he grew to understand how evil she really was. He still feared that she might discover his lie and seek vengeance, but the fear faded the longer he was away from her.

His trapping went well, but he still missed running with his wolves. Occasionally, he spotted a white flash of fur far out in the woods, but when he reached the place, there was nothing but a few paw prints.

One day, while expanding his trap-line, the Huntsman found another small cabin near the foot of a mountain. To his surprise, the Princess sat on a stump outside, surrounded by birds and small animals. She appeared to be telling them a story. His heart glad to find her safe and sound, the Huntsman left before she could see him. He stopped by every few days and saw that she was living with several little men, dwarves, who mined the nearby mountain. They doted on her, and the Huntsman was sure of her safety. But, he continued to watch over her.

Not long after he found the Princess, the wolves began to

join him on his trap runs and bring him larger game. Grateful for their help, he made sure to save the remains of the small animals he trapped for them, even though they didn't need him to feed them anymore.

He lived so for nearly a year, until his routine observation of the Princess went horribly wrong.

The dwarves were wailing, and animals filled the small clearing around the cabin, all mourning in their own way. In the middle of this sad gathering was a glass coffin, studded with the gems the dwarves had mined, and inside lay the Princess.

Even in death, she was beautiful, her hair spread over the white satin pillow, her small hands folded over her stomach, her skin even paler and her lips redder. Quite forgetting himself, the Huntsman emerged from the woods and approached the coffin.

The dwarves stopped him with their pickaxes, their looks fierce. "Who are you?" one demanded.

"I was the Queen's Huntsman," he said. "I knew the Princess."

"She told us about you. You tried to kill her," the dwarf said.

"Yes, to my shame," the Huntsman replied. "I retired as Huntsman soon after."

The dwarves looked at each other, but didn't move out of his way.

"I have been watching you for nearly a year," the Huntsman said. "If I wished to kill her, I could have done so a hundred times over."

The dwarves accepted this grudgingly and allowed the Huntsman to approach the coffin. He knelt beside it, hands folded. "What happened?" he asked.

"The Queen," the dwarf said. "She is also a witch. She disguised herself and brought the Princess a girdle to crush the life out of her. We found her in time and removed it. But she came back with a poison comb. We found her then, too, and nursed her back to health. But this time, the Queen has poisoned her with an apple, and we cannot save her."

The Huntsman lowered his head. "The Queen has succeeded, then," he said. "The Princess is dead."

"If she comes back and finds you here, she will kill you, too," the dwarf said.

"I do not care," the Huntsman said. "I will stay and guard her in death as I ought to have guarded her better in life."

The dwarves went back to work, and the Huntsman stayed. For three days and three nights, he ate nothing, drinking only water, and watched over the coffin. On the fourth day, he heard a merry hunting horn from within the forest and waited, for the game trail would lead the hunting party to the cottage.

In a few minutes, the party emerged from the forest and quieted, struck dumb by the sight of the Huntsman and the coffin. The bloodhounds circled the coffin and set up such a mournful, howling racket it brought the dwarves back out of their mountain.

The leader of the hunting party, a Prince by his garb, dismounted and approached the coffin, blind to all else.

"What beauty," he whispered. "I have never seen one fairer."

"She is the Princess of this Kingdom," the Huntsman said. "Murdered by her stepmother."

"She deserves a Queen's burial," the Prince said. "I would take her to my Kingdom and place her in my chapel."

The Huntsman looked to the dwarves, who conferred among themselves, then nodded. "Take her and treat her well," the leader said.

The Prince beckoned to the servants riding with him, and they picked up the coffin, lifting it to the travois they'd brought to haul game. But, the gems made it heavier than the servants had expected, and one dropped his corner. The coffin struck a rock, the glass shattered, and the Princess tumbled out. As she landed, a piece of apple flew from her throat. She took a deep breath and opened her eyes.

"Your Highness!" the Huntsman exclaimed, kneeling beside her.

The Princess smiled up at him, and he felt her love and forgiveness. "You've been watching over me," she said. He nodded. "Thank you."

"My lady," the Prince said, extending his hand to help her up. When their eyes met, there was no question of their mutual admiration. The Huntsman stepped back and allowed the Princess to mount the Prince's horse.

"Please, good Huntsman, come with us," the Prince said. "I have need of a Huntsman in my Kingdom."

The Huntsman readily agreed. After all, the Queen would undoubtedly find out that the Princess was alive again and make another attempt on her life. He had failed her twice already; it would not happen again. His resolve was firm. The Queen would never again have the chance to harm the Princess, not while the Huntsman drew breath.

He declined when a horse was offered, preferring to run. As he followed the Prince's entourage, his wolves poured out of the woods, following him all the way to the new Kingdom.

***

The wedding was arranged in record time, and the Huntsman and his wolves brought in all the meat needed for the wedding feast. Whenever the Huntsman caught a glimpse of the Princess, she glowed with happiness, as did her Prince.

The Huntsman was not as sure as everyone else that the evil Queen was no longer a threat. He kept a close watch on the roads to the castle and had his wolves do the same. Each passing day only added to his worry and tension, for he became sure that the Queen would threaten the Princess at her wedding. He no longer feared for his own safety, only that of the Princess.

On the day of the wedding, the Huntsman waited near the drawbridge, watching for the Queen's carriage. Sure enough, it clattered across the drawbridge between two other rich carriages. The Huntsman saw the Queen within it, her crown securely on her blonde head. As she passed, she turned her head and her eyes met the Huntsman's for a moment. A shiver ran down the Huntsman's spine at the hate in her gaze.

The Huntsman hoped that the Queen would not interrupt the ceremony, but he stood watchfully in the back of the chapel anyway. As soon as the Princess appeared in the chapel door and the Queen recognized her, she rose with a shriek and drew a dagger from her sash. She ran at the Princess, dagger upraised. The Huntsman grabbed her wrist and pulled the Queen's struggling body close to him, holding her securely though she kicked and thrashed in his grip.

"Unhand me, Huntsman!" the Queen shrieked. "You will release me!"

"No, Your Majesty," the Huntsman replied. "I am no longer your creature."

The Queen screamed louder and attempted to turn the dagger on him, but the Huntsman held tighter and did not allow her to escape. Then the Prince's guards converged on the Queen and took her out of the chapel.

"Are you well?" the Huntsman asked the Princess. She looked shocked, tears standing in her eyes, but nodded. He watched proudly as she overcame her fear and joined her Prince at the altar, where they were married.

At the conclusion of the wedding, the Prince handed the Princess to the Huntsman so the Prince and the King could discuss the Queen's fate. The Huntsman never learned what that fate was, for the Prince kept it from the Princess as not to upset her. All he knew was that the Queen never bothered them again. When the Princess became a Queen herself, she appointed him as her Huntsman. And the Queen's Huntsman watched over her while she and her King lived happily ever after.

Author Bio:

Shiloh Carroll is a PhD student at Middle Tennessee State University, studying the ways in which medieval literature and history have influenced modern popular literature such as fantasy. Her work has also appeared in Trail of Indiscretion and Sorcerous Signals.

Red of the Riding Hood
Tony Peak

Iaise my head from the earth and sniff the pre-dawn breeze. Something wafts through the forest air, taunting me. Something that hasn't entered my home for many years. The hackles rise on the back of my neck and I growl low in my throat. I lick saliva from my lips as I try to contain myself. It's her. After all this time, after all she has done, it's her. Once, when the leaves were still green, I remember her hooded riding cloak was white as snow. So white it blinded those who thought her pure. Now it is stained red, steeped in the blood of my brethren. That is the tint of the garment worn by Red of the Riding Hood.

I lift myself from my haunches and lope past trees covered in ragged bark. Past bushes pricking and tearing at my body. Past memories of the sublime girl I once loved. I go to her, my paws leaving monstrous prints in the earth. Playing the fool, I ate the fruit Red of the Riding Hood brought in her basket. I was still a man then, young and strong. I believed, as all young fools do, that she loved me as well. I recall her succulence; the forbidden flavor of her fertility. I created the first stain on her cloak, drawn from our passion on the forest floor. I still smell our coupling on the breeze as I rush to meet her.

My ears flatten against my head and I howl a challenge. I pant and paw, listening to it echo from tree to tree, cavern to water brook. I know she hears me. No one else is left. It took many victims to dye her cloak the cruel burgundy it is now. I swear I will avenge the rest and myself. I will sink my fangs into her neck. I will taste fruit truly forbidden.

Dead leaves fly into my face as I pursue her scent. My paws claw into the dirt and fling it behind me like my lost memories. It won't be long before I lose them all and devolve into the beast she has made me. With each step, I remember how she came into the forest with sweet fruits and radiant beauty. I was a simple hunter, caring for my aged grandmother in an old woodcutter's cabin. When Red of the Riding Hood arrived, all hunters and trappers vied for her hand. All lusted for her soft skin, her divine smile. None of us pondered why she had come to the forest. None of us refused the fruit from her basket, or her loins.

One by one, we all fell ill. One by one we all transformed into horrific wolf-men, similar to those told in legends around children's campfires. The werewolf, the lycanthrope, the shape shifter—all silly tales, and all true save for the last. Yes, we did hunger for flesh, and yes, the moon was our monthly mistress. The shining disc became as Red of the Riding Hood herself; beautiful, unapproachable, unattainable. Both had control over us. Yet unlike the werewolves of myth, we couldn't change back into men. I cannot tell you how terrible that is. Never again to hold a tool, to wear clothes, or to eat from a bowl. Now my claws are my tools, my fur my clothing, a fresh corpse my bowl.

I bound through the forest, keen to scent her out. She is so close. Spittle and froth fly from the corners of my mouth as I run. I will make her pay. Being a savage beast is just part of the curse she placed on us. The hunger for flesh—human flesh—is what destroyed the sanity of my brethren. It has nearly taken mine, since I lost control and devoured my poor grandmother. Hot, stinging tears fill my eyes as I hurry to see her. I don't blink them away. More kindling—feeding my fiery hatred.

When Red of the Riding Hood returned after our change, she sat astride a steed bred for carnage. A long, sharp, silver blade rested in her grasp. Her first victims were caught unaware, hoping to inquire of her what curse had befallen them. Fools! She earned her name by riding them down under iron-shod heels, or slaughtering them with silver-laden steel. Red of the Riding Hood searched the woods, the caves, the streams. Afterwards, the green, vibrant leaves were stained dark scarlet. Many of my brethren fell—yet many remained. Only later did we realize we were naught but sport for her. Now I race through a dead forest to greet her with claw and fang. She is my sport now.

My ears prick up and I halt, sniffing the breeze again. She's so close she can see me, no doubt. Oh, how sweet her flesh shall taste! How warm her marrow, how juicy her heart! I stand on my hind legs and howl again, mouth open wide with fangs challenging the sky itself. The muscles in my body flex and convulse with eagerness. The priest that lived in the forest once said vengeance was the prerogative of his god, and no one else. Now I know why. Who would want to share something that tastes so sweet? Such ambrosia must be guarded. It must be savored.

Something answers my howl. In the distance, I discern a cry, tingling the hairs lining my ears. A reply to my challenge? She has every reason to be confident. Her sword has slain all wolves in the forest but me. I am the last creature skulking in the nightmares of children; I am the final monster lurking in the forgotten fears of humanity. She knows this, and still comes. I admire her bravery. We were young when this started. The years pass too swiftly for the wolf; every day for the canine is but an hour for the human.

I trot through rotten leaves, tongue lolling from my mouth. Saliva wets the ground in vengeful rain. I slow myself and prepare for the kill. She's on the road; I can hear the horse's hooves. I feel the animal's movements vibrate within the earth. Smell its labored breath. The forest aids me; it is my ally. For years it has hidden me from Red of the Riding Hood. It will not hide her from me.

Through a thicket, I see a flash of scarlet, the wispy white of her mount's tail. Why does she hurry? She has never shied from confrontation before. But, she should flee. Mercy is not within reach of my claws. The thrill of the hunt fuels my legs and I spring after her. The world blurs; never have I moved so fast. Around a bend in the road I turn. Over a fallen tree, I lunge. Out of a bush I burst. She is before me, her bloodstained, hooded cloak billowing like draperies on a window framing the Underworld.

I inch closer and closer. My fangs nip at the horse's flanks, and I taste the barest trickle of blood. The flavor drives me on, running parallel with her steed. I start panting drool as the beast takes over. I revel in it. Why not? She did this to me. She created the monster that I am. Am I responsible for her wickedness? Am I to be held accountable for the travelers I've eaten, for my grandmother's death? Another bite at her mount's underbelly is my answer.

The horse neighs in pain and fright. Oh, such a beautiful song in my ears. Sing for me, you ignorant slave, you ignoble traitor! You who dares bear my foe into my kingdom! As fellow beast, you should aid me. Yet you are in her thrall as I once was. I'll gorge on you after I've finished with her.

Red of the Riding Hood swings her blade down, slicing a burning nick into my back. In doing so she has released the reins of the horse; her other hand clutches something close to her breast. Is it a trophy? A keepsake? I've never known her for the sentimental type. I snarl at her, and finally she deigns to look at me. Oh, such a beauteous face. She hasn't aged a day. The locks of her silken hair are still a burnished red, even after all these years. Yet how many actually passed? She may not have aged at all, the way she appears now. No matter. It is time to end this.

Using my unnatural girth, I ram my shoulder into the horse's legs. The bones in my right forelimb crack and I almost bite off my tongue at the pain. The steed buckles and careens into the road head first, tossing Red of the Riding Hood a dozen paces onto the path ahead. The scarlet folds of her cape settle onto her still form. Rose petals cast down at the feet of a king. I am the king of the forest now. I can partake of my vengeance at long last.

Her scent invades my nostrils, forcing a gush of saliva and horse's blood from my mouth. I take my time and walk slow, though the agony in my right shoulder makes me limp. That is not enough to stop me; it'll heal before the dawn. My victory is near. What could deny me the ritual I have waited countless days to enact? I recall an old proverb my frail grandmother once said: 'every dog has its day'. Shrouded in shadow and anointed in blood, every wolf has its night.

I pad closer, smelling her cloak, her pale skin, her mane of copper hair. I smell my own blood on the edge of her sword, and growl when I see she still grasps it. I bark, spitting out white foam—Red of the Riding Hood still lives. A crimson phantom, she stirs, grunting in pain. A fever dream from my past to haunt me. With trembling limbs and blood-flecked lips, she stands. I let her. Even I would see her die on her feet.

I expect antipathy in her eyes, but instead I spy grief. Deep, heart-rent sadness stirs emotions deep within my being. In her right hand, Red of the Riding Hood holds her blade. In her left, swaddled in the folds of her cloak, is an infant. She tried to shield it with her body during the fall from her horse, but I pick up a scent of blood from it. My ears flatten as the beast in me stands aside for the man I once was. I have never preyed on the young before as none ever enters my forest. What have I done?

I attempt a bark but it escapes my jaws as a whimper. My tail droops between my legs though I try resisting. How can I show weakness now? Not in my triumph! What kind of a wolf am I that I balk at devouring the progeny of humanity? Victory sours in my mouth, rots in my gullet.

Red of the Riding Hood sees the calm come over me, but she doesn't lower the sword. She's waiting. I growl with suspicion. How many of my brethren has she lured into the endless night with such tactics? I shake leaves, dirt, and blood from my fur and stand on my hind legs. I keep sniffing, trying to understand what that scent is. A human child, yes—but not. My human eyes, trapped in a wolf's body, meet hers. She gives me a slight nod of her head. The infant's smell is unmistakable. It is a wolf-child; its wounds from the fall are already healing, as only silver can slay our kind. It is mine. I inhale with vigor as I realize the infant is a girl. My daughter. Cold shame douses the flames in my bestial heart.

Tears come to my eyes, though whether I have offspring or because it has only been a year since the wolf took me, I cannot tell. My old persona takes hold in a way it hasn't been able to for a long while. An alter ego that walked on two legs instead of four; a creature that slept while the moon whispered instead of when the sun sang. A child of the day, not the night. Old memories flood my consciousness. I remember how I arrived in the forest to hide from men. I recall infecting the other hunters and trappers with my lycanthropy. I recall the old woman was Red of the Riding Hood's grandmother, not mine. I remember ravaging the young beauty instead of making love to her. The babe in her arms is the fruit of that first crimson stain.

Only under my daughter's innocent gaze do I understand. The beast fooled me, lied to me, made me believe I was the victim. Humanity's first companion, tamed from the wild, betrayed by my own delusions. Oh, how we all think we are all martyrs, bathed in hate and vice! Yet it is my own hate and the blood of others I drown in, not my own.

Staring into Red of the Riding Hood's eyes, I wonder if there is still a chance. Redemption, in the final moment. I love her, though the beast burns my feelings into cinders of evil. Perhaps I can control it this time. She could remain here and we would be a family! I would instruct my daughter how to hunt, how to...

No. I will not see her gnawing bodies, nor watch her wipe blood from fanged jaws. All I can offer her is crimson puddles in a dead forest or lonely hunts beneath an audience of cold stars. She might have a chance with her mother. Learn to accept the gifts that are given instead of ripping them away in deepest midnight.

I lower myself to the forest road while I still can. I know not when the beast will take hold of my will again, so I make haste. The sun's first rays are creeping through the branches. All this time, the woman I once raped has undone the horrors I loosed into the world, her riding cloak an emblem of her noble cause. Now she has the burden and joy of my child; who may, if reared in the ways of men and not in the forest, grow to resist the beast threatening to overtake us all in the small hours of the night.

I lower my head, though I keep my gaze on the infant. Red of the Riding Hood raises her sword. Yes, it is for the best now. My daughter should never know of me. Her mother cannot allow me to live, to terrorize our child. With the eyes of a man, not a beast, I gaze for one last time at my child, before the blade drops in a final arc of justice and mercy. My daughter of the moon. My Little Red Riding Hood.

Author Bio:
Tony Peak lives in rural southwest Virginia with a wonderful view of New River. His work has appeared in numerous speculative publications and anthologies. When not putting madness to words, he hikes mountain trails, researches Late Bronze Age underwear, or searches for spooks behind reality's grassy knoll. Tony often relaxes with a mug of black tea and a smiling gargoyle that gets naughty with other statues in the house. Check out his website before it's outlawed by the Cabal: http://tonypeak. weebly.com

Pru and the Gunslinger
L.M. Magalas

The godforsaken piece of land known as Kingfisher's Drift was named for the hard case that died there. Billy King, known as Kingfisher, was born and raised in the small town when he was a boy, and so it seemed fitting that he meet his end there. He was hung for his crimes, which included multiple counts of robbery and murder, and became the first resident of Kingfisher cemetery.

Pru knew the cemetery very well from her regular visits there to talk to her mother, and knew the story from her father. He had been one of the young men in the crowd at the hanging and enjoyed telling the story to his wife and child, embellishing in the details. He hadn't told it since he last buried his wife. He hadn't really been the same since.

Pru had come to put fresh flowers on her mother's grave and to catch her up on the news of the small town. She told her how Eli, at the saloon, had gotten over a terrible bout of rheumatism and came back to work to find that the till had been liberated of nearly half a week's earnings. How Sheriff Johnson had been keeping an eye on Madame Porter's house because of a rumor that a wanted man had shown up in town. She always finished by saying how much her and Pa missed her and how they hoped she was happy.

There were plenty of people in the cemetery now. Pru read the tombstones as she passed, and stopped as she always did at the one of a mother and her little girl, around the same time that Pru's mother had died. Pru always felt sorry for them, the little girl especially. The headstone said she died at five. How much living could she have done in such a short span of time?

Pru followed the sun back to her house. As she drew

closer, she stopped. The front door was wide open. Something was wrong. Fearing the worst, she ran inside.

"Pa?" shouted Pru, scanning the room. Chairs had been tipped over and everything from the mantle was on the floor. "Pa?"

There was a bang towards the rear of the house that made Pru stop. Realizing it was the back door, Pru turned and ran. She found her father on the floor, a huddled mass shaking in the light of the setting sun. Panicked, she rolled him over. He sat up with a grimace.

"They took it. They took Maddie's jewellery box. I tried to stop them," he said, fighting to get up, trying to lean on his pistol for balance.

Pru's heart clenched at the thought of her mother's jewelry in someone else's hands. She felt as though she may cry when she suddenly heard voices outside. They were still nearby. Pru's fists clenched. Grabbing her father's pistol, she ran out.

One was already a fair distance away, moving quickly on horseback. The other had just begun to canter when he spotted Pru. A wide and toothless smile broke across his greasy face as he tipped his hat.

"Thanks for the merchandise, little lady," he said. Pru lifted the gun and pointed it at the man.

"Give it back," she said, trembling so much that the gun was shaking. The man's smile didn't change. He began to ride off. All Pru could see was her mother's jewelry box under his arm.

The gun was cold and alien in her hands. Taking a breath, Pru stood the way her father did when he shot cans off of the fence posts. She gripped the gun with both hands and aimed for the man's back. A knot formed in her stomach. He was getting farther and farther away.

Pru took a deep breath, closed her eyes, and squeezed the trigger.

Sheriff Johnson watched Pru carefully from across the table, his brow furrowed in concentration but his fingers drumming the table thoughtfully. The jewelry box of Pru's late mother sat between them.

"Now I know you've explained the situation to me once, but I'd be much obliged if you'd tell me once more, just so's I get it right."

Folding her hands under the table to stop them from shaking, Pru told the sheriff everything that had passed, from coming home and finding her father hurt and the box gone, to the thieves riding away. When she stopped, the sheriff took over.

"So you took your pa's Peacemaker and you shot him."

"Yes, Sir."

"And you shot him from the back porch."

"Yes, Sir," she said. The sheriff sat back in the chair. Pru knew what he was thinking. It was a long way from the porch to where the robber was found. Pru's father took over.

"I'm telling you Sheriff, I'm lucky she come home when she did," he said, "And when she found out they'd taken her mother's jewelry, well she just grabbed my pistol and fired after him. She's a natural shot, that's for sure. Probably could have hit the other one too, 'cept she was worried about how I was doing. No other woman in damn near fifty miles can shoot like her."

Pru stopped, frozen by the words coming out of her father's mouth. She had hardly handled a gun before today, much less fired it. Her father had tried to teach her to shoot, but she'd been so sweet on the critters in her sights that he'd given up. Now here he was telling the sheriff that his daughter was a perfect shot. Pru knew what it was, fatherly pride. She knew he was so relieved and excited about her lucky shot that the words were just tumbling out of his mouth like leaves down a creek, no matter what words they were.

Unfortunately, for Pru, the sheriff appeared to believe him. With a smile, he turned back to her.

"Is that true?"

Not wanting to make a liar out of her father and wanting to seem humble about a skill she didn't have, she gave the sheriff a small smile and nod. Pleased, the sheriff crossed his arms.

"Well in that case, you might be able to help me with something."

***

No matter how many times her father tried to apologize to her, Pru was stuck. As they walked into town, all Pru could think about was what the sheriff had asked her to do. It was terrible. It was unthinkable. Most importantly, for Pru, it was impossible.

They had just reached the general store when Marston Johnson, the sheriff's son, came out. He greeted them both warmly. He looked carefully at Pru, and she knew immediately that he knew all about what she had done.

"How are you feeling?" he asked.

Pru ignored the knots in her stomach, now given to her from two generations of Johnson men, and nodded. "I'm fine, really. We both are," she said in an effort to include her father. Marston didn't notice. He only looked at her.

"Well, if there's anything I can do," he said, "You just let me know." He paused before adding, "You know, it's really something. We've known each other for years and I had no idea what a great shot you are. I think there's something really fetching about a girl who knows how to take care of herself."

Pru dropped her head. When she lifted it, Marston was shaking her father's hand and saying goodbye, hightailing it down the boardwalk, embarrassed.

Within minutes of entering the general store, Pru was approached and crowded by almost everyone in it. They all wanted to know if it was true. Had she really shot that man from such a far distance? She was good with a gun? Were the rumors true about what she was going to do next? Pru's father did his best to yield most of the answers, but the questions still piled onto Pru until she felt she might suffocate. Excusing herself as best she could with a smile, she went outside to wait for her father.

The makeshift alley between the buildings was quiet and shaded, and for the first time since the ordeal started, she felt alone. She sat down and began to cry, quietly at first. Her gentle tears became louder sobs. She dropped her head into her lap, trying to muffle them as best as she could. When she had nothing left, she rested her head against the wall, wiping her eyes.

"You just about finished?"

Pru stilled at the deep voice. Turning slowly, she looked down the alley and noticed a shadow tucked up against a few boxes. The shadow shifted, and in the dim light of the alley, Pru could now see a face under the brim of a hat. She immediately began straightening herself, wiping her face.

"I'm sorry! I didn't see you there."

A smile followed the curve of the hat. "That's usually the idea." There was a pause before he said, "What's your name, honey?"

Pru bit her bottom lip. "Prudence," she said, "but everyone calls me Pru."

"Prudence, huh? Not really fitting, considering how you were carrying on just now." His voice was rough and deep, but not hard. "Now I ain't the most sensitive of men, but it seems to me that when a woman caterwauls something fierce like you, it means she's got a problem. And I wouldn't be doin' my mama proud if I didn't at least ask what your trouble might be."

Pru was torn. It wasn't right to be alone and talking to strangers in back alleys, especially if the stranger was a shadow of a man. Maybe it was because she was scared, or because he was a stranger, but it wasn't long before she told him the whole story of what had happened the day before.

"And now the sheriff wants me to do it again," she said, fighting to breathe, "There's a man at Madame Porter's. He's some big criminal out of Dodge or something. Anyway, he's mighty careful, won't come out of the house. The sheriff wants me to go on in there and kill him. Says that the fella may be a crook, but he's not wont to shoot a lady, much less have time to pull his gun."

"This criminal got a name?"

Pru nodded. "Rance Jordan."

The brim of the hat bobbed. "I crossed his path once before. But just 'cause he ain't likely to shoot you don't mean he won't use them fists of his."

Pru's heart sank a little deeper into the pit of her stomach. Tears came to her eyes and she sniffed.

"From the sounds of it, I'd say you're thinking of watering up your face again. I'd consider it a kindness if you didn't."

Pru swallowed and took a breath, fighting the tears. "I'm sorry. It's just...how can I take the life of a man who hasn't done me or mine any harm? The other man...well, I warned him. He'd taken something of mine and I wanted it back. I didn't want to shoot him. And now everyone thinks...I just don't know what to do." Her shoulders slumped and she dropped her head into her hands.

"I might have a proposition for you."

The nearness of his voice made Pru lift her head. He was still in shadow but was closer, just out of the light. She blinked at him.

"What kind of proposition?"

"A trade. I help you get rid of Jordan, you do something for me."

Pru tensed. "I won't go doing anything that would make my mama ashamed of me."

"Your necklace," he said, "You give me that, and I'll help you take care of Jordan."

Pru fingered the necklace. It was a small silver leaf on a chain, that her mother had given to her before she died. Her instinct was to say no, but fighting to save her mother's jewelry was one of the reasons she was in this mess. Her grip loosened and she unclasped it, holding it in her hand.

"How do I know that you'll keep your word?"

"I always keep my word."

Pru frowned, a thought crossing her mind. "What makes you so sure that you can help me with this anyway?"

For a moment, there was silence. Slowly the shadowed figure began to move forward. Two bright blue eyes and a face worn with time emerged from under the brim of the hat. The two Colt Peacemakers and bullets lining his gun belt caught the light as he pulled open his long and dusty coat.

"Just a feeling I get," he said with a smile.

***

The plan was simple. An alley ran along one side of Madame Porter's. Pru would lure Rance Jordan into one of the rooms that had a window overlooking that alley. Pru would complain about the heat or air and ask Jordan to open the window. When he did, the stranger would be ready to shoot him from his hiding place in the alley. Jordan would be taken care of, Pru wouldn't feel guilty, and the stranger would get his reward.

As she led Jordan up the stairs, Pru felt subconsciously at her bare neck, her muscles tensing beneath her fingers. What if the stranger didn't hold up his end of the deal? Why hadn't she waited until after it was done before giving him the necklace? She thought of the stranger's blank stare, how casually he took the necklace and put it in his pocket. He seemed so cold. What if he didn't show?

Pru felt at the small pistol in her pocket as that last thought crossed her mind. What if she was left alone with the man? Would she be prepared to do the job herself?

The sound of a door closing brought her back. She turned to look at Jordan, who was doing nothing to hide his gaze running up and down the length of her. "Well now," he said, "I must say that while I don't much care for the mousy type, you're just as pretty as some of them other girls in here. And now that we've got this here room to ourselves, it'd be a shame to not use it."

Pru clutched at the pistol through the folds of her dress as Jordan stepped towards her. Between the dryness in her mouth and the racing of her heart, she managed to find her voice.

"You're right, of course," she said, thinking of how Madame Porter spoke to her customers, gentle and airy, "But I was hoping...I was hoping you might do me a favor first."

A smile crossed his lips. "Anything for you, honey," he said, "So long as you do one for me after."

Pru forced a smile as she pointed to the window. "Would you mind opening that for me? I find it awful stuffy in here."

"Not at all," said Jordan, "So long as you don't mind everyone hearing us. Because they will, honey."

Pru clutched the pistol harder as Jordan headed to the window. He opened it. Pru waited for a shot. Nothing. Jordan took a deep breath of fresh air. Still nothing. Jordan even went so far as to lean out the window before pulling himself back in.

Pru's hands were gripping the pistol so hard it was a miracle it hadn't gone off yet. Jordan turned around to face her. Pru prepared herself.

A shot rang out.

Jordan collapsed in pieces. First, his hands dangled limply at his sides. Then he dropped to his knees, his eyes sending up a silent prayer as they rolled back into his head. Then he fell to the floor.

Releasing the gun, Pru ran to the window just in time to see the billow of a coat round the corner at the end of the alley. The weight lifted from her chest and she smiled. When Madame Porter and the others came running into the room, Pru's face still had that look of relief, as though oblivious to the man lying dead at her feet.

***

Pru's relief was short-lived. Anyone with a tongue was using it to talk about what happened to Rance Jordan and the person responsible. Some were critical and others were kind. But, everyone from town and country was in agreement that the world, no matter how Rance Jordan left it, was a better place without him.

Which is why the sheriff, seeing the success that Pru had in dealing with Jordan, asked her to do it again.

His name was Cliff Tucker and he'd been busy. The rumor was that he'd helped with the train robbery just outside of Captain's Creek before riding two days to Kingfisher's Drift, wreaking havoc in every stable and saloon in between. Word was that he was riding in that afternoon.

The sheriff didn't budge. He told Pru to do the same thing she'd done before, and to do it the next afternoon. Tucker would have been in the town a day already, and the sheriff felt that by then his guard would be down, (provided no one tried to kill him overnight).

Pru thought of what to say while the sheriff was talking. She was all ready to politely, but solemnly refuse. Then he started telling her about the things that Tucker had done. How he shot an unarmed man over a poker game because he'd thought he was cheating. How he'd stolen a horse and set fire to the barn so that he couldn't be chased, with four stallions and two mares still inside. How he'd grabbed a little boy on the train to use as protection while he was escaping. By the end of it, all of Pru's words had vanished, and she was in trouble yet again.

***

It had been a waste of an afternoon.

Pru had spent the sun looking for the stranger. She checked the saloon, the general store and every alley in town, and it made her uncomfortable. Young ladies weren't supposed to be spending time slinking down alleys, but that's exactly what she'd been doing. Fortunately, for her, her father had been tending to the horses at the stable all day, giving her the freedom to creep around like a Nosy Nellie. Giving up, she started for home.

She had just passed the last building in the center of town when the door opened.

"Well, you don't look none too happy."

Pru turned to the sound of the voice and found Marston Johnson's figure coming towards her. Pru smiled.

"The heat's just winning me. Thought I might head on home, get some rest."

"Ah," said Marston, "Then would you mind my walking you?"

Pru didn't mind, and Marston seemed glad of it. During the walk back, the two made small talk. Pru asked about Marston's older brother in Copperbend, Arizona, and Marston asked about Pru's father. By the time they had reached the house, Pru felt better about the afternoon and had nearly forgotten all about tomorrow's plans. That is, until Marston brought it up.

"Are you nervous about tomorrow?" he asked.

Pru was caught off guard. Instead of responding, she just looked at him. Marston seemed to understand.

"That's alright," he said, "I would be too. I mean, I'm not nearly as brave as you, but..." he said, pausing, "But I think it's great. You know, what you're doing? I think it's great. I think you're great."

Pru's face warmed and Marston tried to cover his slip-up. "I mean Pop and some others were going to try and drag Jordan out of there for a hanging. But sure shooting, somebody would have gotten hurt or Jordan would've hurt one of the ladies. But then you came along and suddenly we had another chance. Anyway, I just want you to know how grateful we all are that you're doing this."

Every word of Marston's speech added weight to Pru's already heavy heart. She was thankful when Marston decided to leave it at that. "I reckon I better get on back," he said, "Pa's probably wondering where I am. Good luck tomorrow." With a slight tilt of his head and a shy smile, he turned and headed back down the invisible path that the two had walked to her house. Pru watched him for a long moment before turning and entering the house, dreading the sunset that would bring the next day.

She wasn't sure whether to scream from shock or weep with joy from what she found in her house. She very nearly did both at the same time.

The stranger was sitting comfortably in the kitchen with his boots up on the table, his coat discarded over the back of a nearby chair. He tipped his hat at her speechless, open mouth.

"I reckoned you'd come on home when you run out of places to look," he said, holding up a glass, "I also liberated some of the lemonade from your ice box for myself. Hope you don't mind."

Pru quickly recovered. "How long you been here?"

"An hour, maybe more. You know, they're calling you a hero all over town," he said with a wide smile, "Gotta say, it makes me chuckle, being one of the few who really know what happened in that there alley."

The stranger's comment brought Pru back. "Could you do it again?" she asked.

The stranger frowned but the smile didn't leave. "What,

one death weren't enough for you?"

"The sheriff's asked me to do it again."

"When?"

"Tomorrow afternoon. The man's name is Cliff Tucker."

"Ain't he the one who hijacked that Captain's Creek train? Grabbed some little boy ain't old enough to cuss yet, used him for protection?" Pru nodded. The stranger pushed away from the table and stood up. His attention turned to the mantle, his fingers busying themselves among the knickknacks as Pru spoke.

"The sheriff wants it done the same as before," she said. When the stranger didn't respond, she paused. "Please. This will be the last time, I promise."

"Don't go promising things that you got no control over. If another man comes into town next week, you can bet they'll ask you again."

"I'll say no."

"I doubt it. I suspect you don't know how to say 'no' to folks. It's what got you in this mess in the first place, not wanting to go correcting people. You do your name proud, Prudence."

Pru didn't know how to respond, so she watched the man as he moved and shifted the items on the shelf, little trinkets full of memories and years. He stopped at a pile of books. Pru watched as he pulled the top one, a worn and faded blue book. She knew it well. As he turned it over in his hands, she could see the familiar image of the witch on the cover done in gold, flying through the stars. It was a child's book, full of myths and fairy tales. She'd believed in all of that once when she was small. Since her mother died, Pru didn't have much time for reading or believing anymore.

She was surprised when the stranger suddenly spoke. "I reckon you want me in the alley again, same as before." When she nodded, he continued, "And I'll take this," he said, holding up the book before tucking it into his coat, "Ain't got much in the way of reading and I don't want to get out of practice. Nothin' worse for a man than not being able to read."

Satisfied with their arrangement and the lack of speech coming from Pru, he headed for the door. He paused when he reached it. "Word of advice. Don't come looking for me again. I will find you."

With a tip of his hat, he was gone.

***

The stranger was true to his word. The next day, Pru did the same as she had done the last time. Tucker was even more eager than Jordan had been, and quicker to the window. The slide of the glass, a quick pop, and it was all over.

As Pru left Madame Porter's she reveled in the sun, the heat of it warming her tense shoulders. She had already planned her afternoon. She would have a tall glass of lemonade, walk a bit farther to visit her mother at the cemetery, and try to get a good night's sleep. She couldn't remember the last time she'd had a decent sleep. It wasn't surprising how much of an impact the demise of a criminal can have on the guilty conscience of a woman wanting to sleep.

As the house came into view, she stopped walking. Hoping she was seeing things, she squeezed her eyes shut and opened them. She tried again. No such luck. The sheriff's black stallion tied up to their porch post wasn't going away.

She hoped he had only coming to congratulate her.

***

Pru had the words on the tip of her tongue again, and again they dissolved before she could say anything. She tried to think of other options. Her father volunteered, but they both knew it was out of guilt and that he couldn't see anything past the end of his pistol anymore. Even Marston offered to take her place, but his father was not one to be challenged once his mind was made up. Pru decided that she'd gone to great lengths already. She might as well finish. So she agreed, but her agreement came with a price. She made the sheriff promise that this would be the last time. She wasn't a gunslinger. She was a lady, and she didn't need a mother to tell her that was she was doing wasn't very ladylike. The sheriff agreed. One last time, and he'd just about give her anything her heart desired.

At first, she thought she might be able to do it herself. She tried to shoot some cans behind the house when her father wasn't home, but she missed the mark every time. As the hour in question drew nearer, it was becoming harder to ignore. She would need his help. This was going to be more dangerous. Word was getting out and Madame Porter, who hadn't minded the first two times, was getting scared of losing business. The plans had to change. Pru would have to shoot him somewhere else.

She was out of options, and the only one left to her came with a swagger, a pair of Peacemakers and a curved brim. She had a quick walk through town in case he was watching and he found her, just as he said he would. She had just said goodbye to Marston, who had stopped by to offer his services again. She had politely declined.

When she turned and caught a glimpse of a familiar coat on the back porch, she made sure to bring two glasses of lemonade.

***

He didn't interrupt her as she told the story. When she finished she sat back, her eyes fixed on the setting sun. When he still didn't respond, she frowned.

"What do you think?" she asked.

He was rolling a bullet in his hands. He didn't look up, but his fingers stilled.

"I reckon the saloon's our best bet, but it's not going to be easy. The timing's gotta be just right for it to work. And I'll have to be in there, of course," he said. He paused before continuing, "It means you'll have to shoot at him same time as me. If we're even one second apart, the whole thing's gonna come right off the rails."

Pru remained determined. "Can it be done?"

"Which part? Walking into the saloon and shooting Murphy or having two people trying to fire at the same time?" he asked. From her look, he nodded, "Yeah, it can be done. But it's going to cost."

Pru nodded, expecting that comment, "Anything you want in the house is yours. Except my mother's jewelry box. You can't have that or anything in it."

"That friend of yours," said the stranger, "What's his name?"

"Marston. Marston Johnson."

The stranger nodded. "I reckon he finds you pretty fetching. He engaged you yet?"

Pru blamed the sudden warmth of her face on the heat of the sun. "No. And I wish you wouldn't say such things. Marston hasn't said anything to me about whether or not he finds me fetching."

The stranger's lips curled up into a smile. "He does. Fact is, I wager you two are married by the year's end."

Pru frowned. As she opened her mouth to speak, the stranger intervened. "If I do this for you, and I'm right about you two getting hitched, then I want something from you."

"All right."

The stranger turned to look at her with darkened blue eyes. "I want your word that the first child you have, you'll give to me."

At first Pru thought that the stranger was joking and a smile spread across her face. But the seriousness in his eyes and the squaring of his shoulders made the smile fade. Believing his sincerity but not his prediction of her future, Pru nodded.

"You have my word," she said.

The stranger smiled.

***

She would shoot him in the saloon. That was the plan. But, because of her terrible aim, the stranger would shoot at the same time. Pru felt that even with his help, a miracle might be in order.

She could feel everyone's eyes on her as she walked down the dusty road through town. More people than she had ever seen out on a hot afternoon lined the boardwalks on either side of the saloon. As she reached the large swinging doors, she scanned the crowd. Marston and his father were on one side, looking a combination of nervous and excited. Her father was on the other, looking terrified. She gave him a smile, took a deep breath, and pushed open the heavy doors.

The darkness of the saloon forced Pru to pause and let her eyes adjust. As her eyes cleared, she looked around as she'd been told to. A table full of men were to one side of the room playing poker. The piano player was working with a catchy ragtime tune. Three men were sitting at the bar and Eli, the bartender, had just delivered a drink to the lone man at a table just behind Pru. He gave her a nod on his way past the bar to the back room. It wasn't long before everyone else noticed and everything fell silent, the last chord of piano keys hanging in the air. Women like Pru were a rarity in saloons.

"I'm looking for Clyde Murphy."

Everyone stayed where they were, but heads started to turn and eyes began to dart here and there. Slowly, one man raised himself up from his bar stool and turned around.

"I'm Clyde Murphy," he said.

Pru was surprised. He couldn't have been any older than she was, but he sure looked the part. He was lean and smug and held himself up like he was about to swear on a Bible. He crossed his arms and looked Pru up and down.

"Well now, ain't you pretty," he said, "Something I can do for you, darling?"

Pru let the hand that was gripping the pistol fall away from folds of her skirt to her side. With a deep breath, she raised her arm. At the sight of the gun, there was a shuffling of chairs. Murphy's expression didn't change. If anything, his smile grew.

"Pretty nice pistol you've got there, honey. But you don't look much like a gunslinger to me. You're holding yourself all wrong and your hand is shaking. Now I'm sure there's plenty of boys in here who wouldn't mind teaching you how to use that. I know I'd be one of them."

Pru felt blood rushing to her face. She was about to respond when Murphy continued. "Not that I don't mind such a pretty little executioner, but if you're going to shoot me, would you mind getting it done? Otherwise I've got a drink to finish and a fine-looking woman to see."

Pru heard the familiar sound of a subtle and supportive click behind her and knew she wasn't alone. With renewed strength, she took aim. Murphy noticed.

"Okay, honey. If you want to play, we'll play." With a fluid motion, his hand found his hip holster. "Ready when you are."

Pru cocked the gun.

"Wait a minute! There's no shooting in here!"

Both Murphy and Pru turned to Eli, who had just returned from the back room to see the commotion. His gaze fell to Pru. "Take it outside."

Pru swore her heart stopped. "What?"

"There's no shooting in here. You want to have a draw, go outside."

Pru frowned and looked at Murphy, who was smiling

broadly at her. Outside wasn't part of the plan. But his smile turned her stomach, making her think of all the terrible things he'd done, all the children he'd hurt. She'd wished before that she could be brave. Now she had someone to help her do that.

"Clyde Murphy," she said, lowering her gun, "I challenge you to a draw."

Pru watched with some pride as Murphy's expression changed. Within moments the smug, charismatic boy was gone and was replaced with the man she knew was underneath, the man she'd heard and read about. The one who didn't hesitate in killing men, women and children in his way. It was that man who approached her now.

"Don't think I won't kill you, just because you're a woman," he said before strolling past her through the swinging doors and into the street.

Pru took a moment to compose herself as everyone else in the bar rushed out. Turning around, she faced the doors. She froze.

The stranger, who had been sitting in the corner behind her, was gone.

***

Murphy was already standing down the street when she came out.

"I give you ten seconds to shoot," he shouted. He started to count down.

Slowly, all of the confidence that Pru had in the saloon was melting away in the sun. She'd been left alone with all these people watching right now. Surely, they wouldn't let him shoot her. They would have to do something. Wouldn't they? Of course, maybe they'd wait until he shot her. Then they would have something to hang him for.

She imagined herself back on her porch, before this all

started. She watched the man riding away with her mother's jewelry. She raised her arm, the pistol shaking in her hand. Gripping it tightly, she heard Murphy reach three. Then two.

Murphy shouted one. Pru shut her eyes and squeezed the trigger. Two shots rang out.

Two bodies fell to the ground.

***

The doctor wasn't at all surprised that Pru fainted, only that it was fortunate that it happened after she'd fired. He gave her strict instructions to stay in bed, rest, and eat some regular meals. Her father made sure she ate, and Marston came to visit her every day.

Murphy was buried in the cemetery with a wooden cross and his initials, in case some poor unfortunate relative needed to find his grave. As they closed his wooden box, the coroner noticed something interesting. Somehow, Pru's pistol had fired two shots instead of one. Murphy had two bullet holes—one in the shoulder and the other in the chest. Nobody really cared because dead was dead, and so Clyde Murphy was buried and never discussed again.

The stranger didn't come to see Pru after it was all over. She did think of him now and then, when she went to pour herself a glass of lemonade or when she walked by the alley by Madame Porter's. She thought of him at the end of the year when she became engaged to Marston.

Everything returned to normal, and Pru never saw the stranger again.

***

Pru brushed the dirt off her dress, collected from kneeling at her mother's grave. She had just finished telling her mother all of the latest news, about how Leon from the General Store was visiting family, and how the sheriff had retired and his deputy was now in charge. Of course, she had talked about her husband and their baby girl Winnie. Now she was ready to head for home.

She turned and found the stranger instead.

Before Pru could say anything, the stranger spoke. "I've come to collect."

Pru swallowed. "I don't know what you're talking about."

"Seems to me you do. And I expect you thought I'd forgotten."

"No," said Pru quickly, "I just...it's such short notice."

"A promise is a promise," said the stranger, "You gave me your word. I'll be around in the morning to get her."

The stranger turned and began to walk away. Any panic that Pru felt suddenly turned to anger in her stomach.

"No," she said firmly.

The stranger stopped. "What'd you say?"

"I said no. What kind of person are you, slinking down alleys and shooting people and taking advantage of women stuck in unfortunate circumstances?" Pru's voice escalated, "What right do you have to separate a parent from her child? How can you be such a heartless person?"

The stranger began to walk towards her and to Pru's surprise, she didn't move. She stared up into his blue eyes, cold under the brim of his hat. His lips were drawn in a tight line and he barely spoke above a whisper, but it was enough.

"You don't know anything about me. You don't know what kind of person I am, and you don't know what I'm capable of. Tomorrow. Be ready."

Without another word, he walked away.

The world came crashing down around Pru. Dropping to her knees, she began to cry. She wished that she had never made that promise, that she had never met the stranger, or shot the man trying to escape with her mother's jewelry. As her sobs began to cease, she tried her best to push herself up from the ground, but she stopped.

In her tears, her fingers had grasped on to something in the dust. Raising her hand, she found a small chain with a leaf charm in her palm. Pru frowned, turning it over. It looked the same as the one her mother had given her—the one she had given to the stranger. As she lifted her head, something else caught her eye. It was a small blue book, half buried from the blowing dust. As Pru cleaned it, she unearthed the familiar witch on the front cover. Confused, she lifted her eyes to study the headstone at which the necklace and book had been placed.

She recognized it immediately. It belonged to a mother and child, killed around the same time as her mother. She read the epitaph carefully. When she came to the last lines, she stopped. Relief and sadness ached inside of her. Taking a breath, she sent up a silent prayer.

***

Pru was alone in the house with Winnie when the stranger arrived. She had insisted that Marston get an early start on the day and he, trying to please his wife, had been happy to oblige. When she heard the front porch creak and the door open, she took a deep breath and went into the hall.

The stranger frowned. "Where is she?"

"In her crib. A promise is a promise. You may take her."

"Bring her to me."

Pru nodded and turned towards the bedroom. She slowly turned back. "I just had something to say first, if I may."

"Not much I can do to stop you is there?" said the stranger.

Pru took a breath, and wrapped her arms around herself in a hug. "I just want you to know how sorry I am...about your wife and your little girl."

The stranger stilled almost immediately, and Pru quickly

continued. "I wouldn't have understood before. I didn't love anyone and I'd never helped to create something so beautiful. But now I know that if I lost either of them, I would do whatever I had to...to get them back."

Pru took a step towards the bedroom where her little girl was sleeping. "That's why I know that this is hard on you too, taking away my little girl the way someone took away yours. I know that because you lost your own, you'll do right by her. You'll love her like your own. If you can look me in the eye and promise me that, then I'll let her go. Promise me that, Ripley Killsgan."

Killsgan's expression changed. Pru no longer saw a half-hearted gunslinger standing in her hallway. She saw a broken father, angry and forsaken for the loss of his beloved wife and child. No matter what Ripley Killsgan had done after his terrible loss, it would never be as terrible as what he had suffered since losing them.

Without a word, Killsgan turned around and headed for the door. Pru caught up to him on the porch.

"Wait."

Killsgan stopped but didn't turn around. Finally he spoke, his voice gravelly. "Don't ever stop telling either of them how much you love them. Tell them until the day you die. Tell them until they're tired of hearing it, until you're sore and can't talk no more."

Pru nodded. "I will."

He took a step but hesitated. "Oh, and one more thing," he said, turning around to look at her. Pru was surprised to see the smallest of smiles on Ripley Killsgan's face. His smile grew wider as he spoke.

"For the love of the Almighty, teach her how to shoot."

Author Bio:

L.M. Magalas began writing stories on her grandfather's typewriter at the age of ten. Since then she has continued to write and daydream excessively, feeding on the support of friends and family. She is a movie buff and has a special place in her heart for westerns and John Wayne.

Off to Grandma's House
Lawrence Vernon

Brushing a strand of auburn hair out of her eyes, Red shifted her weight on the chair in front of her computer desk. She tapped the number to her grandmother's house on her cell, pressed the phone against her ear, and listened. No response.

A trickle of unease wriggled throughout her stomach as Red hung up and dialed another number. After two rings, a woman said, "Hello."

"Hey, Mom."

"Hi, Red. I meant to call you earlier to let you know that I wouldn't be coming home tonight."

"I figured as much. We had a major snowstorm."

"I know. My flight got canceled so I have to spend the night in a motel. The trip was excellent though. I managed to close a big sale."

"That's nice, but, I'm really worried about Grandma. She's been awfully sick while you were gone."

"What does she have?"

"I'm not sure," Red said, taking a deep breath and rubbing her temple, "but Grandma's all alone and she isn't answering her phone."

"Maybe she's using the bathroom. Perhaps you can try calling again in ten minutes."

"I've been calling all night. She hasn't answered. I'm thinking about going over to her house to check on her."

"Is it still snowing there?"

"No, it stopped." Red stood and strolled over to her bedroom window. She parted the curtains and grimaced at the sight of powdery white mountains that covered the front yard, the street, and the surrounding houses. "But there's a lot of snow out there."

"How are you going to get to Grandma's? They couldn't have plowed the roads yet."

Red released the curtains and returned to her chair. "No, they haven't, but I can take that trail through the woods and be there in twenty minutes."

"Are you sure you should do that?"

"I don't think I have a choice. Grandma is very sick, all alone, and she won't answer her phone. I can't call 911 because they're not going to be able to send anybody over for a while. I'm scared something might have happened to her. I have to make sure she's okay."

"I don't like the idea of my seventeen-year-old daughter walking through a foot of snow in the middle of the night."

Red sighed. "I'll be okay."

Mom became silent for a while. "All right, but please take your cell and call me if anything happens."

"I will." Red snapped her cell phone shut. She left the chair and opened her closet to retrieve a backpack. After shoving several items of clothes and toiletries into the backpack, Red dashed downstairs to grab her coat. Before leaving, she made one last call to her grandmother's house.

Still no response.

With her heart heavy with fear and concern, Red rushed toward the front door.

She hoped Grandma was okay.

***

After drawing her scarlet coat tighter around her shivering body, Red hefted her backpack and waved a penlight in front of her as she trudged through the knee-deep snow. Barren trees reached for the night sky with thin branches like the bony fingers of a skeleton. A full moon illuminated the forest with an eerie glow.

Why didn't I stay with Grandma before the snowstorm hit? Granted, she insisted she would be fine and told me not to worry, but still...

Red inhaled and then exhaled a large, puffy cloud of breath that soon dissipated.

How long have I been out here?

She checked her wristwatch—10:32 PM. Nearly fifteen minutes had passed since she left her house. Red gazed down the trail, a curvy line of crystalline white that snaked through the woods without a single hint of Grandma's house.

A nasty realization struck Red. On a warm, sunny day, yes, it would take twenty minutes to reach Grandma's house, but when one is trekking through knee-deep snow, it was going to take longer than twenty minutes. A lot longer.

"Oh, God," Red cried.

Drawing upon a tremendous reserve of willpower, Red forced herself to press onward. The snow crunched under her boots. A cold breeze stung her eyes and cheeks like needles.

Red stopped and her heart thumped when a howl reverberated throughout the woods.

What was that?

Although she wasn't sure, the howl sounded like it had come from a wolf, but that was impossible. Wolves didn't live around here.

Yet she couldn't shake the feeling that such an animal was lurking in these woods. An image of a snarling beast with black fur, yellow eyes, and sharp fangs loomed within her imagination and filled her with dread.

Let's not get ridiculous. There aren't any wolves out here.

Remember what happened to Dustin Drexel's brother?

Red stiffened as if her muscles had turned to strands of ice. Dustin, a classmate in high school, had a younger brother named Billy. A couple of weeks ago, the police had found the remains of Billy right in these woods. An unknown animal had apparently torn the boy to shreds.

But it wasn't an unknown animal. It was a rabid dog. I remember hearing on the news that the police had caught and killed it.

Maybe it wasn't a rabid dog that killed Billy. Perhaps it was something else.

Of course, it was a rabid dog. What else would it be?

The image of the growling wolf with slavering jaws returned, filling Red with a deep terror and galvanizing her to rush down the snow-drenched trail. The sooner she reached Grandma's house, the sooner she'd be out of this frigid woods with its hungry predator.

A dark figure stepped onto the trail and shone a flashlight into her face. "Hey!"

She gasped. "Who are you?"

"Is that you, Red?" the figure asked.

"Yeah, it's me. Who are you?"

The figure aimed the flashlight beam under his chin, revealing a seventeen-year-old boy with dark eyes.

"Dustin?" Red shook her head. "What are you doing out here?"

"I could ask you the same thing."

"I'm on my way to my grandmother's house."

"In the middle of the night? Through a foot of snow?"

"She's very sick and hasn't answered the phone so I'm going over to make sure she's okay."

"Really?"

"Yes, really. You don't believe me?"

Dustin cocked his head to the side and slid his hand into his coat pocket. "Did you hear an animal howling?"

"Yeah. Did you?"

"I sure did. That's why I came out here. To see what it

was. You wouldn't happen to know what it was, would you?"

"Of course, I wouldn't. Why would you ask me something like that?"

Dustin waved his flashlight at the woods. "You know my brother died here?"

"Yeah, I'm sorry about that."

"You wouldn't happen to know anything about that, would you?"

"Only what I saw on the news. A dog killed him."

Dustin chuckled. "Yeah, that's the official version, but you want to hear something really weird? My parents had an autopsy done on Billy. The doctors compared the bite marks on his body to the jaws of the dog the police killed. The bite radius didn't match. That dog didn't kill him. You know what that means?" He advanced toward Red. "The animal that killed Billy is still out here somewhere."

When Dustin mashed his lips together and his eyes glowed with a fiery suspicion, a tingle of fear rolled down Red's spine and her heart pounded. A click sounded as he fingered something in his pocket.

What does he have in his pocket?

Shaking, Red took a deep breath. "Look, Dustin, I'm really sorry about your brother. If you think some other animal killed him, you should tell the police that."

He arched an eyebrow. "I don't think the police can catch this kind of animal."

"What kind of animal do you think it is?"

Dustin turned to his left. "You live right down this trail, don't you? Not too far from where Billy died."

"Yeah, so?"

"It all just might be a coincidence, but I think it's very strange that when I hear an unknown animal howling and I come out to see what it is, I find you."

"What are you talking about?"

"I think you know what I'm talking about."

Red gazed into Dustin's eyes, and a murderous fury glowed within them. She held up a trembling hand. "Look, I don't know anything about your brother or what that animal was. I'm just going to my grandmother's house. That's all. Now it's really cold out, and she's very sick, so if you don't mind, I'd like to be on my way."

Dustin narrowed his eyes to slits and for one terrifying moment, Red thought he was going to attack her. Instead, he stepped back and gestured down the trail. "You can go."

She seized the opportunity to trudge through the snow as quickly as she could, sparing glances over her shoulder. Dustin stood on the trail, glaring at her until Red rounded a bend and he vanished from sight.

What was that all about?

Don't worry about it. Just get over to Grandma's house.

Red continued on before a set of tracks stopped her. Although she was no wildlife expert, they looked like they belonged to either a large dog or a...wolf? The tracks emerged from the woods and headed down the trail toward...

"Grandma's," she whispered.

Despite her aching muscles, Red quickened her pace; however, running through the snow was like wading through molasses. Relief washed over her when her grandmother's house finally emerged into view.

She rushed up the porch and pounded on the front door. "Grandma, open up! It's me! Red!"

No answer.

"Oh God." While fumbling through her coat pocket for the spare key to Grandma's house, Red noticed the tracks stopped right at the front door. No other tracks left the house.

"Red?"

She turned to see her grandmother in a gown, standing in the doorway. Grandma stood to the side and bade her inside.

"Come in, child."

"Oh, Grandma. Thank God!" Red rushed into the house, enjoying the welcoming caress of warm air.

"My, it's cold out." Grandma closed the door.

"Tell me about it."

"What are you doing here?"

"You wouldn't answer your phone."

Grandma furrowed her eyebrows. "You walked through all this snow just because I didn't answer the phone?"

"I thought something happened to you. Why didn't you answer the phone? I was trying to call you all night."

"I was trying to go to sleep so I unplugged it."

"You shouldn't have done that. You're very sick. What if you needed help?"

"You worry too much. Nothing would have happened to me."

Red studied her grandmother. The old woman looked pale and sweaty as she fingered a hearing aid in her left ear and straightened her bifocals. When Grandma smiled, her dentures glistened under the soft light.

"You don't look well at all," Red said.

Grandma waved a hand at her. "I'm fine. Since you're here, you might as well spend the night. Let me get the guest room ready for you."

Red took her grandmother's arm. "It's okay. I'll take care of it."

"Are you sure?"

"Yes, Grandma. You go on to bed, okay?"

"You're such a dear."

Red smiled.

***

Clad in pajamas and a bathrobe, Red washed her face

in the bathroom sink. After drying herself, she spotted her grandmother's dentures in a glass of water.

I had better brush my teeth or else I'm going to end up losing them someday like Grandma did. That would be horrible.

Red left to get her toothbrush.

***

Red opened the refrigerator and poked around its contents for something to drink. She was hoping Grandma would have some soda, but instead she had milk, orange juice, bottled water, and a clear pitcher of a pink beverage.

What's that? Pink lemonade?

She pulled the pitcher out, opened its lid, and sniffed the contents. After detecting a slight lemony smell, she poured herself a glass, and sipped it.

"Mmm, this is good." Red downed the glass and poured herself another.

While drinking the beverage, a groan sounded from Grandma's bedroom. Red set the glass down, charged over to the door, and knocked. "Grandma, you okay?"

Another groan.

Red cracked the door open and peered in. Her grandmother was laying in bed, reading a book. She widened the door and entered the room. "Grandma?"

Her grandmother faced her. "Oh, I'm sorry, Red. I didn't mean to wake you."

"It's okay. I didn't go to sleep yet." She approached the side of Grandma's bed. "Are you all right?"

Beads of sweat gleamed on Grandma's forehead as if she had just gotten done jogging a marathon. Although Red knew it must be her imagination, her grandmother's eyes seem to have a yellow glow to them.

"I'm fine," Grandma said. "My arthritis acts up sometimes.

It's difficult getting old."

Red turned to her right and spotted the hearing aid and the bifocals resting on a nightstand. "You're not wearing your hearing aid."

Grandma's hand flew to her left ear. "Why, no I'm not."

"And you can hear me okay?"

"I can hear you fine. I guess my hearing has gotten a lot better."

"You're not wearing your glasses either." Red gestured at the book. "You can read that though?"

"I can read it fine. I guess my eyes have gotten a lot better too."

Red pointed at her lips. "Can you open your mouth for me?"

Grandma did, revealing shiny white teeth.

"Do you have a second set of dentures?" Red asked.

"No, my child, I only have one. I can't afford a second pair."

"So how did you get your teeth back?"

"I didn't. I'm wearing my dentures now."

Red shook her head. "No, you're not. I just saw your dentures in the bathroom." Her pulse raced. "What happened to you?"

Grandma stared at Red for a moment before snapping her book shut. "Do you know how hard it is getting old? Every day, something in my body aches or doesn't want to work right. You don't know how lucky you are to be young."

"We're all going to get old someday. Even me."

"I know, but I'm tired of being old. I want to be young again."

"You can't be young again."

"Oh, but I can." Grandma kicked the covers off and sat on the side of the bed. Although Red wasn't sure, she thought a thin layer of fur covered her grandmother's arms and legs.

"I met a man at a carnival who sold me this amazing elixir," Grandma said. "He said it wouldn't make me young, but it would be the next best thing, so I thought I'd give it a try.

"The elixir didn't taste very good on its own so I mixed it with some lemonade, and it did work after a fashion. It cured my arthritis, made me see and hear better, and even grew my teeth back."

Red felt the color draining from her cheeks. "What are you talking about?"

"It does have one nasty side effect." Grandma licked her lips. "It makes me hungry. I tried to suppress it, and I succeeded for a while, but it's becoming harder and harder, and I don't think I can control it anymore." Grandma groaned and placed a hand over her belly which rumbled. "I don't want to hurt you, Red. Please leave before it happens."

"Before what happens?"

"For God's sake, child, get out of here."

"I'm not leaving until you tell me what's going on."

"I can't control it anymore!" Grandma stood up and ripped her gown off. Instead of a naked, wrinkled body, her grandmother possessed a sleek, muscular one with a thick coat of black fur.

Horror burned through Red's body like streams of acid as Grandma's eyes shone a bright yellow, her face elongated into a snout, and her teeth sharpened into fangs.

Red pressed her fists against her mouth. "Oh my God!"

The beast dropped to all fours, reared its head back, and howled. Red fled from the bedroom and into the guest room. After locking the door, she pawed through her backpack, trying to find her cell phone.

A boom sounded at the door followed by a growl. Whimpering, Red emptied her backpack onto the bed and sifted through its contents. Her cell phone wasn't among them.

Red thought back. She must have put her cell phone in

her coat, which was now hanging in the hallway closet. And the creature was between her and it.

Another boom rocked the door, and the wood splintered inward.

With wide eyes and a thumping heart, Red ran over to the window and opened it. A blast of cold air slapped her face.

A crack sounded behind her. The beast would soon be in the room and having Red for a midnight snack.

She lowered her body over the sill and was about to push herself out when somebody grabbed her arm, and pulled. Red crashed onto the ground causing snow to splatter into her mouth and down the front of her robe.

She rolled onto her back and the monstrous head of a wolf appeared within the window frame. The creature growled before Red heard a gunshot. The head of the thing that used to be her grandmother exploded into a ball of blood and bone, and then its body collapsed below the window sill.

"Oh my God." Red pressed her fingers against her lips. "Oh my God."

Dustin yanked her to her feet. "Did she bite you?"

"Grandma changed into a wolf...and you shot her...and... and..."

Dustin shook her. "Did she bite you?"

"No. I got away from her, and..."

"We have to go back inside, think up a cover story, and then call the police. Nobody's going to believe your grandmother was a werewolf. Do you understand?"

Red said nothing.

Dustin shook her again. "Do you understand?"

Red nodded. A fat, wet snowflake struck her forehead. She looked up.

It was snowing again.

***

Red stood in the bathroom, gazing at her reflection. Her auburn hair covered her scalp like a shaggy carpet. Her green eyes, once sparkling and full of life were now empty and void. Even though she was only seventeen, she looked ten years older.

And no wonder. It's been a hell of a week.

After Red and Dustin entered Grandma's house, he checked on the old woman to ensure she had reverted to her human form, and then they cooked up a cover story. When Dustin left, Red shoved all her belongings into her back pack, exchanged her robe and pajamas for her sweater and blue jeans, and then called the police on her cell. Because of the snow, it took over an hour for a patrol car to arrive.

Red explained to the officers that she had come to check on her grandmother because she was sick and wouldn't answer her phone. When she got here, she had found her grandmother dead in the guest room. Red had no idea what happened. A botched burglary attempt, perhaps?

Because Red was still in shock over what really occurred and the police had nothing to indicate otherwise, they apparently bought her story. She also considered herself fortunate it snowed again, covering Dustin's and her tracks outside the window, thus obliterating the only evidence of their involvement.

After attending her grandmother's funeral earlier today, Red felt hungry, but she didn't know what for. She did experience a very curious reaction when she drove past a group of children in a playground though.

Man, they look tasty.

Now why would I think something like that?

Maybe that lemonade...?

Her belly rumbled, and she bit the inside of her cheek. Her canines felt sharper than usual. Her eyes also seemed to have a light yellow glow to them.

Red clutched her abdomen as her stomach growled again.

She was getting hungry.

Very hungry.

Author Bio:

Lawrence Vernon has graduated with a BA in Communication from college in 1991. After working at a series of jobs, he is now employed as a customer service representative for a major cable company. He currently lives in Delaware after spending most of his life in New Jersey. Before that, he spent part of his childhood living in Ohio. He has been writing stories since he was a boy, and his first publication was in his high school magazine. His work has also appeared in several publications like Shroud Magazine, Shadowfire Press, Post Mortem Press, Scars Publications, Pill Hill Press, and Static Movement.

Plain Sister Pretty: A Japanese Tale
Heather Whittington

Much as I want to, I can't be jealous of my twin sister. Even her name says it all: Akemi, it means 'bright beauty'. Her black hair shines like silk, her face is pure white without rice powder, and her lips tinged red without stain. Laughter and intelligence glow in her night-black eyes. She's maidenly but not timid, graceful but not brittle. Her feet are tiny, her hands slim, her kimono hugs a figure supple as a willow tree branch.

I was named for my love of dancing: Maiko. My parents gave me such a pretty name to hide the fact that, especially when standing beside Akemi, I'm plainer than empty parchment. My hair is dull, my figure square, my complexion riddled with imperfections. The only time I inspire anything other than pity is when I dance, but as the daughter of a *samurai*, I have little time for that.

My days are spent learning how to run a household to please my future husband, learning *bushido*, the warrior's code, so I can teach my future children, and training with the *naginata* so I can defend my husband's home in his absence.

All of it utterly boring.

Technically, I'm older than Akemi by a few minutes, but she is treated like royalty. Even the *daimyo* my father serves, Jimyoin Daiki, has commented on her beauty. His eyes watch her with the interest of an indulgent father; his oldest son, Jimyoin Takehiko, is looking for a bride. The *nakodo*, or matchmaker, warned against this choice, suggesting the daughter of another *daimyo* to cement an alliance of peace. Her words fell on deaf ears.

The marriage contract was made within a few weeks of the *daimyo's* expressed interest. Nothing less than the best would do for his son, even the daughter of his own *samurai*, lower rank and all.

The wedding was atrociously comical in my eyes. My parents sunk most of what they had into her dowry, and still they managed to pull off the most opulent of ceremonies. The bride's white kimono shimmered with embroideries of cranes and clouds. Wearing my best maroon kimono wrapped with a thick tan obi, I helped her navigate the voluminous white folds, hiding my amusement under a mask of polite disinterest.

Takehiko appeared handsome enough, though his nose was too flat and eyes too close together for my taste. I hoped with all my heart that my twin would be happy.

Towards the end of the ceremony, a handful of white birds flew over the congregation, flapping feathers loose from their wings and squalling like fighters. From the look on the *daimyo's* face, this was not part of the proceedings. From the back of the crowd of spectators, a path formed ahead of the most gorgeous woman I'd ever laid eyes on. Though her bright red kimono puddled around her feet and trailed behind her, she moved without assistance and without a single misstep. Her face radiated with an unearthly gleam, like the sun hid just under her complex headdress of red and white. She bore in her hands a pair of slippers made of gold cloth embroidered with spun gold thread. I wished I could see her feet; I wondered if they were smaller than my sister's.

The woman smiled, holding forth the slippers to the *daimyo's* son. "I saw your wedding procession pass, and what I saw in you pleased me greatly," she said to him. "Please take these as my wedding gift to you."

Takehiko accepted the slippers solemnly, handing them to his new bride. "Please, remain and celebrate with us so that we may thank you for the kindness you've shown us."

But the glowing woman smiled, clucked her tongue at the white birds still flapping overhead, and left the way she came, sinking into the crowd like spring rain into the dry earth. The birds followed her until they seemed to blend with the puffy clouds in the sky, disappearing from sight.

Everyone exchanged glances, murmuring about the identity of the mysterious woman.

***

After the ceremony, I tried to relax into the normal routine of lessons, chores, and occasional secret dances in empty rooms, but my mother, still blossom pink with the triumph of her youngest daughter, increased her efforts to make me more graceful, more desirable as a wife. She kept me hopping from morning to night. I ground my teeth in frustration, but smiled lovingly whenever my mother yanked on my shoulders to make me stand straighter. No matter how plain and undesirable I may be, no one can say I'm not an obedient daughter.

I expected no more visits from Akemi; running the household of the *daimyo's* son consumes most of one's time. Before a month passed, she appeared at our door with her attending girl, her normally smooth skin puckered with worry, and two spots of high color in her cheeks. I invited her in and shuffled off to fetch the tea. Akemi's girl slipped the sandals from my sister's feet and remained seated in *seiza* just outside the door. I could see her shadow through the closed paper screen.

I brought the tray of tea and cups to the low table, tucking my kimono by my ankles as I lowered myself to the floor. I placed the tray on the table without spilling a drop or rattling a dish. "You're getting better at this, Maiko-san," Akemi said, her lashes hiding the amusement in her eyes.

I smiled. "With you married, Mother has no one else to hound about propriety. I must bear all of it alone." I poured the tea, reveling in the pungent scent of jasmine and oranges, and offered it to her. She accepted with a murmur of thanks. After a moment of silence, I asked, "So what brings you back here? I thought all the wonders of the *daimyo's* riches would enrapture you forever."

Akemi smothered a giggle. "As blunt as ever, I see."

"Plain girls with pretty sisters don't have to worry about softening words until the sister is gone." I cradled my cup in my palms. "I guess now I have to start worrying."

A line etched itself between Akemi's perfectly arched brows. She placed her cup on the table and folded her hands upon the rich pink and peach flower embroideries on her cream silk kimono. "I have a favor to ask."

My eyes opened a little wider. "A favor, is it?" I, too, set my cup on the table. "Please feel free to ask, my sister."

"My husband..." She stopped, biting her lip.

"Yes?"

"He's...he's not well."

"What do you mean?"

A sound like a small sigh escaped. "The first week he was the perfect husband. Very attentive, very busy with duty, but always a kind word for me."

"And now?"

"Now, he sleeps most of the day. When he's awake, he speaks incoherently." She swallowed. "He stopped sharing my bed. I'll never get with child this way. And I know that's my first duty as the wife of Jimyoin Takehiko, the *daimyo's* son." I heard the anguish rise in her voice.

"How very strange." When she said no more, I asked, "What is it you wish of me?"

She clasped her hands in front of her. "I know it is much to ask, but you are the only one I can turn to. I want you to come to our home as a servant girl. I will say I hired you myself. I want you to tend his rooms, and see for me with your own eyes what—"

"Indeed, you do ask much of me, Akem-sani," I said,

holding out a hand to stop her spill of words. "I could not do such a thing. The shame to our parents would be great. You would lose your position in your own house."

"But I could help disguise you! No one would know! We could say you are visiting our aunt in Osaka." She leaned forward, eyes heavy with desperation. "Please, say you will do this for me. If you don't, I may have to end my life in shame for bearing no children!"

I studied her, unaccustomed to seeing her out of sorts. The change to her looks startled me; she seemed older now. I pressed my lips together.

"Please," she begged one more time.

I took in a slow deep breath, composing myself so she would not see my fear. "All right."

***

So together we concocted the story of visiting my aunt, and I informed my parents that very night. They were agreeable, especially my mother; she thought that my aunt's stern influence would be good for my instruction.

I packed few things, and left the next morning on my horse with my father's favorite retainer riding beside me. Hachiro served my father as long as my sister and I had lived. He sang songs with us, taught us the bow and arrow, and even snuck us the occasional sip of sake. I hoped I could trust him now.

When we were out of sight of the village and alone on the dusty road, I pulled up the reigns of my horse. "Hachiro, I must confess something to you."

"Indeed," he answered, a smile playing beneath his black mustache. "You've been fidgeting on your horse ever since you mounted."

Quickly I told him the story Akemi related to me. His heavy brow furrowed deeper and deeper as I spoke, until he was almost frightening. I told him of our plan, and he huffed like an angry dragon.

"And what do you expect me to do? I am charged with your safety."

"I need you to go on to our aunt's, but not to announce yourself. Conceal yourself within the village and waylay any messages coming from my parents to check on me." I waited on tenterhooks for his answer. I saw the refusal in his eyes, so I jumped in. "This is my sister, my other half. I will do what I must to ensure her happiness. With or without your help." I smiled at him. "Your help would make me safer."

He snorted, looking back and forth along the road. "There is truth in what you say. All right, I will help." He glared at me, setting my flesh rippling with fear. "But if you fail, I will behead you myself."

My smile widened to a reckless grin. "Agreed. And I will clean your sword for you beforehand."

***

Though I didn't ask him to, Hachiro helped me cut my hair with one of his sharpened knives. When he finished, my hair curled around my cheeks. Hachiro's fierce expression altered as he looked at me.

"What?"

"I hate to say it, but the short hair is becoming. It softens the angles of your face, and the hair looks brighter." He grinned at me, showing teeth.

I made a face at him, and slipped off into the deepening twilight to the *daimyo's* village.

Ducking behind a clump of bushes, I exchanged my fancy blue silk kimono for a dowdy one of brown and gray. For once, I blessed my plain features, for I required no other disguise; no one ever paid much attention to me.

My sister met me at the gate. As she ushered me past the guards, she informed them that I was the new servant she brought from her father's village. They studied me, the intensity of their gaze making me cower, but they let me pass with no objection.

"I've already told my honorable father-in-law and husband about you. You will tend to Takehiko's rooms, fetch water and tea, and launder his clothes." Akemi fiddled with the folds of my ordinary kimono, her eyes filled with worry. "I know you will discover what I need to know."

I reached out and squeezed her hand.

Searching Takehiko's rooms while he was out one evening, I saw he lived in a much simpler manner than his father—no ornaments, no draperies, no perfumes or incense. I began to think the man more boring than myself, if that were possible, for a rich man's son. The only thing that came to my attention as I poked around was the pair of golden slippers given to him by the mysterious lady at the ceremony. I leaned over and examined the slippers. While the gold embroideries still shone with perfection, the soles were worn thin, scratched and dirty. I noticed stains of grass around the edges, odd for a pair of shoes worn for sleeping.

My brain whirled as I pondered my discovery. I concealed myself in the room he used for calligraphy, directly next to his sleeping quarters.

It wasn't long before Takehiko returned from checking his father's troops. He yawned with a wide-open mouth, saying nothing to his wife. He refused his supper, and immediately went to his bed. I watched his shadow play on the paper screens that divided the rooms.

No more than two hours later, with the household retired for the night, I saw the shadow rise from the pallet and slide along the wall to the door. I heard it open. Then the shadow moved down the hall. I followed the scent of sandalwood from his freshly laundered clothes. Just before he turned a corner, I caught a glimpse of gold at his feet; he wore the golden slippers.

To this day, I'm unsure as to how we arrived at the meadow; the village is surrounded by fences, huts, animals, and samurai. I believe goddess magic concealed us and led us to the meadow surrounded by willow trees and filled with violets that vibrated with a shade of purple unknown to me before. The flash of gold kept me on Takehiko's trail. When I heard beautiful voices blending in harmony, I hid behind a clump of bushes.

Takehiko kept walking straight up to the glorious white figure in the center of the meadow, whose presence rendered the use of lanterns pointless. She filled the air with a luminescence pearls and diamonds would envy. It was the mysterious woman from the wedding ceremony! The figures surrounding her shone with their own bright colors, men and women smaller in stature, but just as hard to look at for a long time. I found myself shading my eyes whenever they started to water.

"Ah, Takehiko, you are late this evening!" The woman stood head and shoulders taller than all the others. Takehiko, not a tall man to begin with, seemed to grow as he got closer to the party. When he reached the white woman, his head was even with hers. "Let the music play!"

Invisible stringed instruments struck up an elegant tune. The figures partnered up, beginning a dance pattern I recognized as one usually performed by geisha. My eyes widened. I knew the lady now; she had to be the goddess Benzai-ten, the patron goddess of geishas, dancers, and musicians!

My feet itched to join them as they moved and spun to the music. After a while, the goddess picked up a *shamisen* and began to play. Takehiko knelt before her, listening rapturously.

Just as the sky began to lighten with the first hint of sun, the white goddess set aside her *shamisen* and lifted Takehiko to his feet by raising two fingers in the air. "It is time for you to return. Speak not of this to anyone."

I wanted to slip away before him, but I needed Takehiko to guide us back into the village safely. I waited until I was sure none of the heavenly beings were looking before I crawled away from the bush and ran, hunkered as low to the ground as my kimono would allow.

***

My sister sought me out as soon as she rose from her pallet in the morning. "I know it is unlikely, but have you learned anything?"

I smiled at her. "Indeed, my sister, I have learned more than your imagination would accept as real. However," I continued, holding up a finger to stave off more questions, "I believe I can fix this situation. I cannot say anything to you as yet, for that may prevent a happy resolution." I frowned, touching my fingertip to my lips. "I may end up disappearing for a short time."

Worry sprang onto Akemi's beautiful features. "What do you mean? Are you sure you should—"

"I may not have a choice. I will deal with the consequences when they arise." I bowed deeply to her as another servant rounded the corner, shuffling along the smooth wooden floor in her stockings. "I will attend to you as soon as I can, Akemi-san."

She had no choice but to accept the situation. She returned to her room.

***

That night I waited until Takehiko settled into his pallet with a gusty snore. I glided into the dark room, avoiding the shafts of moonlight from the front opening of the home. I knelt, silent as death, and lifted the corner of the blanket, exposing his feet. Sure enough, the golden slippers glittered even in the dark.

I can't explain how I wrested the shoes from his feet without waking him. I was rather amazed myself—especially worried as I was that he would begin his sleepwalk before I succeeded. As soon as I held a shoe in each hand, I slipped from the room into the hallway, releasing my breath in relief. Once I was outside, I pulled the golden shoes onto my own feet, briefly admiring the winking gold threads of embroidery. They actually made my clunky feet look small and dainty.

Standing still, I felt a great urge to walk. I followed the urge, placing one foot in front of the other in measured steps. My brain felt shrouded in mist, like I was on the verge of falling asleep. I shook myself awake each time, until I noticed that I wasn't really getting anywhere. I allowed my mind to drift, and seconds later I found myself in the meadow, the heavenly figures milling under the willow trees before me.

The scent of violets almost made me sneeze, but at least it also woke me up. The shoes carried me right to the feet of the goddess, who sat in a chair made of the twisted branches and trunks of several willow trees. Her black-lined cat eyes widened as she looked me over.

I lowered my face in a sign of humble recognition. "I know who you are," I told her.

The glowing woman smiled, her slim fingers smoothing the edges of her white outer kimono. The color left spots on my vision, as if I'd been staring at the sun. The spots matched her blood red inner kimono and molded lips. "Indeed."

"You are the goddess Benzai-ten."

She inclined her head, closing her eyes a moment. When they snapped open like a fan, she leaned toward me and placed those ice-cold fingertips under my chin, forcing me to look at her. "You are plain. But you are brave." She sat back. "Why is it you are here and not my beloved?"

"Because I followed Takehiko-san here last night. His wife is very distressed at the behavior of her new husband." I lowered my gaze to the violets crushed beneath her sandaled feet.

The goddess chuckled, sending a wave of fear crashing down my spine. "And why should I care what a mortal woman feels."

"Because he is her husband." I kept my eyes on the violets, praying to my ancestors for help. "Would he come here on his own if not under the influence of these golden shoes? What chance does a mortal woman have against the powers of a goddess?"

Benzai-ten chose not to answer. She watched me with those penetrating eyes.

"If you will leave him to his wife, I will dance for you," I offered.

She smiled. "I promise nothing. Let me see you dance."

The other heavenly beings moved away from the center of the meadow, leaving a small group of *shamisen* players near the edge. With tiny steps, I walked to the center and held my hands up. As the players began strumming their instruments, a fan of gold appeared in my open palm. I clutched it before it fell, and began the dance. My feet slid through the violets without a sound. A warm breeze caressed my face, stirring the heavy flowered scent in the meadow. As my arms floated in the night air, the sleeves of my kimono lengthened into drapes; the color transformed to a deep red that gradually changed to black at the bottom. Heavy gold embroideries trailed along the fabric like a fast growing vine, forming shapes like buds and leaves. My dull black hair swept up into a tall, domed headdress accented with gold sticks. I wished I could see myself as others could.

At the last twangs of the *shamisens*, I snapped the fan closed and sank into a deep bow. The audience murmured its appreciation. I tilted my head to look at the goddess; she seemed pleased.

"Very well," she said. "You have my leave to return to your home and say goodbye to your family. Tomorrow night, you will put on the golden slippers and come back to me to dance for my pleasure. For eternity."

I smiled and bowed to her once more.

***

In the early morning rays of sunlight, I returned to the house of my sister, who stood with her husband in the doorway. He looked angry.

"You have stolen my shoes," he began.

I held up my hand to silence him. He sputtered at my impertinence for a moment, then stopped out of curiosity.

"My sister brought me here out of her deepest concern for your welfare."

"Your sister..." Confused, Takehiko glanced at his wife, who kept her head down in shame.

Lowering my hand, I continued. "You were a changed man after a short amount of time. She asked me to discover what the reason was. You see, these shoes were given to you by the goddess Benzai-ten." I lifted the edge of my kimono just enough to allow the gleam of gold to wink. "They brought you to her every night to dance and listen to her play and sing."

Both Akemi's and Takehiko's eyes widened with shock. I knew they didn't believe me now, but I held proof hidden in my sleeve.

"I followed you the night before last, Takehiko-san. I witnessed this with my own eyes." I gave him a comforting glance. "I saw you were not under your own control, but that of the goddess. That is why you remember nothing."

Akemi made a small sound of sadness, but did not cry. Takehiko's face tinged red. "And how do you expect me to accept such blasphemy as truth?"

I nodded. "Last night I took the shoes so that I could confront the goddess myself. I danced for her so that she would spare you. She agreed to leave you in peace with your wife." I withdrew the gold fan from my sleeve and knelt on the floor with it lying across my palms, offering it up to him as though submitting myself to his sword. I bowed my head and waited for Takehiko to take it.

He did, fingering the delicate carvings of the handle. He snapped it open, gasping at the bright glow, and traced the gold lace patterns. Snapping it closed again, his dark eyes flicked to his wife, who gazed on the fan with reverence.

"It is her gift to you, to apologize for distressing your wife." I raised my head. "And tonight I must return."

"What? Why?" The words burst from Akemi's mouth. She quickly shut it, expecting a harsh word from her husband for speaking without permission, but Takehiko paid no notice.

"I made a deal with the goddess after I danced for her." I smiled sadly. "He may remain here with you, but I will return to the goddess to dance for her."

"For how long?" Takehiko asked.

"Forever."

This time all the training in the world couldn't prevent the tear slipping down Akemi's cheek. "Maiko-san," she whispered.

Takehiko's forehead shone with perspiration. He seemed to be searching for words. "What...what will you do now?"

I folded my empty hands. "I hope you will allow Akemi-san to accompany me home. I wish to say goodbye to my parents before nightfall."

Takehiko grunted, rubbing his chin as he processed the situation. Soon he nodded, and Akemi gave him a grateful smile.

***

Akemi and I returned to our parents' home to tell them the unbelievable story. It took a while to convince them that I was not unhappy with my fate. I had no husband, no prospects.

My mother admitted I was a horrible housekeeper. I made my father promise he would not punish Hachiro for assisting me in my ruse.

That night, I placed the golden slippers on my feet and lay on my pallet, closing my eyes to sleep. A moment later, I found myself back in the violet meadow. As I moved through the crowd of glowing figures, the intense gaze of a handsome young man caught my attention. He smiled at me as I passed. I gave him a tiny smile back.

The goddess waved her hand at me, once again transforming my dowdy clothes into sumptuous garments. As I danced for her, a look of contentment spread across her perfect features. Again, I saw the handsome man watching me as I twirled my fan in flowing circles. His eyes burned with a sort of fire I'd never seen in any man unless he was looking at my sister. But this man looked at me, and me alone.

My heart leaped with joy.

Author Bio:

Heather Whittington lives in Alaska with her husband, three cats, and two dogs. She teaches fitness classes and martial arts by day, and performs in local musical theatre productions and writes stories by night.

Gretal
Ashley Hendricks

I was not born here, in this cold, windy place where the trees touch the sky and the river runs silently below ice. Perhaps this surprises the traveler? Perhaps he sees the old transparent skin of my hands, shudders at the purple veins you see bursting forth, and think this is the disease of this arctic place.

It is a much more complex science than that, I am afraid.

My mother gave birth to me in the woods—a fair-haired woman struggling in a dark, humid place. She was alone, and she ripped up her skirts as she fell back into the soil. The dirt moved around her, trying to catch her—hoping to help. Her thin lips whispered words that would help me to be free, and her to live.

A massive tree with ancient writing held her firmly with its low branches, a midwife to help her. She strained against it, her back brushing against the wood. Finally, I was released to this world and she held me.

How could I know that she was so beautiful? How could I know that she had run from the accusation of witch? Have I anything to recount as I opened my new eyes to the world?

Only the sunlight through the branches.

Only her cheek that she put to my heart.

***

By the time I walked, I knew that ours was a special life.

Travelers, lost children, thieves would sometimes come upon our home made of twisted roots and tree trunks, but they did not belong to the woods.

The children that stumbled into our midst could not read each other's thoughts nor turn rain to sunlight as my mother could. Though my mother fed each passerby, she almost did so out of pity that they could not see past their own eyes. She always sent them on their way, warning that they must never again get lost in the woods.

Occasionally a young man would make his way to our door. They all seemed the same though their names changed over the years. My mother fell in and out of love as was her habit, but they always left after spending time with her. And though they promised, every one of them, to return, we knew it would not be so.

No one could ever find our cottage twice. My mother assured me that any man, woman, or child could only find a witch's door once by grace.

***

The word *witch* is strange to me; even now I do not believe that I ever was one. My mother brewed potions and we danced around fires. We read and wrote at a time that women did not, does that make a witch?

I think rather, we were chemists, experimenting with the life that surrounded us. My mother seldom called us witches; she said we were merely observers. That we must observe at all times, that we must try not to interfere.

She spent days examining different plants and soils, and I, even at a young age, spent my days capturing all I could on paper. I ground flowers to make dye. I sharpened lead against the rocks of the river.

In this way we passed years. And in those years my mother did not age.

We spent the days boiling roots to aid our health and reading out of great books. We recited our own poetry to each other and learned to cook everything that one might find in this land. She brushed my long red gold hair and tied it up with ribbons and jewels.

We achieved what so few mortals ever do; we were complete. We were happy.

***

My mother could usually tell if children were running or lost in our woods, but I cannot be sure if she knew of the two tramping through the forest. They were loud, snapping twigs and calling to each other. Their voices were unlike I had ever heard, they were rich, tinted by travel and life.

We stood outside of our home, her with a broom in her hand, glancing thoughtfully at the direction of the sound.

The little girl tumbled out the brush first, as if she had been pushed. Her dark hair was messy and long, falling into her blue eyes. Her golden skin shone with the dew from the morning, and her lips were perfectly sculpted. I could not tell if she was mortal child, and I knew my mother was wondering the same.

She was slight, but fearless, and she smiled wide for the two of us.

The boy came next, and though his look was the same, he had none of her impishness. He looked rather embarrassed, catching the girl by her wrist and moving in front of her.

"We apologize for intruding," the boy said, sounding like a small prince.

The girl laughed.

My mother looked at the two with a smile at the corner of her eyes, "Well. Since you have ruined our morning, won't you come in for something to drink?"

"Yes, thank you," the girl answered formally, with the same grin.

She dragged the boy by his hand and followed my mother

into our small home.

The girl ate feverishly, as if it had been years. Tearing into the chicken with her white teeth and gulping down the tea we brewed.

The boy was more subdued, but he followed.

My mother looked at the girl shrewdly, as if she would know her secrets, but she did not have to pry. At once the girl looked into my mother's eyes and said, "My name is Gretal and my brother Hansel, and we are looking for our mother. They said she ran into these woods." She spoke so assuredly and earnestly that my own mother sighed and looked at me.

"Why would your mother run into the forest alone?" my mother asked.

Hansel shifted in his chair, embarrassed. "We have no clue."

"Our mother is a dancer," Gretal spoke up. "And sometimes she hears music where there is none, and must follow it. She does not fear being alone," she said, almost angrily.

We lived so outside of any normal society, that such a thing would be common to us, but my mother seemed to understand at once that the two children did not belong to that simple life. She viewed them as something else all together, they shone for her as jewels might and she pressed the girl to tell her more.

"We travel everywhere and see everything," the girl bragged, trying so hard to impress my mother, for already she loved her. She reached into her collar and brought out a medallion of gold, so thin it might have been paper, so heavy I was surprised it did not hurt her. "This is from the temples in Egypt, we stood at the doors as our mother danced inside. When she was finished a woman burst out and put this into my hands, and told me my mother had danced in a hall of spirits and cleansed it." She bit into her lip, and then said quietly, "She only dances, and she can do nothing else." The admission brought tears to her eyes, but she smiled, as children are prone to do.

"Have you seen her?"

We had not, and surely we would have noticed. But my mother was intent on finding her, and so left me to look after the children and made her way into the wood.

"I might take long," she warned me before kissing my face. "But do not worry, I will come back."

I did not worry about my mother, who could bend trees just by asking. But I did worry about watching such children.

I had never been around this kind of child before. They seemed so much younger than I was, but they were self assured, graceful. Hansel's manners were impeccable but Gretal's were almost invisible. She stared, pointed, and slurped her stew. Smiled all the time. Above all else, they were fearless.

It seemed we settled into a routine the first day my mother was gone. We would wake and prepare breakfast together, Hansel and I would eat little and Gretal would eat hers and then finish both of ours.

Gretal would play outside while Hansel and I read aloud to each other.

They would watch as I would boil roots and make elixirs to calm this or that. We were silent with each other; I regarded them as small specimens. The natural world held so much that I might explore, that two children did not really bother me so.

Hansel liked to follow me through the forest and I made him somewhat of a pupil. I would explain the different plants, the fauna. He could memorize quite anything.

Gretal could not be persuaded to come with us; if she was made to, she would follow and pout. Stopping ever few moments to lie down in the grass or pick flowers to wear in her hair.

She liked to spin until she fell over, but had the natural balance of a cat. She would leap from branches and land on her toes.

I sat once, under a tree sketching, when she tumbled out of the branches.

I sighed heavily.

She smiled brilliantly at me. "You're a good sketch," she said. She peered into my book. "Do you ever draw people?"

I paused. Yes. I sketched people occasionally. But always as an afterthought, by memory. I captured those that had passed through our lives, but the images were always blurry and half remembered.

I surprised the girl and myself by laughing. "Never one that is so changeable," I said, clearly guessing her motive.

Gretal laughed and stood up on her toes. "Like this?" she asked.

"Try and hold it and I will sketch it."

I think, perhaps, any artist will tell you that something quite amazing happens when you begin a piece that captures, and it was so in that moment. I have never been the kind of witch to make things happen, I am only an observer, as my mother made me, but I think that I helped her to stay on her toes. It was natural to her, but maybe I slowed the wind and maybe I kept her distracted with a butterfly. I don't know. But I must have sketched her for hours, her small, highly arched brown feet, and the toenails so even and perfect.

When the light was fading she finally fell to the floor with a laugh. "See. I can do anything," she said, laughing.

In that dim light I forget her mortality, and I quite agreed with her.

Time is so strange to me; I can never say how much of it has passed. It runs forwards and backwards and in circles around me.

***

My mother did not return alone, she dragged a woman behind her.

We three were outside and when Hansel saw them

approaching he shouted and ran towards them. Gretal ran after him, her hand in mine.

The woman was wrapped in blankets; my mother looked seriously at me, calmly told me that I must boil her herbs and get her bed ready. My mother looked so alive and alert, and I nodded at her.

Hansel helped us carry the woman to the bed while Gretal only paced back and forth, once my mother undid the blankets, however, Gretal flung herself onto the bed and held on to the woman.

The woman on the bed was beautiful, she had high-sculpted cheeks and such a lovely face, but she was thin and cold. By her side, Gretal looked robust and almost like a cherub come to kiss a saint.

My mother got out a huge book, and began to read to herself, quickly. "What is her name?" she asked Gretal.

Gretal pushed away her mother's dark hair off of her forehead. "I can't," she whispered, miserable. "I mustn't tell anyone her name."

I glanced into my mother's eyes. We knew the custom— we did not speak each other's names. They are powerful words, and would give power to those that knew them.

"Delia," Hansel whispered.

"Oh," Gretal sighed, and for the first time looked so wretched she seemed another child, "Delia," she whispered into her mother's hair.

I do not know how to cast spells; I think the whole thing silly, really. But my mother knew old words, she came from another time. She sent the children to wait outside in the woods. They must be out of the house. Hansel was dutiful, and kissed his mother on her forehead, but Gretal had to be practically beaten to loosen her grip. She looked into my eyes and then she went bravely.

My mother was soon glistening with the effort to save the

woman, and we both moved as if following unspoken orders. Unobtrusively I laid my hands on the woman's frail shoulders and she gasped.

I could see her life as clearly as I could see my small garden just beyond my window. It seemed as if her window to her life had come alive.

Delia. The gypsy queen. The ghost dancer. Mama. She had many names, and each one carried a weight as they were given to her.

She followed the music she heard. She could see it, rising and falling like lava onto ice, melting and burning its way through each surface. Delia could hear music when people spoke and if their songs were sad how she wept.

Delia had followed a song into a forest, and she didn't think it would ever release her. She was sweating, moaning, it demanded to be heard.

My mother forced a liquid down her throat and we both watched as she grew limp, then fell asleep.

***

The days that followed were lovely. We were easy with each other, all of us. Delia was interesting, beautiful, and had lived a strange and large life that her children seemed to see as legendary. They treated her as a deity, perhaps, and were bashful in their worship.

But my mother saw her as she was, and they grew close. One woman, placed forever to watch life pass through and the other made to pass through life. My mother marveled over Delia's jewelry, each piece from another place. Delia had a story for each bracelet, each ring. One ring was sculpted out of iron and had a completely white stone pressed into the whole round of it. My mother thought that especially beautiful.

She left one morning, holding both my mother and me.

Kissing both of us on our faces and saying how grateful she was. How she loved us. She was as alive and as changeable as a flower, and quite as frail as one as well.

We were observers, only. And we needn't have been fortunetellers to know that the next crisis was just ahead of them, but we said nothing.

Hansel thanked us profusely, seemingly sure that all of his mother's troubles had been cured by us but Gretal was infinitely more aware.

"Are you coming?" she asked my mother.

My mother only kissed her atop her head and went back inside our cottage.

She looked at me then, and smiled as she always did, and it was touched with a sadness that made her older, and I realized that for all her courage and charm, she was just a few years behind me. "Can I come back?" she wondered to me.

I had never told anyone that they could, if they tried but I did not hesitate. I reached into my pocket and gave her the blue stones that will shine even at night. "Leave a trail behind you and you may find your way back if you ever choose."

The three walked into the morning and only Gretal turned to wave a final goodbye.

I never thought I would see any of them again.

***

Life continued for my mother and me—travelers came and went. We fed them well for their tales of the world and sometimes I would take to a visitor and fall in and out of love.

I wandered away once—I married a farmer and sewed and gossiped with other woman. I sketched in the morning.

I suppose the end of this tale was supposed to come there but it didn't. The man I married was quite a lot like me and one day he chose to wander out of his own story. I went back to my mother and told her about the life I had left. She nodded, amused. I understood that she had lived and left many lives herself.

And time passed as it always does.

One day a hunter came upon our door, bleeding from an attack of some wild animal. He was tall and broad, with blue eyes that my mother could not ignore. His manner was polite, soft. He fell in love with my mother at once, and maybe spent his entire life thinking that she was only a dream.

He built a house adjoining our cottage and there my mother lived as husband and wife with her love.

I spent most of my days alone, sketching and then eventually painting the world I lived in. I thought mine to be a perfect life. I thought that, perhaps, because I could not even imagine anything might be missing.

***

She came upon my door at dusk, knocking loudly.

I was painting by candlelight, just brushing colors onto a stretched canvas, meaning nothing.

I knew her the moment I opened the door.

She was taller, but still slight and smaller than me. Her cheekbones high the way her mothers had been. Her eyes were darker now, but still a disconcerting blue, framed by long dark eyelashes. Her mouth still appeared to be perfectly drawn on her, her lower lip generous on her brown face. Even in the dark, she looked as if she was made of gold, sculpted to stand guard in an ancient temple. Then she smiled and I saw that impishness had not faded.

She moved slowly, so that I could stop her if perhaps I did not remember her, and put her arms around me. I could feel her lips fluttering by my face.

"Gretal," I said and I laughed for it seemed strange to say her name.

Her soft laughter echoed mine.

"Come in," I said.

Gretal walked into the cottage she had barged into when she was a child and looked around.

"I was hoping you would remember me," she said, a hint of apology in her voice.

I thought then that I could not have forgotten her in a thousand years. She sat down next to the fire on the floor and immediately looked up at my painting.

"All these years, I remembered your sketches," she said. She sounded peculiar to me; her words were not touched with the malice and sadness of others I have known. "Everything you drew you made so beautiful."

I sat beside her on the cold floor, something I had never done before. I could feel heat coming off of her in waves, and I imagined that Delia had felt that every time she heard the music.

We sat silently together for a long time, Gretal looking around at my paintings and me looking at her.

"My mother is dead," she said after a while.

I merely nodded at her; death is not surprising to me.

She was about to speak again when my mother walked in.

Gretal jumped up and rushed at my mother, hugging her.

My mother laughed and threw her arms around Gretal, "My girl!" she sighed. "You're freezing!"

Gretal laughed back at her and then looked at her hands. "You're married!" she accused, grinning.

"Come, let's get you fed and warmed."

I followed the two out, just behind them, a thought on my mind that had not crossed my lips.

Bray was a good man, affable and amusing at every turn. He met Gretal with little hesitation, he thought her to be like us, ethereal and immortal in some ways.

We sat around a table and drank and ate, and laughed.

Bray talked about the world he had lived in, hunting deer

and then being attacked by a stag.

"I was only asking for it," he laughed. "And it brought me here." He grew serious. "It was the luckiest thing that has ever happened to me," he told Gretal.

"When I was six, my brother and I came to find my mother. It turns out that her running away into the forest was the luckiest thing to happen to me as well," Gretal answered him with a smile.

My mother and I looked at each other over the table, both of us amused that she felt that way.

"How is your brother?" my mother asked.

Gretal gave a small shrug and a smile. "He's studying at the monastery," she answered. She suddenly laughed. "He is well, and happy."

My mother touched her hand suddenly. "And you?"

She paused a moment, collecting her thoughts. "I am well and happy also," she answered slowly. She looked at Bray and said apologetically, "I wouldn't want to bore you."

Bray smiled. "Oh I have heard so much of the gypsy children that stumbled into my love's life—I would like to hear the rest of their story."

Gretal smiled at that. "There isn't so much," she said, but I knew that she lied. "When we left here we joined another show, Mama was still dancing for the spirits. In the show there was a priest that bled at the palms, and how Hansel loved him! They read the bible together at meals and after a while, he convinced Hansel to go the monastery that had cast him out. He went, and well, how could anyone not take to Hansel?"

My mother was frowning. "And your mother?"

"She is dead," Gretal answered. She brought out the iron ring and placed it by my mother's hand. "She asked me to bring this to you. It has taken me a long time, I am so sorry," she said though I did not know if she was talking to my mother or to hers.

I could hear my mother's churning thoughts and I glanced

at Gretal, prompting her.

She sighed and then, in front of a complete stranger and the women in the woods she loved, she told us of her mother's death.

"Perhaps it was a year after we left? We traveled with gypsies that she had known when she was younger, and we lived for a while by the sea. We had just begun to travel again when we wandered into one of those forsaken villages that prizes superstition over entertainment. My mother was always beautiful," she told Bray. "And others were always jealous in the gypsy camps." She shook her dark thoughts away. "She was ousted as a witch," she said. She smiled at me and I saw the way she looked when she was only a small girl, tinged with sadness.

My mother drew a sharp breath. "By another gypsy?"

Gretal nodded her head. "It is not proven," she said. "But it is thought that another dancer put the thought into the villager's minds. Not that my mother ever tried to disprove it."

"And they killed her," my mother said slowly.

"No," Gretal said. "She walked into the ocean. She left me a letter and her jewelry, and she just walked into the ocean." Tears threatened her lovely face then and she tried hard to smile them away. "They would have. As it was, I was taken and questioned, and only after the priest threatened retribution was I released. We all wept that we could not give her a proper burial, but we found her body on the beach." She spoke now, a grief in her voice that was roughened and painful to listen to. "We laid her out, her ankles crossed. We do this so that we might kiss the ankles of a dancer," she explained to Bray, although neither my mother nor I had known of their customs. She smiled again, and I imagined her crossing her mother's ankles and kissing them delicately. Weeping into the dark hair of her goddess.

"Who is this dancer that did you such evil?" my mother asked.

"Her name is Vindia, she was my mother's shadow."

"Do you worry that she will try to harm you next?" Bray asked.

Gretal laughed then, suddenly and sweetly. "But I'm not a dancer," she said. She looked into my eyes.

"What do you do then?" I asked her, for I could remember her grace, her natural rhythm.

"Tight rope walker," she answered.

***

I meant to go quickly to bed that night and stopped only a moment to look in on Gretal, but she was awake and sitting up. Looking back at me.

Her hair had fallen loose over her shoulders, over her face. I walked into the room and sat on the bed.

I wanted to tell her how sorry I was that she had lost her mother so soon, how I wished she had come back before now so that we might have taken care of her. How I worried for her in world.

Instead, I was silent, feeling the heat coming off her even in the cool of the night. She touched my hair. "You look exactly how I remember you," she said.

The garment she wore fell loose and thin around her, and I felt things I had never felt in my entire life.

It was unlike any feeling I had with any of the men that had visited. None of the coy words and awkward fumbling of clothes and belt buckles.

I might have spent my entire existence dumbfounded as I sat next to her. But she moved, again so slowly that I could stop her if I wished. She got close enough to me to put her face directly in front of mine, our noses touching. Her warm sweet breath was flowing into my mouth as she searched my eyes. I stared at the blueness of her eyes, her perfectly structured face. Her golden hands held my face and when she brought her lips to mine they were firmer than I imagined them. Sweet, but firm.

She kissed me softly, first, and then more desperately. I touched her shoulders, finding her shoulder blades angular she was so thin. I ran my hands on her back and felt scars there. She did not flinch but she stopped then, allowing me any exit.

I had a choice then. I could turn away. I could deny her and myself. But I kissed her back.

And in doing so was lost to any other love for the rest of my existence.

***

Loving her allowed me to lose myself in a way. Being with her was uncalculated, unstructured. I loved her that she was the daughter of Delia, the gypsy nomad; the sister of Hansel, the little prince now in a monastery. I loved that she was a tight ropewalker. But most of all I loved that she was Gretal. That she always smiled even when she cried. That she was passionate. That she could not hide her emotions.

Also in loving her I knew things about her that she could not have said out loud.

I ran my fingers along the gnarled scars on her back and I saw how she was whipped in the square of the village that had cost her mother her life. I saw Hansel sewing up the wounds, tears in his eyes falling onto his beautiful sister's ruined skin. I felt the bruises she had gotten on her travels here. How she had climbed trees to get away from dangerous men, how she had fought hunger and thirst to deliver her mother's ring. I saw her as a tight ropewalker, dancing along the wire, laughing, skipping, and pirouetting. I saw in her that she did not hear music as her mother did, that her grace was a source of joy and that she felt guilt that her mother had not had the same luxury.

She had been loved from afar, young men asked for her hand. A prince even made the humiliating trek to the gypsy's show to try to woo her away. She had never been touched by a man and would never be. Her world was one occupied by women. Her mother had made herself immortal by walking into the sea. She had given her daughter an image, a moment, that would forever cement in her heart the lovely yet cracked glass that was their life together. When she was young, she saw her mother saved by two women who personified all that was good in her young eyes.

I knew also, that she lived in the world and could not leave it to hide as Bray had done. She thought the world full of beauty and wonder, and yet it all circled back to me.

The witch in the wood.

She thought me the most beautiful thing in the world, and so her thoughts always followed her blue stones back to the cottage.

***

She was merciless with my sketching, demanding that I paint and draw at all hours. Gretal did not know anything of art, but then, neither did I. Our own standards were constantly created and reworked. She would leave and then return with paintings, some priceless, some wretched. I would learn from them. I only asked her once, if I might see her walk on the tight rope.

Gretal looked away thoughtfully at the trees in the forest. After much convincing Bray fashioned a tight rope, or what he thought was one.

Gretal assured us that it was perfect, that she could never fall. I watched her climb the tree and then leap onto the rope as if she were as light as a butterfly. She arched her feet and did a running cartwheel, smiling big. We applauded and cheered for her, and when she came down finally, her face was streaked with tears though she laughed.

My mother held her and asked her what was wrong.

Gretal burst into laughter, the tears coming faster, "It just feels so good."

If we are lucky, we get to have that feeling. It settles just when you are doing something you love and are passionate about. It resonates when you come to know that not only are you good at this, you are invincible.

Gretal may have been the best tight ropewalker that ever lived. Though she was modest, I believe that she knew it might have been a possibility for she had never seen anyone do the things she could.

I loved her and hated her when she was most in her element.

I loved that it woke her and made her feel alive, and I hated that she was so small and the drop was so deep.

***

She was away often, and we missed her when she was gone. We had formed a family, solitary as all of us were; we were content with each other. My mother and I could sit in silence for weeks, and Bray was consistently reading and writing. He had gone from a hunter who might have died in the woods to an author who loved to write in them.

Gretal came in on us and we were flooded with the light and loveliness that breathes in the world. She was the best part of the existence we had, unspeaking, renounced. She brought Hansel occasionally when he would acquiesce to being kidnapped from his studies.

He laughingly told us the stir that Gretal caused when she came to the monastery, that she liked to skip stones in their holy water and almost got him thrown out. But he could not deny Gretal anything, and he found that he had a home with us, as well.

***

Gretal only asked me once to follow her out of the wood and see her show. She was humble when she asked, her lovely eyes down looking up through her dark eyelashes. "I'm going to do something I've never done," she said. "And I want you there to see it."

When I told my mother she did not object, only looked at me straight in the eyes as she always did. "We cannot know the future," she said, and it seemed as though she was sad for a moment, but then it passed and she readied me for my trip.

Gretal chattered the whole way out of the wood, telling me about the show. The outside world was not unchanged since when I had left it, but her world was something I had never seen.

The show was small but curiously famous. Their odd wonders drew an audience from miles away.

The priest who bled from sacred wounds and then healed himself sat atop a high wall so that everyone might see.

A fortuneteller swore to tell my future as I walked through.

I laughed as Gretal sheepishly pointed me to the show's Witch, who sat on a lavish chair staring at everyone who passed. Gretal smiled at her and she winked back.

There was no act or creature that surpassed Gretal to the audience. Even the fortuneteller would watch from an opening in the tent. Taller than I have ever seen and wider then I can imagine the wire stretched. It seems as she climbed that she would disappear and belong to the night.

But then I could see her slight frame against the background of black, and her face closed to the fear that destroys men.

Gretal began slowly on the wire, but then danced, and jumped, leaping into darkness, landing on one foot. She turned cartwheels, and spun pirouettes. She turned over onto her hands and walked the rope with only her fingers.

There was never any net below her, never any harness to catch her.

As the audience cheered in rapture, the Witch sighed disdainfully to me. "They love her," she said, jealously sad. "They love her that she has no mystical origin and can do the things she does. As if my nature is not enough for them."

They did worship the Witch for her predictions, her voice. They feared the psychics. They were frightfully curious of the abnormalities. But yes, they loved Gretal, loved that she was a self-made miracle, I suppose.

When the show was over she would sleep in my arms, my lips on her forehead.

I was constantly fascinated by this show of curiosities. I walked from tent to tent, peering in on the wonders and the lies the gypsies sold. I grew fond of their old Witch—as un-magical as she really was.

She gasped once when we accidentally brushed hands and hurried me into a seat.

Holding my palm open to her she said, "I don't normally do this. The fortuneteller gets angry when I do—but I just had to tell you that I see a young man in your future. A king!" she breathed.

I tried to hide my smile, aware of her loneliness, her facades. I nodded as she told me of the imagined life I might live when my king showed up at the show. Over her open fire and her props, I wondered out loud her age.

She grew silent and sad, reaching under her table and bringing out a flask. Sipping gin and hiccupping, she said that she was very old to work in such a place. That she had left a husband and two children behind in a small house deep in the country.

Gretal walked in quietly and sat beside her, listening to her as well, holding her hand as she cried.

She spoke of a sickness that had killed three of her five children—a sickness that denied them sleep and peace. Whispering, she admitted their small faces deteriorating in front of her. How they slept finally, as beautiful as they had ever been in life. How she had fed them poison to make it painless.

Her husband had loved her and hated her for the act. He didn't trust her around the children he had left.

A woman left her husband one day and joined the carnival and became a witch.

I sympathized with her. I was a witch that left my small paradise to see the world through a carnival's kaleidoscope. Her confession made me wonder how many of the others were merely hiding inside a disguise—hopeful to discard their old lives and wounds. Choosing, instead, the kinds of abrasions that fit nicely into categories.

Looking at Gretal across the witch's table I imagined her old. I thought of her golden skin fading, becoming paper thin, filled with veins. I saw her back hunch and her legs become weary.

When we walked out of the tent I grabbed her hand quickly, and she turned, a small smile on her face.

I was not prone to affection. I never had been, but I wanted to draw her into me suddenly and kiss her perfect lips, her nose. Kiss the thin eyelids.

We stood inches apart in the night, her looking at me and wondering.

Like a man might, she brought my wrist to her lips and kissed the bridge that led to my hand.

"I was only thinking you are going to be an amazing old woman," I said, in a rushed whisper.

She laughed out loud, shaking her head. Her eyes were so full of love that night, standing in the bruised twilight, holding my wrist.

I had no other way of telling her that I loved her. I did

not have the words. I could not weep over her, but I wished then that I could. That when she was old we could remember my passionate pledge of love so many years ago. I wanted to give her that. But she was Gretal, and kind and easy in a way very few people on this earth are—and she demanded nothing and accepting everything from me as if it were a gift.

She linked arms with me in a girlish and merry way, hurrying me along.

I thought I had never felt happiness such as that moment.

I felt that no matter what misery resided in the tents we passed that we were a part from them forever, and it was not I, an ageless real witch, that shielded us, but rather this fragile young girl that kept all sadness at bay with her relentless smile.

***

Vindia was a beautiful dancer, not unlike Delia in her looks—though where Delia was angular; Vindia was soft, rounded out. That she had hated Delia was obvious.

One night the witch and I sat drinking and I listened to the carnival gossip. I was sketching her with no real purpose in mind, except knowing the woman wanted company.

"A man asked Gretal to marry him yesterday," she told me conspiratorially. "He is desperate over her, asked her twice!" She shook her head. "That girl would be lucky to end up with such a man—richer than a sultan," she crowed.

I had to smile over this, Gretal's beauty and kindness prompted all sorts of proposals—and she was endlessly surprised and gracious.

The witch clucked as she recounted Gretal's refusal.

"But we're still waiting for yours to come, dear!" she assured me.

It was then that Vindia came to join us—her eyes as dark as ravens. There was something coldly attractive about her, a steeliness that radiated out of her body. Through the tips of her fingers. When she spoke her voice sounded like diamond gravel, lovely and cutting.

"I've been wanting to talk to you," she told the old witch pointedly.

The old woman sighed, though it was clear she loved the attention.

Vindia offered her upturned palms, a warmness flooding her cheeks. "Won't you tell me if he will come back?"

"I've been teaching this one all about the dark arts," the witch said dramatically, pointing at me. "Give it a try," she urged me, not being able to resist a wink.

I tried to refuse but Vindia became affectionate to the idea.

"Come now, are you going to travel with us and never find a calling?" she chided me, her palm more insistent in my face. "Any story will be better than the one she's been telling me for the last year," she laughed.

I do not know how to read palms, or to even pretend. I took her hand with both of mine and looked into her eyes, burning coal just behind her pretty mask.

When I touched her hands, I knew that she had told a young man who had fallen in love with her that Delia was a witch. And the cause of plague. I knew that she had danced in many fairs and had seen much of Europe.

And I knew when I looked into her life that she had rejoiced when Delia had taken her own life—that she had given up her guilt.

There was so much to see in her. So much loss and grief; so much love that had been washed away, leaving her like the stripped stones on a quarry.

I could only swallow and say sheepishly, "Well. It looks like he's coming."

She tore her hand away and clapped, smiling. She threw

a coin on the table and left us with a laugh.

***

When I lay with Gretal that night, I lit a lantern and propped up on my elbow, looking down at her. In the light, she looked ablaze, glowing like a star. She opened her eyes and looked at me, slightly turning to face me.

"I want to weep for your mother," I told her, curious over my own words. "I want to cry for you and I want to hate the woman that made her do it."

Gretal thought over my words and then nodded. "Yes. I know you do. And that you would if you could." She faltered over her words, and then sat up. "There is so much that you don't know about this life," she said. "So much that is wrapped up in the traditions of it all. The superstitions," she corrected herself. She began playing with my long hair, wrapping a red golden cord around her fingers. "I wept so over my mother," she said. "It felt like my lungs had been ripped out of me. Not just because she was dead. We all die." She smiled. "Well, most of us, anyway." Touching my cheek gently, she went on, "Not only that she was gone. That she had walked into an ocean. She was—sometimes-miserable," she said, and it was the only time that I ever heard her say anything that wasn't worshipful of her mother. "We have a superstition; when we are burying the dead we kiss a dancer's ankles, but we also kiss the last hands that touched her—even if they are violent, wretched. I think there's something left of them there," she said.

I saw then—they revered the flesh that had last held their loved ones when they breathed.

She squinted. "I regret that she didn't want me to hold her as she left this place," she said. "I know I couldn't have let her; and she would have known it too. But it hurts that she left the world with no one holding her, as if no one would anchor her." She paused and looked at me then slowly shut the lantern to die.

Gretal fell asleep quickly but I could not for the longest time.

***

She soon became passionately obsessed with something other than our time together. She was secretive, enamored, and always overflowing with excitement. Gretal couldn't contain herself to sit down and eat, let alone spend hours on end walking and talking with me. When I held her I felt her buzz with energy, when we kissed I could hear her blood pounding through her veins.

I could never begrudge my love passion, though I wondered about it. But she wanted to keep her secret and so she did until she was ready to share it. She worked tirelessly in the large tent that held her tight rope. She came to bed late, covered with bruises and shaken. She reminded me of a tiger cub that is being taught to hunt, she was getting scratched up by her lessons, but they were making her fearless.

One day, I knew it was time. She winked at me and beckoned me to follow her. Gretal had such little pretension that this made me laugh and want to indulge her. I saw that three tight ropes had been fashioned, at least a foot away from each other.

We stood in the ring and looked up at them together.

I imagined the crowd that would come, the applause, and I tried to imagine what it felt like to be Gretal dancing between three tight ropes.

We made love on the floor in the ring.

In my arms she was feverish and pulsing like a beating heart.

The carnival was alive with anticipation. Gretal's act was drawing fans out from hundreds of miles. They all began to work slavishly on their own arts, and I sketched and painted the scenes I captured there.

When the priest told us that he had gotten word that Hansel was coming, Gretal demanded even more of herself, sometimes forgetting to change out of her sweat soaked clothes when she came to bed. I didn't know to be jealous of her passion, I could not deny her that mindless joy that it gave her. I know it when I paint. Only when I paint. I gently dressed her bed and would demand she eat, but in other ways it made me adore her more.

I painted her once on the tightrope. A portrait that has seen centuries come and go. She stands in red, her feet plied at the middle of the rope. Her eyes are half closed and her head is tilted back, her golden throat exposed. She might be anyone, except for the way her lips are slightly opened, the shadow of a smile around the corners of her mouth. She was never without that happiness, that innocent longing.

I painted it from memory. After she was gone.

***

Hansel arrived a few days before she was to perform her new act. He was dashing and charismatic still, but his lessons had chastened him in a soft way. He thought longer before he spoke, and when he did only said something kind. I saw him through Gretal's eyes, her glorious brother who she loved. Her better mannered, smarter half. They were beautiful together, as lovely as they had been as children. Echoing each other's loneliness and grief over their mother, but also lauding their youth and resilience. He taught Gretal prayers and she sang him songs, he brought her prayer beads and she wore them in her hair. He could not chastise her; he loved her too much to ever say an unkind word to her. I watched them, endlessly sketching as I had never sketched in my life. They were inspiring, truly, to view, and I did believe that everyone who saw them felt the same.

I was fleshing out one of my sketches in the dying light of the day when I heard voices. Living among the people of the carnival I was not shy with them, or they with me. Arguments were held outdoors, spectators watched unashamed.

She whispered first, "I know you came back to see me."

"I did not," he said back firmly.

"You did! I've missed you," she said miserably.

I turned and I could see the woman try to put her arms around the man; in that last light I was blinded suddenly, blinking hard.

"You came to see her," she said flatly.

"Yes," he agreed. "I did come to see her." He spoke kindly, but without apology.

"I loved you," she hissed. "I loved you so much."

He sighed back. "I never felt that for you," he admitted. "But I do want for you to be happy, I want for you to let go of..."

"How could you ever love me," she seethed, and now others were staring at the two in the clearing. "You only ever loved your whore of a sister," she spat.

If he had not been studying to be a man of God, I think that his twitching hand would have slapped her across the face, but instead he only shook his head in sadness and disgust.

"I regret you," he said, his voice cold and sharp.

It seemed our whole small colony, except for Gretal, had seen Vindia and Hansel, and though none of us spoke of it just then, we were all chilled by the dancer's face as she stared at his retreating figure.

Because she had not witnessed it, I felt I had to tell her

every detail.

Gretal listened, thoughtful and amused.

"Did you know?" I asked.

She shook her head but then said, "I didn't know they were lovers. But I'm not surprised by it." She glanced at me. "No one would be surprised if we announced we were lovers, though they may not know it out right."

I had to laugh at her, and her complete honesty.

"We all live by different rules here," she said. "That is why we don't just go live somewhere."

"Ah," I breathed, "but you don't hate him that he was with her?"

She gave a small smile and shrugged her shoulders. "I love you," she said. "I have no more left to hate anyone with."

***

Gretal did not mention Hansel's trespass again, and when she saw her brother she tried to be especially jovial, doing an impression of me sketching that made us both tear up. He was tender from the argument and his own past but soon was soothed by his sister's happiness and youth.

Quickly, now. This moment.

***

The tent was packed in with people and creatures, all overflowing into the ring. The tight rope shone like strung diamonds, and with a gasp all saw that there were three ropes, set now two feet away from each other.

She began as she always had, lightly and slowly, and then suddenly she leaped and spun between the ropes, dancing back and forth between them. Women cried at seeing this, and even I was caught by her grace, her beauty, her belief that made her body adhere to her wishes.

It seemed she did this endlessly, joyfully. Dancing. Spinning. Loving this.

And then she stopped on the middle rope, feet in a dancer's position.

She was so small suddenly; so fragile I did not know how the applause did not throw her off her mission.

She looked at the crowd and found my face, my eyes, I waited—my breath held. And I loved her again. All the lives in all the world pointing to other directions could not move me.

I loved her for being a tight ropewalker. I loved her for refusing to see ugliness in abnormalities. I loved her that she was Gretal—daughter of a gypsy queen.

She smiled then, so beautiful that if I could have wept I swear, I would have.

The crowd hears the rips before she feels them, the first wire snaps and she dives for the next one, we sigh, thinking it part of the act. But then the second goes and she leaps to the third.

I see it before she feels it, and she finds my eyes. It happens so fast. She does not wait for it to break.

She arches her back, sailing through the air.

Her head thrown back and her eyes and lips slightly open.

She falls into forever.

***

I am the first to touch her, to cradle her broken body. Her arm is bent and her legs are grotesquely broken. There is blood flowing from her mouth, but she is still breathing, sharply and not for long. She is broken everywhere.

Where is the priest who sits on a wall with his internal stitching kit, if he cannot put her together who will?

Where is my immortal mother who knows how to undo

this damage?

But only her witch is there in the round with her.

The light of the moon creeps into the tent, hitting her face and she looks as eternal as a goddess, as mortal as the child she is.

Was I to know that there was such beauty in this world? Did I believe it?

I can only feel her fingers brush my lips with her blood.

And see

Only the moonlight through the cracks of the tent

Only her cheek that I put to my heart.

***

I was the last to touch her.

As was custom they displayed her, and one by one, those that loved her came to pay their respects.

They touched her brow, and then kissed her crossed ankles, as delicately as butterflies.

I was the last to touch her.

And so, as custom dictated, they would kiss her ankles and then my hands.

Hansel's lips feel like Gretal's on my palms, and if I could, I would have wept. His guilt has forced him into despair and he cries out against my hands.

Vindia's are chapped with murder and jealousy; I can see her slicing small imperfections into the wire.

I see her plan to kill my love. What good is this telepathy in hindsight? What good are these witch powers without Gretal?

The first hundred felt like nothing, but by morning the skin on my hands were chapped and thin.

By the next week my hands bled, but they kept coming, and I could not refuse them.

When each would lean in and their lips would meet my

hands I would get visions—one after another, their lives, their loves, their heartbreak. Gretal. The connection always led to Gretal, over and over. I wanted to scream in agony to stop and to never stop. That I might continue to see her through memories that are not my own.

But the procession does end.

And my own memories are raw—like my hands.

I walk into the night and never return.

***

I watch the traveler leave. Afraid and enchanted all at once back into the cold, away from my diseased hands. I think for a moment of following, taking nothing and starting again, and perhaps one day I will. But for now I can only sit, looking at my hands, remembering.

Author Bio:

Ashley Hendricks writes dark fantasy and young adult fiction. She is simultaneously conducting research for her upcoming young adult fantasy novel and teaching high school in New Orleans.

His Melted Heart
Sylvia Hiven

Heinrich had forgotten everything about his existence before he arrived at the toy chest.

He knew there had been twenty tin soldiers in the beginning, neatly cradled in a flat box, their paint lustrous and each of them with a musket tucked at their sides. They had been a proud troupe, and each man had been like a brother to him. Their little Mistress had played with them plenty, staging glorious battles and heroic quests for them to display their skills and courage. It had been a grand time.

As the years went by, his brothers vanished among the rest of the playthings. Some fell onto the floor and were swept up by an eager broom. Others decided to venture out into the nursery on their own, and never returned. It did not take long before Heinrich was the sole survivor of the troupe.

Heinrich felt lonesome then, and often sat alone in a corner of the toy chest, pitying himself for his tragic fate.

But Black Bart would not have it.

"Don't look so down, soldier," the cowboy said, gently poking Heinrich with his spurred boot. "You ain't been here for more than a few years. You got all your parts and your paint ain't peeling yet. And our Mistress doesn't care about you enough to play with you, so you get to sit here and relax, day after day. What you got to be sad about?"

"My brothers," Heinrich replied. "I was not meant to be alone."

"Ah, you fool. I ain't seen my horse for five years. Some grubby little hand grabbed Drifter right out from under me at a birthday party once, and I've been solo since." The cowboy shrugged. "Loneliness ain't so bad. And as soon as you meet someone, well...you've chased that loneliness away, haven't you?"

Heinrich looked up at Bart. The open—albeit toothless—grin splitting the cowboy's scruffy face was clear in its intention—it meant to say that Heinrich wasn't alone anymore. And while having Bart as company was a nice distraction, it still did not give Heinrich a purpose.

That purpose came into his life in a pink box.

***

The velvet box, decorated with glass beads and pearls, was placed on the vanity table across the nursery. Heinrich did not pay much attention to it at first. The box just sat there, gleaming like the mother-of-pearl hairbrushes and beaded combs strewn about it. Heinrich was a practical man, and saw no attraction in such a pretty, useless trinket.

But the day that the box opened up, he began to believe in beauty.

From the belly of the box, a goddess rose, accompanied by a soft tune. Her graceful arms were raised above her head, reaching for some invisible treasure in the air. Her slender neck was bent, and her face upturned in a longing expression. Perched upon one leg, and with the other outstretched behind her, she twirled around to the gentle music.

And each time she spun, Heinrich's world stopped.

"Hold your horses there, soldier," Bart said, rolling his eyes. "You'd be wise to forget about that one. You ain't never gonna get next to the likes of her."

"What is she?" Heinrich asked, still staring in awe.

"She is a *ba-luh-reena*," Bart said, spitting out the word as if it had a foul taste. "She lives in a box of jewelry and pearls and gold. She ain't never gonna come down here into our chest. That girl is art, not a plaything."

Despite his contemptuous tone, Bart's eyes betrayed him. They gleamed with admiration as well.

Heinrich and Bart watched the ballerina for many months. Their little Mistress opened the box several times a day, letting the ballerina out of her velvet prison. Each time she appeared, unfolding her rosy limbs, it was like watching the budding and bloom of a perfect flower.

It was true what Bart said: the ballerina was certainly not a toy. But where Bart was proven wrong, was his claim that she would never leave her pink box.

Despite the ballerina's loveliness, she eventually lost her appeal to their Mistress. One winter's day, Heinrich and Bart watched in horror as the ballerina was plucked from her home and carelessly manhandled by the Mistress' hand like a rag doll. When the child had finished her rough play, she did not bother to put the ballerina back in her box. Instead, she just discarded the beautiful creature into the toy chest with a shrug and disappeared out of the nursery.

Bouncing off the head of a soft teddy bear and crashing against the nutcrackers so hard that their wooden limbs rattled, the ballerina tumbled into the bottom of the toy chest. She landed before Bart and Heinrich in a mess of limbs, blonde curls and tulle, a cry of discomfort escaping her lips.

"*Mon Dieu,*" the ballerina lamented. "Oh dear, oh my!"

Heinrich was by her side immediately. "*Fräulein,* are you alright" he asked.

She pushed her unruly locks out of her face, revealing a pair of large eyes, blue and bright as stars. Whoever had created her had put much love into chiseling the delicate landscape of her face. Every curve of her features was perfect.

"Yes, I am fine." She tilted her head, and looked at him with curious eyes. "I am Isabelle. What is your name?"

"Heinrich," he replied, helping her to her feet. "And this is my friend, Bart."

The cowboy stepped up to them, tipping his worn hat. "It's a pleasure to meet you, miss," he said. "Sorry that you had to be dumped here with us, but...here you are."

Despite the happiness twirling around his heart from just being in Isabelle's presence, Heinrich felt a sudden sting of concern. "Yes," he said. "I don't know if you can get back to where you came from, and this place is certainly not as beautiful as your jewelry-laden box."

"Oh, I wanted nothing more than to get out of there. If I could have plucked myself from that box and thrown myself into this toy chest, I would have." Isabelle still stared at Heinrich with a gentle smile, her china-blue eyes drilling into him and down into his very core. "I have watched you from afar for a long time, Heinrich. I am so glad to finally meet you."

Never had Heinrich's tin heart patted faster than in that moment.

***

For the first time in years, Heinrich felt every inch a soldier.

His mission was the sweetest yet: providing for Isabelle. He convinced Bart to help him build a shelter in a corner of the toy chest, constructed with parts from an erector set and with a discarded silk handkerchief draped over it for privacy. They found a pin-cushion on which Isabelle could sleep. A gleaming thimble became her table. They even found a buckled lid from a snuffbox, which they propped against the wall so that Isabelle could practice her *relevé*, *retiré*, and *plié*.

Each time they brought Isabelle a new item to add elegance to her sanctuary; she thanked them both with a kiss upon their cheeks.

But her lips always lingered on Heinrich's cheek for just a heartbeat longer.

One evening, as the two of them had said goodnight to Isabelle and left her alone in her little home, Bart nudged Heinrich playfully, his eyes twinkling like pieces of polished coal. "You're a lucky soldier, my friend," the cowboy said. "I think that the girl fancies you."

Bart's words made Heinrich lose his breath. "Do you think so, truly?" he asked, unable to contain his delight.

"It's obvious. You could bring that girl dried rocking-horse dung, and she would love you for it."

"We both bring her gifts," Heinrich said. "She appreciates us both, I am sure."

"Ah, I could paint myself purple and stand on my head, and she would not notice me." There was a hint of sadness in Bart's face, but a devious smile chased it away. "You're the man for her. You should go alone to her, and show her how else she can make use of that bed you built her, other than getting her beauty sleep."

Heinrich blushed. "You should not speak like that about Isabelle," he said. "She is a beautiful, honorable girl, and she deserves respect."

"Come now, soldier. You ain't trying to tell me that she doesn't make your blood rush when she kisses you goodnight, are you?"

Heinrich opened his mouth to launch another protest, but nothing came out. After all, Bart was right. Just looking into Isabelle's eyes made him feel like his insides were on fire. He was certain that being truly close to her would heat his core and melt him back into the lump of tin from which he had once been created.

And that, he mused, would certainly be a death worthwhile.

***

Isabelle was as charming and enchanting on the inside

as she was on the outside. Heinrich found himself completely spellbound by her. Many days, Heinrich would watch Isabelle as she stretched and bent before her makeshift mirror. Sometimes she would dance for him, becoming *Swanhilde* or Aurora and bring passion and grief to his heart with her performance. Other days, they would sit on the pin-cushion in her little sanctuary and talk for hours. Isabelle would tell Heinrich about all the places she had seen from her box, and Heinrich told her about the brothers he had lost since he had arrived at the toy chest. He had never been able to talk about that loss with Bart, but Isabelle seemed to understand his pain.

"Heinrich, my dear friend," she said. "I am so sorry about your comrades."

"It is not easy, being alone," Heinrich replied. "A man is nothing without his friends."

Isabelle took his hand, squeezing it tightly. "I am your friend now, *cheri*," she said. "Is that not something?"

Such devotion played in her eyes, and each time she looked at him like that, Heinrich's impulse was to pull her into his arms and kiss her. However, something inside of him told him that he had not deserved her yet. He was just a simple soldier after all, and she was a beautiful ballerina. He had to prove himself first. He just did not know how.

Heinrich's hesitation bothered Bart to no end.

"You're an idiot," Bart said to him. "If you ain't gonna make a move on her, perhaps I will. I know how to show a girl a good time. And that pretty lady sure looks like she needs one."

Heinrich glared at his friend. "This isn't the Wild West, Bart," he said. "Isabelle needs to be courted properly, like a lady."

"So court her." Bart was silent for a few moments. "You know that old dollhouse on the other side of the nursery?"

Heinrich knew of the dollhouse. He had seen it through a crack in the corner of the toy chest. He pondered it often, wondering what sort of treasures he could find inside to bring to Isabelle, but inevitably gave up on the idea for the sheer impossibility of it. After all, he could not get out of the toy chest. Even if he made it to the other side of the room, how was he to bring anything back with him?

"I know what you are thinking," he said to Bart. "You think I should go over there and bring Isabelle some special gift."

"Girls like gifts," Bart said with a shrug. "I'm sure you could find her many pretty things there. It would show her that you can provide for her. You could ask for her hand, get down on your knees, or whatever you chivalrous types do." He nudged Heinrich, again with a mischievous glint in his eyes. "Then she would be yours to have, in any way you want her."

Heinrich sighed. "But it is not possible," he said, looking upwards toward the towering wall of the toy chest. "I will never make it. I can't even get myself over the edge of this place."

Bart smiled. "Well, you are lucky," he said. "Because your best buddy happens to know how to get you over there."

***

For the first time, Heinrich realized how fortunate he was to have made friends with Black Bart.

Sure, the cowboy grated on him at times. He had a bad temper and an uncouth mouth, and he stunk of tobacco and sweat. It also bothered Heinrich how often Bart's eyes trailed over Isabelle's slender body every time the three of them were together. But now, as Heinrich was facing this impossible task, Bart was the one making it possible.

Bart convinced one of the tattered teddy bears to help push Heinrich as high as possible towards the edge of the toy chest, and got a rag doll to give up the silk sash in her hair. He tied it around Heinrich's waist, tightening it with thorough knots and loops.

"I can lower you to the other side, and pull you back over with it when you're ready to come back," Bart said. "You and whatever treasures you find for Isabelle. I heard that there's a mirror in that dollhouse. A real mirror; one that would show her reflection perfectly. See if you can find it."

And so, Heinrich ventured outside of the toy chest for the first time since he had arrived in it.

When his boots landed on the floor of the nursery, he felt as if he was a warrior treading unknown territory. He untied the sash from his waist, and wrapped it around his musket so that it would not accidentally get pulled over the edge and eliminate his only way of return.

"Psst." One of Bart's black eyes appeared in a crack in the toy chest. "Don't be too long now, you hear? That ballerina of yours is bound to wonder where you went eventually. I'll try to cover for you, but don't be draggin' your feet! Good luck!"

With Bart's encouraging words urging him on, Heinrich turned around and began his journey.

Making his way across the wooden floor was not as easy as Heinrich had expected. He had to jump across many wide cracks between the floorboards, and being made from tin, it was not always easy to move swiftly. The sunrays that streamed in from the large window moved rapidly with him—it was almost nightfall when he arrived at the dollhouse.

Stepping inside of it, however, Heinrich realized that the trek certainly had been worth his while.

The dollhouse was a palace, full of treasures. Whatever creatures had inhabited it were long gone, likely lost much like his soldier brothers, but all of their belongings had been left untouched. Room after room was decorated with elegant furniture, rich curtains and glittering chandeliers. There was a sitting room with cushioned chairs and a silver tea set on the table. Entering the bedroom, he came across a four-poster bed, covered with soft bolsters and pillows.

Heinrich walked through the rooms, wide eyed, his heart aching at all the beautiful things that he wanted to take back with him. What really caught his attention was the mirror that hung on the wall in the first floor hallway. Its glossy surface was smooth and even, and surrounded by a golden frame. The moment he laid eyes on it, he knew he had to have it for Isabelle.

After pulling the mirror down from the wall, Heinrich peeked out through one of the windows of the dollhouse. Eve had fallen, shrouding the nursery in darkness, lit up only by the crackling fireplace. Heinrich hesitated. The mirror would not be easy to transport across the floor in the darkness, with the cracks between the floorboards surely making the task harder. On the other hand, waiting too long to see Isabelle again made his heart ache. He did not want to waste time.

He managed to carry the mirror down from the dollhouse and onto the floor. He trembled, both with exhaustion from the effort and from the cool night air that slipped up through the cracks between the floorboards. He pulled the mirror halfway across the floor, but that was as far as he could manage before he had to sit down and rest.

The fireplace, spreading its gentle warmth into the room, flickered its light down upon him, making him sleepy. He slumped down beneath it, resting his tired head against the edge of the mirror. He lay there, embraced by the fire, pretending it was Isabelle's love warming him up. It did not take long before sleep pulled him under.

He dreamed of Isabelle, and of being encased in the heaven of her arms.

***

As soon as Heinrich woke up the next morning, he realized something was wrong.

He felt dazed and out of balance. Opening his eyes, he could barely see anything. He blinked several times, trying to clear his vision, but the world still looked blurry and skewed.

The treacherous warmth of the fireplace had cost him dearly. He had fallen asleep too close to the flames, and the heat from it had melted parts of him. Lifting his hands close to his face, he stared at them in horror. The fingers upon his hands were nothing but bubbled lumps.

He leaned over the mirror and stared at his reflection. His face was completely malformed. His nose was merely a nub and his mouth was askew. His eyes were nothing but black slits. He opened his mouth, attempting to utter a gasp of horror, but no sound pushed out from between his molten lips.

He was a monster. Would Isabelle want him now? Was her heart pure enough to see the sacrifice he had made for her, or would she turn away in disgust at the sight of him?

She must see me, he thought bravely. *She must know that beneath this melted mess, I still love her.*

Getting the mirror to the other side of the room had been hard before, and now, when his limbs were nothing but scorched lumps, it was nearly impossible. He dragged, pushed and pulled it across the uneven floor boards, putting all his might into it. His back, legs and arms ached.

When Heinrich finally arrived at the base of the toy chest, his tin face sweating and his arms and legs shivering with exhaustion, he found to his terror that the sash was no longer hanging over the edge.

He frowned. He remembered distinctly tying the sash to his musket, making sure that the weight would be enough to keep it available to him upon his return. Bewildered, he leaned the gilded mirror against the side of the toy chest. He stumbled around the wall of the chest, searching for the crack in the wall through which Bart had talked to him the previous day, hoping that his friend would be there to help him.

Despite his ruined eyes, Heinrich found a crack eventually. When he pressed his melted face against it, he found himself peering into Isabelle's sanctuary.

Isabelle was there, sitting on her pin-cushion bed. She looked as beautiful as ever, her curls framing her face like a halo, splashing golden light into her fair eyes. But those eyes were grieved and filled with tears.

"*Je ne comprend pas,*" she said. "Why would he leave me?"

Heinrich realized that Isabelle was not alone. Bart was there with her, standing at the edge of the room, his tattered hat in his hands. He wrung it desperately.

"Isabelle, I don't know," Bart said. "Heinrich was always weak of character, with a treacherous heart."

"But... I thought he loved me." The tears in Isabelle's eyes waited no longer; they fell over her fair cheeks like clear pearls, making trails of grief across her face. "I thought he was going to ask me to be his."

"Heinrich was always fickle, all the time that I knew him," Bart said, approaching Isabelle where she sat upon her makeshift bed. "He didn't know what he wanted. I think he was afraid. Perhaps the feelings you had for him scared him so much, he ran off."

Bart's words made Isabelle weep wildly. Large, crystal tears rolled from her eyes, and her gasps of grief made Heinrich's heart ache.

However, his heart did not ache for long. Black Bart moved closer to Isabelle, sitting down next to her and wrapping his arms around her tender shoulders and looking into her eyes deeply. Heinrich felt his insides crumble apart.

"Isabelle," Bart said. "You're the most beautiful woman I have ever seen. You shouldn't waste your tears on Heinrich. He could never appreciate a woman like yourself. He's just a boy. You need somebody that can take care of you. A real man."

Heinrich watched in horror as Bart leaned closer to Isabelle, seeking her peach-colored lips with his fleshy, cracked mouth. But Isabelle turned her head away, rejecting his advances.

"I am sorry, Bart," she said in a quiet voice. "But I love Heinrich, and I always will."

Bart's black eyebrows jutted together like two severe storm clouds. "You silly girl," he growled, taking hold of her wrist. "You searched every corner of the toy chest for yourself, and you know that soldier is gone! He doesn't want you, and he ain't coming back. And here I am, making a decent proposal. You'd be wise to take it, and not be an obstinate mule about it!"

She struggled against his grip, her tears falling faster. "Let me go," she sobbed.

But Bart did not care about her plea. "Fine," he said angrily. "If you don't give willingly what I want, then I will take it."

He took hold of her other wrist, and pushed her down upon the pincushion. Isabelle squirmed beneath Bart's touch, clawing desperately at him, but the cowboy only laughed as he tore her dress into shreds of silk and tulle.

Then, for a moment so terrible that time seemed to stop, Bart raised his gaze and looked towards the crack where Heinrich was watching. Their eyes met.

Heinrich tried to scream, but no sound came across his molten lips. Bart's lips, on the other hand, curled into a devious smile. He shot Heinrich one last, acid look, and then he closed his eyes, burying his face in Isabelle's soft neckline and mumbling with satisfaction. Heinrich had lost part of his sight, his sense of touch, and his ability to speak, but the cowboy's words were still painfully clear.

"Mine," Bart mumbled. "Mine, finally."

Author Bio:

Sylvia Hiven lives and writes in Atlanta, Georgia. Her fiction has appeared in over thirty publications, including Daily Science Fiction, PseudoPod, Flash Me Magazine, EscapePod, and others. She also edits the speculative fiction e-zine LingerFiction.

Apple of My Eye
P.L. Dugad

The first thing the woman did upon waking was reach for her two children. They were not truly hers, but they were beloved to the man who was beloved to her, and so she loved them as unequivocally as he did. Anxious for their safety—for there was nowhere they might have hidden but the forest, and the forest was full of darkness even at noon—she wanted to call them back to her. But the woman had been careless and slumbered far too long; she could not remember what names to use. Never mind; they had nowhere else to go. Surely, they would return soon.

She smiled, imagining how she would greet them once their feet pattered the floor, hesitant, knowing that they had been naughty. Her voice would scold them for their reckless behavior, though her hands would belie her callosity; it was impossible that she might resist hugging them tightly, smelling the sweet scent of childhood in their hair. How could she beat their simple-minded youth out of them? The world was harsh enough as it was; they would grow up and leave long before she was ready no matter what. She had to preserve their innocence as long as was possible. And so, the woman waited, and let the faint tendrils of a happy anticipation tug her expression into a more pleasing shape.

Seated near the doorway and the bitter draft of a ceaseless winter, she allowed herself to sink into the subtle heat of nostalgia, substituting it for the impotence of the stuttering embers in the stove. She remembered how it was when she had first met the woodcutter. He had been overflowing with a hurt so potent that she had felt it even as she hid in the darkest depths of her home, the forest. Even to her unwilling ears, the cries of his wounded mind had rang out louder than the cries of the tree he had felled that day. The habit of a lifetime, the hatred of the careless prodigal children of nature, was swept away. Yet, it was no surprise, that her revulsion for men had turned so rapidly to love. Was it not love, after all, that had made her turn away from the ways of men, long ago when she had chosen her solitary path? For eons, she had thought it would end there, in the hollow of the enormous tree that was her home and whose whispers comforted her when the vestiges of loneliness threatened to force her back into the life she had forever forsaken.

Then he came, and he needed her. Not as the witch of the forest, a mystery who dealt in potions and black curses to those who could pay, but as a woman. A living, breathing mother to the children so recently orphaned and a wife for the widower who found himself adrift, bereft of anyone to care for him. When she first sensed him he was a pitiable thing, this wide armed man who had been burnt brown from head to toe by his labor. His cap of dusty hair was unruly and in need of a cut; his brown eyes had melted into a constant suspicion of tears.

The witch reached within herself and found the small core of humanity she had never been able to kill, though she had tried so many times, and let it expand, let it take over her being. For him, she was a woman. In the small church, paned with costly windows of stained glass—that were the pride of the six villages it serviced—she stood, fearing not the sight of the god these people worshipped. His casual vengeance meant nothing to her. At the altar she stood, and said her vows with as much heart as she had once put into ending the lives of his kin, and she became a woman. Nothing more, nothing less.

Once they were joined, they returned to his poor hovel. He apologized many times in as many ways as there were cruelties, but she always told him he was foolish to worry so. "I have married you, and it is you I want, not a great house," she said. She could have mentioned the poverty of the tree she had lived in, but the memory of its whispers was a treasured one, and she had never told him of the years spent mothering the forest, protecting it from the viciousness of his kind.

They had met so innocently one day, by the whim of a chance she had contrived, at the edge of the forest as he was leaving with his axe and empty hands. Again and again they met at the edge of the forest, for she could not leave its boundaries without withering in those days; she was already weak so close to the human world. At last, when he took her hand she was freed of her compulsion for nature, free to become his, to become domestic and conventional. He had never asked her where she had come from, nor had he questioned the fact that her side of the church was empty, though he had had his children and cousins and parents all to visit, and for that she loved him more than anything save the thought of the melancholy that her presence would cure.

When the sadness continued into the first days of their wedded life, she knew it was but the shock of novelty, and the guilt that he had somehow betrayed the dead woman who had borne him his children. Sweet things they were, a boy and a girl, as blonde as he was and she was not. Well behaved to her face, they never questioned her authority or her right to stand at the stove their true mother had once occupied, baking sweets that perfumed the two bare rooms where they lived.

At night, the children held each other in fear, and at school in the village, they were always whispering with each other and with their friends. The woman had no knowledge of this, for they kept it from her; but the woodcutter knew. He had held them when they were born, and nothing they did could be a secret from him, try as they might.

"Such kind-faced children," she always told her husband, seeing now that the darkness in his mind concerned them. He must not worry that they were not hers, for they did nothing to show it, they were never insolent. And, as it were, she was unable to bear children herself; but this she did not tell him, for she did not wish to draw any attention to the truth of her being. Yet all her cautions were naught; fear mushroomed in her mind, that he doubted her, supported by the distraught ivy spreading in his mind. She allayed those concerns, too, by being as gentle with the children as is possible without being nothing more than a complacent observer to their mishaps and misdeeds. If she had never raised a hand to them then she would have been worse than violent; she would have been neglectful.

For the boy's birthday—it came back to her, his name was Hans—for Hans' birthday, the woman swallowed the last of her pride and residual love for the forest. She went to the village, taking care to avoid the huts that still stank of the loam that only grew where no sunlight fell, and begged for butter and egg and sugar, that she might make something special for the boy who had so little. To her former home, she went next, picking the best of the late summer apples. Merciless, she shut her ears to the keening sorrow of the trees that had borne them with so much hope for future germinations.

Thus equipped, she made the finest pie there ever was, and though it smelled so good, and there was little enough food even then, she did not eat of it. For she saw the hunger of the woodcutter and his growing son, even that of the little daughter. And she told herself that her sacrifice would forever persuade the woodcutter of her fidelity towards his children. She loved apples so much; she loved the crunch between her teeth and the way the tart juices dripped into her mouth. It was inconceivable that her pained belly and starved expression should pass unnoticed.

Yet he continued to worry, and the shroud that hid his happiness grew no thinner, and her anxiety forced her to confront him. "It is nothing," he said. "Nothing" it was, so many times, so many nights, until he came home one evening.

It was later than usual; the sun had long since descended into the mountains, even the faintest glimmers of twilight were but a memory to trouble the diurnal soul. She had had ample time to prepare his meal and, of course, to worry. The food itself was a cause for worry. There was so little; the children had eaten the crusts she had given them, and the bird she had coaxed into an oven and baked for them (though not in their sight—the little girl would never have abided eating a creature whose lively eye she had fallen for, the woman knew). Pressing her stomach ever inward, the woman had gruel from the tiny bones of the bird, but it was barely a mouthful; she was saving the rest for her husband. She knew, however, that a hard day's labor would not be tempered by so little.

And there was nothing she could do but sit and stew in her own traitorous thoughts—until he entered the door, so silent and tired that he made less noise than the passage of wind.

She stood at his side and watched him eat, watched him sit at the table until he realized there was nothing more. It bothered her deeply that she might have helped him, long ago, with the use of her artistry as one skilled in the ways of the forest. Afraid, knowing that she must broach the subject soon; the woman peered at his drooping face. She saw that his weariness was not merely the result of his work.

"What ails you so?" It was the five hundredth time she had asked the question, and for the five hundredth time he would have said "Nothing." But the sight of the children huddled beneath a blanket, thin and small for their ages, and the emaciated woman standing there so expectantly, giving him all her love in the hopes that his reciprocation might somehow fill her empty belly, and the poverty of his situation crushed him into the ground. The only way he knew of to escape the inevitable suffocation was to snap, and snap he did; after he dragged her outside and a small ways away so that the children would not hear. He did not want to worry them.

When he first laid an arm upon her, she knew something was amiss. The vigor of his grip was a shocking thing; it murmured with violent, unfulfilled desires. She looked to his eyes for answer and saw the pettiness that she had always told herself was not there; it had always been no more than hunger, or exhaustion, or desire. The lies she told herself were no longer enough. Still the woodcutter's wife insisted on believing that her sacrifice had not been in vain; that the bestial animosity thrilling in every line of his body was not beyond redemption.

And then he started speaking.

He cursed himself, cursed his ancestors, cursed the land so cruel to make him live in such misery, and worse besides, drag others down with him. Tears fell from the man and the woman alike and mingled on the ground, salting the earth. She had not known the depths of his shame. It did not matter, she repeated to him so often and so thoughtlessly; but it did, it always had. He could not abide the appearance of their poverty; every un-mended shirt, every jutting bone was a slap in his face. Had she the power to change it?

As when she was a witch, the human had not completely disappeared; so now, there was witch inside her. He looked into her eyes and saw the glint. He slapped her full in the face with all the strength of his right arm. The woodcutter screamed a single word, hoping the dark silhouettes in the moonlight would echo the force of his hoarse voice into her astonished skull.

"Witch!"

Holding her cheek, she struggled to her feet, head ringing from the blow and the unfairness of the accusation. In the past, she had borne the hatred with pride and a straight back; it had been true enough then. But his continued tirade was not one she had ever heard before.

"Did you think I would marry a woman of unknown origins so easily? Did you think I would not suspect your refusal to leave the forest, or your avoidance of the villagers? Even the children know! Do you not hear their whispers when your back is turned? Witch, you were to help me! Does your kind not eat children?" (Some did, and relished the flavor besides; but she had never, and his words were an outrage.) "Could you not have rid us both of those two hungry brats? Starving and Sniveling, they should be called, their lives are worthless to us!"

She stared at him in horror; she had mothered a forest, and would never harm her own, even if they threatened her. "They are your children," she said, afraid that the whisper was too little, too late. It was, and would have been even if she had swallowed her fears when they had first met.

"I cannot see them suffer like this," the woodcutter said, and now he was sobbing, body as limp as it had previously been hard. "Witch, you must, you must do something to rid us of them—do not tell me what it is, for I do not wish to hate you." *What was* this, *then?* she wondered, and a malevolent suspicion about the nature of his late wife's demise clouded her own judgment. "But please, please, I beg you to let us live together, by ourselves, in a hut that will soon enough be larger than we had ever dreamed. Let us feast, too, every night; we'll never go hungry again. You are starving, I know, look how your eyes stare. We will eat—you would like that, would you not?" Her husband was, all of a sudden, the most tender of men.

He kissed her on the same cheek he had slapped with such alacrity, thinking his saliva might somehow take the sting away. But, as it was too late for him, so it was too late for her. Witch he had called her and witch she would be; but not as he wanted. She would not be an enemy to children; she would be a mother again, the mother of all those who needed her protection.

That following morning, he left in silence before dawn, ashamed to face the consequences of the decision he had forced upon her. The hours of sunlight passed without remark, and evening swept its velvet cloak over the sky in anticipation of the delicate dusting of stars. Still he did not return. Not even when it was so late that the children had insisted she light a candle, their only precious one, that he might see the way back.

It was the dark of the moon. An inauspicious time, all said, although never without the bright glare of the sun for protection.

The three of them—mother, boy, and maid—waited until the dawn of the following day. But, no one came to them; and they were far enough from the village, living closer to the woods than the other superstitious folk would dare, that no one knew of their sadness. The woman had no friends and the village mothers would not let their children near the accursed hut; they were alone in their misery.

When the slavish anticipation grew unbearable, the woman sighed, tied back her hair, and made a loaf of bread from the last of their grain.

"You must search for him," she told them. "I cannot come with you, for someone must stay here if he does return, and as it is you are of his blood and will have a much easier time of the search than I would."

The children nodded, and went in silence, not knowing that she had already wiped his name from her memory. For what use is the name of a dead man?

She pitied them, and feared for their lives; her protection could not save them from everything that lurked in those woods. Darkness set, and neither children nor woodcutter appeared— although if the latter had, she would have removed his head with her sharp, sharp knife. That was the only way to deal with a walking corpse.

At last, human fear took her over; she could wait no longer, and tucked the knife into her wide belt before leaving. A finger's-width sliver of moonlight cast an eldritch glow over the scene; every pile of leaves or dead branches was supernatural that night. Yet she was unafraid. The woman had no need of pebbles or mere breadcrumbs to mark her way, and no need of worry no matter how deep she wandered. Although she did not know where her children were, she was as wise as any woman was and knew where they would be. Her footsteps never faltered.

It was in the darkest depths that she found them, weeping. In life, they had feared what their father might do to ensure they did not die of hunger, and the purpose with which he had brought such a bride to their home. In death, he was dearly beloved, and missed, and all the epitaphs ever written for all the gentlest men. Seeing the broken form of the woodcutter was too much for the children, and almost too much for the witch-woman. She controlled herself; it would not do to smile at the corpse, axe embedded in its surprised chest, and at the tree, larger than the belly of a king's oven, too proud to wear even a single nick upon its surface. How could he have anticipated its defiant bark that had turned his own weapon against him? The man laid there, an object of pity; but she cared not. Her eyes were only for his living progeny, as yet untainted by his vicious mind. They were shivering in their thin clothes, too afraid to stay warm.

"Come home," the woman said, and wrapped her arms around them. They did not resist, but nestled closer to her; they needed the heat and the comfort.

More than someone to comfort, they needed someone to provide, though; and she could not, tainted as she was with the whispers and dark looks of the villagers. If she had dared attempt her herbal arts, the children might have noticed, and connected the strange death of the woodcutter with her fearless ventures into the forest. Anything she could bear but their hatred. She bore the days when empty bellies rumbled from a week of scavenged crumbs, the times when they were too weak to stoke the fire that was a necessity, as the days grew ever shorter. And she refused to be anything but a woman for their sakes.

They managed for a time, somehow, but without the woodcutter, the trees engulfed their little hut; and the others did not care much. Occasional bundles of bread and fresh milk that were with the blessing—and threat—of the village priest stopped appearing on their doorstep, and soon there was nothing left to sate their hunger. With the turn of the season, the last berries disappeared, and soon there was nothing to sate their hunger. The three of them were starving, starving and cold; the snows of winter fell vengefully, the ground a taunting white blanket of sparkling sugar that melted into ice water when their greedy mouths sucked at it.

Before long, there was nothing left for her to offer them but the emptiest of solaces, a cruel but desperate illusion built from the last dregs of her love. She enchanted the house to smell of and even appear as gingerbread, gumdrops, candies—foods so rarely seen by them that they were a wonder. It was no wonder, however, to nibble at the most delectable of sweets and taste nothing but varnished wood.

Hans and little Greta would die of hunger, and she might, too. She could not let them, or herself, pass from the slow starvation tearing at their guts. For she was a witch, and they were the apple of her eye.

Author Bio:

Priya Dugad enjoys folktales and horror and is always looking for ways to combine the two. She graduated from the University of Chicago with a BA in neuroscience, which has given her all sorts of insights into writing. Previous publications include all kinds of little on-campus entries, as well as a surrealistic piece in Grasslimb. She can be found online at sciencebitch.tumblr.com.

The Rise And Fall Of Jack Hill, As Told By His Mother
Arthur Bangs

The following narrative comes from the diary of a Mrs. Helen Hill, née Helen Worthing, and was discovered in the back of an armoire in Yonkers, New York, home of the prominent historian Joseph Jacobs shortly after his death in 1916. The alleged diarist Mrs. Hill purports to be the mother of the notorious Jack Hill, and tells an improbable account of his rise to power. The mystery surrounding Mr. Hill's early years, fuelled in part by his own reticence concerning the same, makes the account of great historic significance. The early portions of Mrs. Hill's diary chronicle the day-to-day life of a poor (but evidently educated) woman and her shiftless twenty-year-old son. The excerpt below begins with the entry dated March 28, 18--. Note: The text is reproduced in its unedited manuscript form, including emendations made by the author.

***

March 28: Pease porridge for supper again. Milky hasn't given milk in three days; I suppose it's my fault for giving her a name that would invite this type of irony. She's getting old and we don't feed her as well as we should, but it's strange that she would dry up so suddenly. Without her milk, we have no income, and without any income, we'll soon starve. I'm afraid we'll have to sell her if she doesn't produce soon.

***

March 31: It has been nearly a week now, and still nothing

from Milky. We have no choice but to sell her. Jack is going to bring her to the market tomorrow.

Perhaps we can use the money we make selling Milky to set up the spare room for a paying lodger. Maybe the responsibilities of a landlord will prompt Jack to finally do something with his life.

Oh, I'm deluding myself with such words! He'll never amount to anything. Forgive me, Lord, for saying such a thing about my own son, but it's the truth. We wouldn't even be in this situation if Jack had bothered to learn a trade. I tell him over and over again that he comes from a long line of respectable and hard-working folk—at least on one side of his family—but before I even finish talking, he already has that faraway look in his eyes. Then he just shrugs and grins at me just like his father once did before he passed away.

For all my pains to raise him right, Jack is becoming more and more like John every day, dreaming of greatness but not lifting a finger to achieve it. He spends hours on end lying in the meadow staring at the clouds. And when he comes in for dinner he rambles on about the most preposterous things that he's going to do—such as building a hot air balloon and flying to the moon, or travelling to the sixth century by means of the administration of a sharp blow to the head. In my worst moments, I have considered offering my assistance in the latter endeavour. Never mind the patent absurdity of such fantasies: even if they were possible, would they put food on the table? Why couldn't he at least dream up some practical impossibilities? It's a pity that he couldn't make money from such fancies. He spins a tale as fine as his father could, and his stories have helped us forget our hunger on those days when there wasn't enough food on the table. But we cannot live on foolish dreams alone, and when the story ends, we find ourselves once again facing the harsh reality of life.

Before retiring to my room this evening, I went out to the

shed to bid farewell to Milky. I've never described her in my diary before, so I will do so now. She's a black-and-white Holstein, about five feet from hoof to shoulder, with eyes that can pierce the soul. She looked up when I stepped into the shed, slowly blinking at me and chewing her cud, but in that once impassive gaze I now saw judgment—and condemnation. She knows we're planning to sell her.

Standing before her in that ramshackle shed, I was suddenly overcome with guilt. It's our fault that she's no longer giving milk! We never fed her well enough, though we ate little better ourselves. We neglected her, both physically and emotionally, treating her as nothing more than a milk-cow, when she has been so much more. She gave everything she could to keep us alive all these years, and now that she's no longer of any use to us, she'll be sold and most likely slaughtered for her meat. I cried aloud at the thought, and before I knew it, I had my arms wrapped around her neck and was bawling like a child.

I wish I could say that I cried solely out of concern for Milky, but it wouldn't be the truth. Though a part of me wept in penitence for what we have done to her, another part wept out of fear that selling her would only delay our inevitable ruin.

***

April 1: That foolish, impulsive boy! Jack returned home this evening, and when I asked him how much money he had received for Milky, he smiled and held out his hand. In his palm were several beans. They were shaped like English beans, but shone a bright emerald green.

I looked up at Jack, then at the beans, then at Jack again.

"What's this?" I asked.

"Magic beans. I traded Milky for them."

That's right: Jack Hill—the great-grandson of Bartholomew Worthing, one of the shrewdest merchants who ever lived—traded the family cow for a handful of beans. Milky's meat alone would have given us enough money to live on for weeks—God forgive me for speaking of our Milky that way, but it's true—and he comes home with beans!

"What are we going to do with a pile of beans?"

"Grow them, of course."

I would just as soon eat them and be done with the whole affair, but he suddenly has it in his mind to become a magic bean farmer! I would have told him not to waste his time if I hadn't been so surprised to hear him say that he planned to actually work.

An even bigger shock came when he in fact did work, if one could call digging a few shallow holes in a spot of dirt behind the cottage and dropping beans in them "work." When he had finished, wiping the sweat of five minutes labour off his brow, he stared down at the ground as if expecting beanstalks to sprout at any moment. Eventually, that familiar faraway look appeared in his eyes, shining as emerald as the beans themselves, and he wandered off to the meadow to stare at the clouds.

So much for Jack the farmer.

Oh Lord, what will we do now? I'm afraid to tell Jack this, but I've been considering Herbert Cooper's marriage proposal. The man is a revolting beast and his children are a pack of urchins, but at least he would provide for me. It's better to be a cooper's wife than to starve.

I can hardly believe what I've just written. Helen Worthing, daughter of one of the most prominent shippers in the country, marrying a boorish cooper! Helen Worthing, who had her pick of suitors from all over the country. The lovely Helen Worthing...I *was* lovely once, some would even say beautiful. I'm still young, not yet forty. I haven't lost my figure, and there are only a few stray strands of grey in my auburn tresses. The Lord knows I've aged well, considering all that I've been through. Is Herbert Cooper really the best I can do?

And what would happen to Jack? I doubt Herbert's offer includes free room and board for a ne'er-do-well stepson who is too lazy to become a cooper's apprentice.

***

April 4: I don't know how, but he's done it! Jack dragged me out of bed at dawn to look at the bean patch, and they've sprouted! Not just sprouted—burst! The plants are already a foot high, and show no sign of slowing their growth. They truly must have been magic beans for Jack to get them to grow, and so fast!

Jack hurried off to town after breakfast, taking with him what little money we have left. I demanded an explanation for why he was going, but he just gave me that grin of his. It's now evening and he still hasn't returned. I hope he hasn't gone off with those friends of his to waste the last of our money in celebration, just because he got some beans to grow.

***

April 5: We fought last night.

Jack came home well after midnight, and to my surprise, he *wasn't* drunk. However, most of the money he had taken with him was gone. He didn't explain where he had been all day or how he had spent the money. Instead, he told me not to concern myself about it, that soon we wouldn't have to worry about money any more.

"Why?" I asked him. "Are you going to get rich selling magic beans?"

I told him that if he didn't find some way to earn a living that I would accept Herbert Cooper's marriage proposal and he would be on his own. Oh! He flew into such a rage, telling me that "that dirty cooper" was below me, below our family, and that he would make Herbert regret it if I ever mentioned his proposal again. Dear Lord, how he frightens me sometimes!

He eventually calmed down, and asked—pleaded—for a few more days. He said that the bean plants were growing so fast that he would be able to harvest them soon.

I relented. What else could I do? I must admit that I felt a flush of pride when he said that our family was too good for Herbert Cooper. Could it be that my son has found ambition? Can I hope for so much? I only fear what will happen when his plans—whatever they may be—come to nothing.

***

April 11: It has been a week since the beans first sprouted, and the vines have already flowered and sprouted more beans! Jack was full of excitement this morning, hopping around the little patch collecting the fruit of his labour, such that it was. I never thought I would see the day when he would not only engage in work, but actually take joy in it! Perhaps the Lord has heard my prayers after all, and this is a sign of better things to come.

I asked him if we would celebrate by preparing some beans for supper, but he just grinned and shook his head. What he did next came as a bit of a surprise. He put on his best coat and picked up the sack of beans.

"What are you doing?" I asked.

"I'm bringing these to town."

"Why on earth are you bringing them to town? Bring them to the farmers market and see if Ben Anderson will buy them. You might not get much from him—it's a small crop, after all—but you're not going to get any more in town."

"Just trust me," he said, and then headed out the door.

"When will you be back?" I called out to him as he starting walking down the lane.

"Later!" he shouted back.

It's almost time for bed and he still isn't back.

***

April 12: Jack came home late last night flushed with drink and carrying a sack of money the size of a small loaf. The last time I had seen so much gold was when I was a young girl and one of Father's ships had come in.

I had some difficulty getting the story out of Jack—he was slurring terribly and he kept falling asleep in the gold he had piled on the table. Apparently, he had found someone who had a taste for magic beans, and upon consummating the transaction, Jack had celebrated with a night on the town.

Who could have known that there was someone in this world more gullible than Jack? I asked him about the man who had bought the beans.

"Ogre," he said, wiping some drool from his chin.

"Ogre? You sold the beans to an *ogre*?"

He grinned. "Yep, sold'm t'ogre. Ogre said I gotta bright future'n beans."

Jack clumsily poured the gold back into the sack, somehow managing not to drop any onto the floor. Then he stood up slowly, leaning heavily on the table to steady himself.

"I'm goah beh,' he said, and staggered into his room. He's still in there, snoring loudly, and I don't expect him to wake up before noon.

***

It's now evening. As expected, Jack slept well into the afternoon. When he finally awoke, he crawled to the table and began counting his money. I asked him how much was there, but he just winced and rubbed his temples.

"Don't worry about it, Mother," he said. "I'll handle our

money from now on." He handed me a gold crown. "It's almost supper time. Go to the market and buy the biggest goose you can find."

I had half a mind to hit him with the skillet for his audacity, but at the sight of the money and the thought of having goose for the first time since Christmas, I simply took the money and put on my cloak and bonnet.

As I walked along the lane to the market, the scent of the first primroses of spring in the air and the gold crown growing warm in my palm, my thoughts on the matter grew milder. Maybe I'm being too hard on him. After all, he did bring all that money home; we now have enough to keep us fed for months, and more than enough to buy Milky back, if it's not too late.

I just wish I knew how he really got all that money. The idea of a bean-eating ogre is simply too preposterous for words.

***

April 13: Jack went into town again last night. He had been quiet all through our supper, as if deep in thought, but when I asked him what was on his mind, he simply replied:

"Beans."

I hadn't thought anything of it at the time, but soon after I had completed last night's entry, he opened my bedroom door and stuck his head into the room.

"I really wish you would knock, Jack." I told him.

"Sorry. I'm heading into town. Don't stay up."

"Now? But it's nearly nine o'clock! What business in town demands that you be there in the middle of the night?"

"*My* business," he said, and shut the door.

He didn't come back until this afternoon, when he arrived at our doorstep in a horse-drawn cart driven by another man. As the man unloaded a bale of wire and a pile of lumber, I asked Jack what all of it was for.

"We're going to have a proper fence for our property, like respectable folk," he said. There would even be a fence for the bean patch. "We can't let any wild animals—or greedy neighbours—eat into our profits," he said with a wink. The man set to work, first building a fence that surrounded our property, and then one for the bean patch. Jack strolled about our yard like a country gentleman, watching the man work but not helping him.

Just as the man was finishing the fence for the bean patch, two more men arrived in a cart. It looked as if they had raided an apothecary, for their cart was filled with a variety of oddly shaped glass containers, scales and heating implements. The men seemed very agitated, but then Jack gathered them around him, and though I couldn't hear what he said, I knew that he was enchanting them with one of his outlandish tales, for as he spoke their looks of apprehension faded into a dreamy calm. Jack has always had a golden tongue, just like his father, but its potency normally lasts only as long as it is moving. To my surprise, it was not the case this time: when he had finished speaking, the men nodded and returned to work without comment. As they passed by I saw that they had faint smiles upon their faces, but lurking behind their eyes I saw...well, the only word that comes to mind is madness. As if what propelled them in their labour was the same lunacy that makes a dog howl at the moon. I had often thought that if Jack could only develop a sense of purpose to go with his gift for speech, he would become a great success. After seeing what he did to those men, I'm now frightened at such a prospect.

The men unloaded the cart, bringing the equipment into our spare room. When the cart was emptied, Jack and the men went into the room and shut the door behind them. They didn't come out again for a couple of hours. Listening outside the door, I could hear voices and things being moved about. It sounded like Jack was doing most of the talking, while the others simply grunted short answers. It was after nightfall when they finally emerged from the room. One of the men installed a couple of metal brackets on the door, and Jack looped a padlock through them. He then gave the men some money and sent them back to town in one of the carts.

***

April 21: I last wrote a week ago. It has been so busy around here that I haven't had any time alone during which I could write. I once wrote whenever I wished, but lately I've noticed Jack watching—appraising—me, and glancing at my diary. When I think now of some of the things I've put in here, some of the things I've said about him...what would he do if he read them?

I keep my diary hidden now, and only write in it when I know he's not around.

The bean patch has produced a second crop already. Yesterday, Jack's three men from town returned to help him with it. I don't like them at all. They are courteous, if unpolished, saying "How do you do, ma'am?" to me and "Yes, Sir" to Jack, but there's a derisive tone in their voices when they say it, as if we are all parties to a conspiracy and the pleasantries are a source of amusement to them. Even worse is the look they give me, like that of a lazy wolf regarding a sheep, as if my continued well-being depended upon their indifference.

Instead of taking the crop to town again, they brought the entire batch into the spare room, which Jack has kept locked all this time, and closed the door behind them. Jack must have installed a second lock on the inside, for when I tried to go in to see if they wanted anything to eat, the door wouldn't budge. A few seconds later, the door opened and Jack stuck his head out of the room.

"What is it?"

"Is there anything you need? It's almost supper time," I said.

"No. Don't disturb us, and *do not* try coming in here again. Understood?"

I was so shocked at his tone that all I could do was nod like a fool.

"There's a dear," he said. "We'll probably be in here all night, so there's no need for you to wait up."

They were indeed up all night. In the early hours of the morning I was awakened by the sound of excited voices coming from the spare room. It continued for some time before fading into silence. It was even longer before I was able to fall back asleep.

The next morning they emerged from the spare room, looking dishevelled and fatigued, but beaming with accomplishment. Jack gave his friends instructions of some sort and they went off in one of the carts. Jack remained behind, locking the door to the spare room and going outside. He placed his head under the water pump and doused himself, then shook the water from his head as if he were a dog. I stood on our front step watching him. Running his hands through his dirty blond hair, he looked at me.

"I have to go to town," he said. "Do not let *anyone* into the cottage. When I leave, lock the front door and don't open it until I return."

I glanced at the new locks he had installed in the front door.

"But I was planning to go to the market to get a small bird for supper."

He shook his head. "Make do with what's in the larder. I'll be back later."

Night has fallen and Jack isn't back yet. Where could he be? I don't like any of this. I don't like the secrecy. I don't like the fences and locks on the doors. I don't like the men he is bringing around here.

I don't like being alone in the dark.

This will sound foolish, but I wish Milky were here.

Before he left, I asked Jack about buying her back and he laughed.

"That dried up old cow? She's likely to be in a stew by now, though not one I'd want to eat!"

I was too stunned to even respond. How could he be so heartless?

Milky's gone forever, and I feel like a prisoner in my own home. All I have left is this, my diary. I will close for now and return it to its hiding place, where he'll never find it, under the pile of hay in Milky's shed.

***

April 22: As I write this I am staying as a guest at the Curling Vine Inn. It is one of the finest inns in town, and Jack has rented its biggest suite for me. Because the town is built on a tableland and the inn is at the town's edge, the rooms on its southern side offer picturesque views of the surrounding country. In the gloaming, a mist has descended onto the plain, blanketing everything below the town in soft white. Sitting here looking out the window, I feel as if I were high in the clouds, in an ethereal place far removed from the drudgery of our life in the country.

I wish I could go back.

Jack returned to our cottage this morning with a stranger. Jack called him a "hired man," but by his appearance "highwayman" would have been a more accurate description. He looked like he had spent the past several days in the wilderness and had the stony expression of someone who has committed a lifetime of unspeakable acts. The hired man lowered a couple of empty trunks from the cart and brought one of them into the spare room. Jack disappeared into the room for twenty minutes, then came out again and had the hired man load the trunk back onto the cart. He then brought the other trunk into my room. Jack told me to pack.

"Where are we going?" I asked.

"To town. We're moving up in the world, Mother."

The hired man trudged into my room and threw a filthy sack and an old musket onto my bed.

"All of my life's possessions are here! I can't fit it all into a single trunk!"

Jack locked the spare room and looked about our small cottage. "Just pack clothes. You won't need anything else in our new home. Besides," he gestured to the hired man, "Fitzwilliam will watch over everything you leave behind, and you can send for anything you need later."

I followed him out the front door. "But—but I need more than just my clothing."

He stopped short. "Oh! How could I have forgotten?" He walked into the shed. "You wouldn't want to leave this behind, would you?" he said as he came back out, pulling my diary from its leather pouch and leafing through it. Reading the last entry, he looked up at me with a mock expression of hurt on his face. "*Heartless*? Mother, how can you say such a thing about your own son? And after all that I'm doing to make our lives better. It really is unfair." Then he smiled and handed me the diary.

He left me here at the inn a few hours ago, promising to return once he had finished some business. He added that he was also going to inquire about purchasing a townhouse "fitting for people of our station."

***

April 23: I have just had the most frightful experience of my life—my hands are shaking so much that I don't know if this is even legible. I'll write everything that happened with as much attention to detail as I can. I must put everything down right now—because if I don't do it now, I don't know if I ever will.

Jack arrived in my suite this morning as I was sitting to breakfast. He greeted me with transparently false warmth and chatted as if we were still living in idyllic poverty out in the country.

"How was last night's business engagement?" I asked stiffly.

"Oh, incredible, Mother, simply fantastic!" he said, but just as he seemed about to say something more, he stopped. His smile faded, and instead of continuing his train of thought he proceeded to break his fast, stuffing his mouth with toast and consuming most of the tea. I ate quietly, unsure of what else to say to him.

"Say, what *did* ever happen to father?" he asked suddenly.

I spilled my tea. "Your father?" *Why was he asking this?* I thought to myself. *I've told him a thousand times.* "He left us when you were an infant to—to find a better life for us..."

Jack snorted. "A better life for *him*, more like it." Seeing my reaction to this comment, he leaned across the table and spoke in a gentler voice. "You never heard from him again, did you?"

"There was an outbreak of cholera that year. Many people died," I murmured as if by rote.

He stared at me in silence for a while, and then gave me a condoling smile. He pitied me! It was all that I could do not to scream at him. I would have preferred it if he had laughed at my folly, but instead he pitied me.

He continued to watch me as I struggled to calmly finish my breakfast. As time passed, however, he grew more and more agitated, and eventually he left his chair and began pacing the room. After several minutes of this, he put on his coat.

"I have business to attend to," he said. "Please stay here,

if you don't mind." As if I had a choice. "If you need anything, just ask the innkeeper and he'll provide it. I'll be back in the evening."

He turned and left the room before I could say a word.

I spent the day in the suite's sitting room, reading the innkeeper's Bible. Shortly after sunset, while I was finishing a passage in the Book of Judith, there was a knock upon the door. Before I could answer, the door opened and a man entered.

He was massive. Not that he was exceedingly tall—he looked to be only a little over six feet—or obese, for that matter; in fact, he carried his weight rather well. But he *was* thick, especially in the middle, and tapering off towards the head and feet. Whatever it was, his appearance gave me the impression of immense, almost monstrous bulk. He was dressed in a fashionable light brown gentleman's lounge suit that indicated wealth, good taste, and possibly indolence. He removed his bowler hat and bowed, revealing hair that matched the colour of both his suit and hat.

"Good evening, Madam Hill," he said. "Forgive my impertinence in calling upon you without permission, but when I heard that you were in town I simply *had* to pay my respects and would accept no refusal." He lowered himself into the settee facing me. It barely contained him.

"I am known by my associates as Ochre," he said. His jade eyes glimmered merrily at me and a smile exuding charm emerged from the fleshiness of his face. A shiver ran through my body at the sight of it. What was it about this man that could cause such a reaction within me?

"It is nice to meet you, Mr. Ochre. Do you have a first name by which your friends call you?"

"No, just Ochre." He gestured to his hat. "It's an affectation of mine. Ochre hat, ochre coat... do you know, I even own an ochre carriage!" He laughed softly.

"To what do I owe this pleasure?"

"I'm a business associate of your son, Jack. In fact, I would go so far as to say that I'm a mentor of sorts to the boy. Has he mentioned my name to you?"

I suddenly recalled Jack's drunken ramblings about the 'ogre.' "He has, although he neglected to tell me that you were his mentor."

Ochre's smile faded, and he held out his hands in an exaggerated gesture of helplessness. "Ah, well. Young men these days! Ha-ha! Yes, I suppose he does underestimate all that I've done for him. You see, I helped him get his start in the magic bean trade."

I nodded. "You're the one who bought the first crop from him."

"*First* crop, eh? Interesting..." Suddenly there was the glimmer of a faraway look in his eyes—not unlike Jack's—and then, just as quickly as it had come, it was gone. "It's true, I was the one who bought the, ah, *first* crop from your son. However, I was actually referring to the *very* start. It was one of my employees who bought your, ah, Milky, from your son with magic beans. He also told Jack about the exciting opportunities to be found in the magic bean industry." He saw my sceptical look. "Jack hasn't explained to you the *magic* of magic beans, has he?"

"No, he hasn't. I assumed that he and his associates were all simply deranged."

"Deranged! Ha-ha! How very charming! You see, Madam Hill...may I call you Helen? You see, Helen, the essence of magic beans, when distilled into an elixir and imbibed, can create a feeling of transcendent euphoria. New vistas are opened, fear and worry disappear, and dreams take tangible form—or at least they appear to. When one is under the influence of magic bean essence, it's as if one's deepest, most heart-felt fantasies have come true. Unfortunately, this effect is only temporary, and its absence creates a great thirst for more." Mr. Ochre smiled again.

"But fortunately for me and your son, this means that the trade in magic bean essence is a very brisk and a *very* lucrative one."

This all sounded ridiculous. "But why did you choose Jack to grow beans for you?"

"Ah! That's perhaps the most fascinating thing about magic beans!" Ochre said, leaning forward and speaking with the passion of a businessman. "Anyone can distil the magic beans, but not just anyone can grow them. It takes a person of a certain—how shall I say it?—*quality*. Believe me, I've tried hiring yeoman farmers to do it, and the crop was useless. No, to grow magic beans one needs an idle dreamer, a wanderer if not in action then at least in fancy. That's why magic beans are so rare. It isn't easy getting such a person to do any amount of farming, even with such a quick-yielding crop. I needed someone with the right disposition who was in such desperate straits that he would have no choice but to put in the requisite effort. That's where our Jack comes in. Once I found out where he lived, it was simply a matter of procuring a concoction to dry up Milky and waiting for Jack to come to us."

"You mean that Milky wasn't even—" I stopped short, fighting a growing desire to throttle the man. He was responsible for all of this. He sent Milky to her death! At the same time, I realized that someone who could admit to such an atrocity so casually might be dangerous. Forcing myself to remain calm, I asked him: "But how did you know about Jack in the first place?"

Ochre leaned back and looked at me, an amused expression on his face. "How indeed? The answer to that is so simple that I'm surprised—no, *hurt*—that it hasn't occurred to you already. Have I really changed that much in twenty years?"

That smile, those sparkling green eyes regarding me with derision...

It was John. Twenty years older and greatly changed, but without a doubt, my husband sat before me. I had so many accusations, so many demands, but all I could muster was a single word: "Why?"

He ran a hand through his hair. "Why did I leave you? Or why didn't I tell you that I was here in town? As for the first, you should hardly be surprised. From the start you knew what type of person I was. It was my carefree ways that so attracted you to me, after all. Alas, my hopes that seducing and marrying the daughter of Cornelius Worthing would grant me a comfortable, toil-free life were dashed when in a fit of respectability your father disowned you. Rather inconvenient, that was. Oh well, *c'est la vie.*"

I couldn't believe what I was hearing, even though he was simply telling me what I had suspected for years.

"Once little Jack was born, I knew it was time for me to go. But no sooner had I set off to find my fortune than I met a little man dressed like a country bumpkin standing on the side of the road. He gestured toward me, and when I approached him, I saw that he was holding a handful of beans. Speaking with a strange accent, he told me how they were 'the food of the fair folk,' and offered me untold riches if I would serve as his apprentice for just a few days. Intrigued by his proposal and having nothing better in mind to do, I followed him into a valley, one that I haven't been able to find since…"

As he spoke he seemed to look right through me to a faraway place and time. I knew that look too well, having seen it on his face when he first courted me, and on his son's face countless times in the intervening years. Despite the hatred I felt for the vile man sitting before me, I found myself drawn into his words, the soft, rich sound of his voice entrancing me just as it had so long ago.

"It was a strange place, like something out of a dream. It was October when I left you, yet the valley we entered seemed to be in a state of perpetual springtime. The trees were in full bloom, and in the meadow of the valley floor there were all kinds of wildflowers—forget-me-nots, buttercups, lady's smock. But there was something else about the place that was...unsettling. My first night there, sitting before the fire in the campsite the little man had set up, I felt as if I were being watched—yet not once in my entire time there did I see a living creature other than my companion. The following morning, he handed me the beans and told me to plant them in the soil by the stream running past our camp.

"We spent the next week together, the little man and I. He wasn't much of a conversationalist—any time I asked him about himself and where he came from, he would evade my questions, instead talking about the beans with a passion bordering on obsession.

"I laughed when he explained the effects of the elixir to me. 'Can I try some to see for myself?' I asked him. He shook his head. 'One cannot salt the sea.' He often spoke in such riddles, but over the next few days, as I watched our bean patch sprout, flower and bear fruit, I came to understand his words, to feel the truth in them. It was my *imagination* that was making the beans grow so fast, that was giving them their magic.

"At the end of the week the beans were ready to be harvested. Out of nowhere he produced an ancient set of alchemical components and he showed me how to make the elixir. We stayed up late into the night, distilling the beans and preserving their essence in little stoppered vials. I woke up the next morning and he was gone—but he had left behind a few vials of the elixir and a pile of beans from the crop we had grown together. I gathered these things and left the forest as quickly as I could, unsettled by the thought of being there alone when night fell.

"I made my way to town, reinvented myself as a 'procurer of remedies' and left the name 'John Hill' behind me. John Hill had a few creditors who were well past the point of accepting simple monetary compensation for the repayment of old debts. Besides, the last thing I wanted was for a Mrs. Hill and son to discover my whereabouts and show up. So, Ochre was born."

He paused, and the spell of his story was broken.

I leapt from my seat and struck him across the face with all my strength, but it was as futile as smacking a wall. He grabbed me by the shoulders and threw me back into my chair. I glared at him as he straightened his suit, my body frozen in shock from the violence I had forced upon it through my actions. "I gave up my family name, my wealth, my status, my future—*everything*, for you, and you left us to die!" I spat my words at him like venom. "Do you realize what our lives have been like for the past twenty years, struggling just to survive?"

John shrugged in a gesture of feigned helplessness. "Surely you can understand my situation. Here I was, an enterprising young man with a crop that could make me a fortune. Why would I burden myself with a wife and son when I would be rich enough to marry the finest woman in the country, or better yet, keep as many mistresses as I please? As you may suspect, I chose to do the latter." He chuckled. "Of course, that was *before* I learned the limitations of the magic beans. You see, wandering is for the young, and over time I grew too used to a life of comfort. I'm no longer a young man, and have too many years," he patted his belly, "not to mention too many pounds, to go off wandering anymore. And as for idle dreams, what does one dream about when living a life of wealth and comfort? I needed Jack because my elixirs were losing their potency."

"Why didn't Jack tell me all of this? Why didn't he tell me that you were alive?"

"Because I didn't tell him, *Sweetheart.*" I hadn't been called that in twenty years, and to hear it now galled me. "I wasn't looking for a *partner*. I was looking for someone who would do all the work while I reaped all the profits. The problem is that Jack didn't just inherit his father's imagination: he also inherited my cunning. He bribed one of my less-than-faithful employees who knew the method of distillation and he has now

set up his own magic bean essence manufactory in your cottage."
John leaned forward, his hands steepled before him. "Which
leads us to the reason for my visit."

I laughed. "You're a fool if you expect me to help you after
what you did to us."

"Oh, your *voluntary* help won't be necessary. Holding
you hostage should be sufficient," he said with a smile.

Up to that moment, I had felt only disgust for my former
husband, but it wasn't until then that I fully realized just how
dangerous he was. With a surge of fear, I quickly arose and
stepped toward the door.

John waved his hand nonchalantly. "Don't bother, Dear.
I have one man in the hall and another downstairs."

I sat back down slowly, my fists balled so tightly that my
hands throbbed in pain.

"That's better. Now, we are going to wait here until Jack
returns, and then we'll have a quiet little chat. I've sent some
men to fetch him for us. They should be here at any moment."

There was a knock at the door.

"Ah! Perfect timing! It's our son, come home to his Mother
and Father!" John slowly raised himself from his seat and went
to the door. When he reached it, he turned to me. "Now be a dear
and don't do anything stupid." Reaching inside his waistcoat, he
pulled out a small pistol, and then turned the doorknob.

The door burst open, and John flew across the room and
into the wall, his weapon flying out of his hand and clattering
across the floor into the corner.

Jack entered the room, followed by his three friends.

"Hullo, Mr. Ochre!" Jack boomed. "Or should I call you
Dad?"

John looked down at Jack's hands, and his face turned
pale. Following his eyes, I saw that Jack was holding the splitting
axe from our home in the country.

"Now, now, son," John said, raising his hands in

supplication and forcing his best smile. "There's no need to get carried away. Your mother and I were just talking about how proud we are of you—"

"So proud that you never admitted to me that you're my father?" Jack asked, brandishing the axe and slowly approaching John. "So proud that you ran out on your wife and son, leaving them to die? So proud that you have armed men accost me in the street?"

"What are you doing with that axe?" I cried.

Jack gave me a look that chilled me to the core. "Stay out of his, Mother. This is between me and him."

John pressed himself against the wall, glancing at his pistol in the corner, well out of his reach. "Jack...you and I can make a lot of money together..."

"I can make a lot more by myself," Jack said.

"Please, Jack..." John said, "You can't do this to me...I'm your father..."

Jack raised the axe over his head. "Wrong. You're my *dead* father."

With a rage-filled bellow, John pushed himself off the wall and charged at Jack, but before he had taken two steps, Jack swung the axe and planted it deep into his chest, the impact throwing him back against the wall.

John opened his mouth, and for a moment, I thought he was screaming, but I soon realized the sound was coming from my own mouth. John stared bewilderedly at the axe jutting out from his body, the crimson gushing down his ochre waistcoat. Looking up at me, he made a gurgling noise, blood bubbling from his mouth, and then collapsed to the floor.

The scream dying in my throat, I looked from John's twitching body to Jack, who was standing over him, his fists clenched, glaring with unspent anger at his dead father.

Before I realized what I was doing, I set myself upon Jack, clawing at his face and shrieking at him.

"Mother! Calm down!" Jack grabbed my wrists and forced me into the settee where John had been sitting moments earlier. "Help me with her!" he shouted to his associates, who rushed forward and held me down. Jack stood up and backed away from me, visibly shaken but trying to compose himself.

"You murdered him!" I screamed as I struggled in his men's grasp.

"Don't you understand that I just saved your life?" he said, running a trembling hand through his hair.

"But he was your father!"

"My father?" Jack laughed. "Are you defending this scum? A man who left his wife and newborn son to die?" He wiped a drop of John's blood from his cheek with his handkerchief. "Our neighbours in the country told me about him running out on us. I didn't want to believe them. I told them they were liars, that he was dead, just as you had told me. I wanted it to be true as much as you did, but it was all a lie." Pointing to John's corpse, he said, "You wanted this as much as I did, Mother." He walked up to the body and kicked it. "I wish he were alive so I could kill him again."

I didn't answer. I wanted to tell him that no one should be murdered, no matter how evil they were, but I couldn't. I realized then *why* I had attacked my son, why I so despised him at that moment—it was because he had killed John *and I was happy that he had killed him.*

Seeing the horror of this realization written on my face, Jack ran to me, grasping my hands and caressing them frantically.

"Mother, don't look at me like that!" he cried. "It's all over! Everything's going to be okay now, I promise. We're going to be rich, and happy, and you'll never want anything! Here," he said, pulling from his coat pocket a small glass vial containing an emerald liquid. "Just drink this and you'll feel better."

"No!" I shrieked, struggling against the men's firm grasp.

"Keep that poison away from me!"

"Poison? Please, Mother," Jack said softly, "I would never poison you. You're suffering from hysteria. This will calm your nerves." As I continued to struggle, he tightened his grip on my hands. "Henry, help me."

The one called Henry grasped my head and forced my mouth open. Jack popped the vial open and poured it down my mouth, then covered my mouth with his hand. Feeling myself choking, I swallowed.

Jack slowly lifted his hand from my mouth and smiled. "You'll feel better in no time." He looked at his men. "You can let her go now." They let go of me and stood back. I lay motionless on the settee, physically and emotionally overwhelmed by the entire ordeal.

"We're going to leave Mother alone so that she can rest. But first, get rid of *that*," he gestured to John's body, "and have a maid clean up the mess immediately. Give her this," he said, handing a pile of coins to one man, "and tell her that if she says a word about this to anyone she'll end up just like him. I'll take care of the innkeeper."

The men dragged John from the room, the axe still sticking out of his chest. A few moments later a maid came in and started scrubbing the blood from the floor, sobbing as she did so.

Jack brushed off his coat, glancing at me from time to time. "A calming effect comes first, although its efficacy will be sorely tried by tonight's events." I stared up at him without responding, a thrall to his detached, clinical manner. "Your anxiety will fade away eventually, replaced by pleasant thoughts. Hmm..." Looking down, he reached under the settee and picked up John's hat. He placed it on his head, setting it at a bit of an angle.

"What do you think?" he asked, grinning like his father. I didn't answer.

He disappeared from my view, and when he returned he pushed a book into my hands.

"Here, Mother. It's your diary. You can write it all down if it makes you feel better." He stood up and moved to the door, his form becoming indistinct and his voice fading almost to a whisper. "When you read it again years from now you'll realize how this was all for the best." Then he was gone.

Now I sit here, writing this and awaiting the full effects of the elixir. I have tried to put it all down exactly as I remember it. I'm afraid that the elixir will rob me of this night, and for all of its horror, I do not want to lose this memory. This cannot be forgotten.

Jack did this to me. My own son. I've raised a monster, one even worse than his father. How did this happen?

He told me that he did all of this for us, so that we could have a better life. He was willing to do anything for a better life, even murder his own father.

But...but...

But he *has* done it, hasn't he?

He has become powerful...important...wealthy...just like I always hoped he would. He's no longer the idle dreamer...he's a man of action. And those weren't simply dreams, but dreams of our future, dreams that are coming true! I admit it, I complain about him to no end, but surely, there have been far worse sons. Because of him, we'll never go hungry again. Because of him, we'll be highly respected in society...and I'll wear the latest fashions again, and attend balls like I did as a young woman... and Jack will marry a fine girl and have strong sons and lovely daughters, my grandchildren...and I'll spend the rest of my days in comfort and happiness, the proud mother of Jack Hill, the most famous man in town.

Someone's knocking at the door! That must be Jack coming to take me to our new home. What a wonderful son! I am such a lucky woman...very, very lucky indeed...

***

The April 23 entry is the last in the diary.

Historians have debated the diary's authenticity for years. Those who argue in its favour cite the diary's historical accuracy, particularly its references to the family cow: the last word Mr. Hill reportedly uttered on his deathbed was "Milky," the meaning of which was a mystery prior to the discovery of Mrs. Hill's account. Those who doubt the diary's legitimacy note that while there are historical records of a Ms. Helen Worthing, daughter of the shipping magnate Cornelius Worthing, as well as records of several John Hills (predominantly aliases), living in --------shire around the approximate year of Jack Hill's birth, there is no record that a Mrs. Helen Hill, mother of Jack Hill, ever existed.

Author Bio:

Arthur Bangs lives in New York City with his wife, two cats and an apartment full of books. He has been a lawyer and an academic, and he is currently completing his certification to become a high school English teacher. In his free time he reviews books for sffworld.com and writes weird fiction. His work has appeared in Darkest Before the Dawn.

The Stepmother's Tale
Sally Anne Croft

They call her beautiful Snow-White, but what's beautiful about a child with white skin? It's unhealthy. She had no colour in her cheeks. Her red lips looked like they were painted on, and her hair, though a lovely, silky-black, was rarely combed and styled properly. She was allowed to run wild in the castle, but wouldn't ever go outside in case it spoiled her whiteness.

I did my best, though I was not her true mother. She was only a year old when I married her father, the King, but, as she grew up, the child defied me at every turn. No matter what I did in order to please her, she ran away crying out that I was trying to kill her so her father would give me all his attention instead of sharing it with her. How silly!

Personal appearance is very important to a queen. Beauty is our main, if not only, asset. The best advice my own mother gave me was to always look my best. She gave me a magical mirror, which I consult each day, asking if I am beautiful. Vain, perhaps, but I see it as my job, almost, to set the example to the women in the kingdom.

***

I tried to encourage Snow-White to take an interest in her appearance, but she was too independent, and made snide remarks behind my back.

As she grew older, I could see she was becoming a beautiful woman, though still far too pale. My mirror agreed, saying though I was beautiful, Snow-White was fairer. Of course, I felt a pang of jealousy, but her beauty would be good for the kingdom, encouraging wealthy, handsome princes from all over the world to come and court her.

I sent for my huntsman and asked his advice for how to get her outside, and bring some colour to her cheeks. He thought that, given her wayward nature, she might go out if I suggested she was right to stay indoors, protecting her beauty.

Sure enough, as soon as I put this plan into action, Snow-White decided she just had to get some fresh air. I insisted that Jack, the huntsman, went with her, as the forests are full of wild beasts, and they would see such a young girl as a tasty snack.

She kicked up a fuss, of course, saying it wasn't proper for a princess to be alone with a man, least of all such a common brute, in the woods. I told her that her servants could go with her, so she decided against that. Really, the girl is impossible!

Well, he took her out into the forest, and showed her birds' nests, animal dens, secret pathways and magical pools. He really did his best to entertain her, but she soon became bored, and while he was stalking a boar to kill it, the naughty girl ran off. It wasn't Jack's fault. He brought me back the boar's heart to have cooked—my favourite meal.

***

Well, you can guess what the gossips made of this. I send my beautiful stepdaughter out into the wild woods with a huntsman who comes back without her, but with a heart, and presents it to me like a trophy.

Word soon got round that I had ordered him to kill her and to bring back her heart for me to eat! Can you imagine people actually believing such rubbish? Well, they did, and I was accused of being a witch and an evil stepmother.

The king, as you can imagine, was beside himself with grief. The child reminded him strongly of his first queen, whom he'd loved very dearly. He was going to send out all his soldiers to search the land for her, but I thought that would frighten the girl, and all the peasants, too.

"There is an easier way to see if she still lives. I shall ask the mirror who is the fairest." And that is exactly what I did. The mirror answered that Snow-White was living in a glen with seven little men—and was a thousand times fairer than me, which I didn't like much, I must say. Still, it was comforting to know she was well, and being looked after.

Her father's rage was terrifying. "My daughter! My beautiful little girl! Acting as a housemaid to a bunch of men! Who are the villains? I'll have them all thrown in the dungeon! I'll have them strung up on the ramparts! Send out my soldiers! Oh, my poor girl!"

"I shall go and find her, my dear. I shall ask where there are seven little men living in a glen, and I will go there to get her back."

***

I borrowed clothes from an old woman, as my own were not suitable for roaming the wild woods, and I thought the peasants would be afraid if they saw their queen standing at their cottage doors. My maid came with me, and two male servants to carry our provisions, and a few trinkets as a reward for anyone telling us where the girl was living.

We rode over seven mountains before we heard any news of the seven dwarves living in the glen. I ordered my servants to wait nearby with the horses, ready to grab her and take her home. Taking the basket of trinkets, I approached the neat little cottage, glad that she wouldn't recognise me in this form of dress. I didn't know if the little men were inside the cottage, and wasn't going to take a chance.

I needed her to come out of the cottage alone, so I called "Fine wares to sell. Fine wares to sell," as if I were a peasant woman peddling goods.

Snow-White came to the window and said she'd been ordered not to open the door to anyone.

Well, I couldn't bear to see the girl kept as a prisoner in this little cottage. Her hair was a mess, and her clothes were a disgrace.

In my basket, were laces of pretty colours, and I could see she wanted one of them, so I held it up to the window.

"I could lace you up now, if you like. It wouldn't take a minute, and just think how pretty you'll look."

***

She opened the door, and I laced her bodice to a fitting shape, but just as I was about to grab her and pull her out to the waiting horses, my maid came running to the door, crying "The dwarves! The dwarves are coming! They are carrying shovels and pickaxes!"

"Oh!" Snow-White cried. "You've been sent by my stepmother!" and slammed the door in my face.

And do you know what the wretched girl did next? Because she thought the dwarves would be angry with her for letting me in, she laid herself on the floor, hardly breathing. They thought her bodice was laced up too tight, and cut it, and Snow-White made up the story that I'd tried to kill her by doing up the lace far too tight for her to breathe.

Her father was beside himself with grief that his little girl was living like a servant to these men, so I promised to go again to try and fetch her back.

The next day, I asked the mirror who was the fairest in the land, and was relieved to hear that it was Snow-White. I dressed as another peasant carrying her wares to sell. The same servants came with me across the seven mountains to the little cottage.

"Good wares to sell. Good wares to sell," I called out again. Snow-White came to the window and said she'd been ordered not to open the door to anyone.

In my basket this time, I had a beautiful comb, and I could see she wanted it.

I held it up so she could see it better.

"I could comb your lovely black hair for you now if you like. It wouldn't take a minute. And just think how pretty you'll look."

***

She opened the door, and I combed her hair to a neat style, but just as I was about to grab her and pull her out to the waiting horses, my maid came running up to the door, crying "The dwarves! The dwarves are coming! They are carrying shovels and pickaxes!"

"Oh!" Snow-White cried. "You've been sent by my stepmother!" and slammed the door in my face.

I couldn't believe this had happened again. This time, she laid herself on the floor, hardly breathing. The dwarves saw the new comb and pulled it out of her hair. Snow-White then made up the story that I'd tried to kill her by pushing a poisoned comb into her hair.

Her father, the king, was even more grief-stricken, and made me promise that I would succeed in bringing his daughter home the next day or he'd call out his soldiers.

I again went to ask the mirror who was the fairest in the land, and was relieved to hear it was Snow-White. I dressed again as a peasant woman with tempting rosy apples in my basket. Taking the same servants over the seven mountains, we made our way for a third time to the little cottage.

Again, Snow-White came to the window, saying she'd been ordered not to open the door to anyone.

"That's alright," I said. "I will just leave you one of these lovely rosy apples, and be on my way."

"No," she cried. "Don't leave me anything!"

***

"Do you think it's poisoned?" I asked her. "Here. I'll cut this one in half and eat some, so you'll know it's perfectly safe. I'll have the white side, and you take the sweet red half."

I sat down where she could see me, and cut the apple. She licked her lips as she watched me eat my piece.

"Oh, I want the apple," she said, and reached out to take the red half.

"Now, Snow-White. You and I are going to have a little talk." I said. She gasped with fright.

"I am your stepmother, and I've come to take you home. Your father is a strong king, but when he is alone in his chamber, he cries with grief every night."

Tears ran down Snow-White's cheeks. She bit on the apple to try and hide her sobs, but a piece got stuck in her throat. As she began to choke, my maid came running up to the door crying "The dwarves! The dwarves are coming! They are carrying shovels and pickaxes!"

Now, I'm not the nervous type of woman you occasionally see, who simpers and cries for little or no reason. However, knowing how Snow-White had portrayed me to her friends, made me afraid of meeting them right now, with the girl choking on a piece of my apple. I therefore decided to leave them, praying "As white as snow, as red as blood and as black as ebony, this time the dwarves will need to bring you back to life again."

I knew I could not go back to the castle again. How could I face her father, and say that his beautiful Snow-White was dead?

I went to a castle on the other side of the forest. The king there welcomed me, and I told him what had happened.

"Tomorrow morning, I shall send my son to the glen to see if Snow-White is safe. But for now, you need to rest."

I slept very badly that night, I can tell you. With the first light, I heard the clatter of hooves in the courtyard, and knew the prince was on his way to the forest.

I missed the comfort of having my mirror telling me Snow-White was more fair than me, and though the king showed me every kindness, I couldn't enjoy anything, and I felt I had to return home and break the news to her father.

Before I spoke to my husband, though, I went to my magic mirror.

"Mirror, mirror, on the wall, who is the fairest of us all?"

'You are now the fairest of them all.'

I fell to the floor in a faint, and my maids had me carried to my chamber.

I should have felt thrilled that I was the most beautiful lady in the land again, but I couldn't. Not like this. Even though Snow-White and I had never been close, I still had tender feelings for my stepdaughter.

The following day, I felt strong enough to get out of bed, though I still had no idea how to tell the king about the death of his beloved daughter.

A messenger was with the King. We were being invited to a wedding at a castle across the mountain, and I didn't want to spoil the king's pleasure, so decided to wait before telling him the awful news.

***

I dressed in my finest clothes and costliest jewels, though

took little pleasure in it. As a matter of habit, I went to my mirror and asked who was the fairest in the land.

'Oh queen, though you are of beauty rare,
The young bride is a thousand times more fair.'

Another woman fairer than me? Impossible! I was impatient to get to the wedding and view this bride for myself.

Well. You can imagine my surprise when I saw it was Snow-White, alive and well!

She told me how the prince had seen her laying in a glass coffin, guarded by the dwarves, and became smitten by her beauty. Apparently, there was an accident when the coffin was moved, and the jolt dislodged the piece if apple stuck in her throat, and she was able to breathe again.

She made a stunningly beautiful bride. Her white cheeks were flushed, and her hair was dressed with flowers and jewels.

Snow-White made me a present of a pair of flame-red shoes. The soles were as strong as iron, and made for much dancing.

The minstrels began to play, and the bride and groom started the dancing. It was a beautiful wedding, and I danced and danced until I fell down, exhausted and had to be helped to our carriage to go home.

Author Bio:

Sally Anne Croft lives in a beautiful seaside town in south-west England. When she can drag herself away from the beach, and ignore the weeds in her garden, she enjoys a love/hate relationship with her computer—which is definitely female with permanent PMT and a strong aversion to authority. Her work has appeared in Flair News, People's Friend, The Lady, The Music Teacher, 'Devils, Demons and Werewolves' anthology (Bridge House Publishing), and online at The Story Slot and WriteInvite.

My Dear Plastic Man
William Knight

When the doorbell rang, Mrs. Rigby was sitting on the balcony, drinking a glass of sugarless lemonade and watching the far-flung specks below. From the seventy-second floor of the Archmore Apartment Block, the commuters on the ground looked like a band of scurrying ants.

She smiled in anticipation as she maneuvered her mobility scooter around a potted lacebark elm. For once even the discordant notes, wafting through the reverberating floorboards, weren't enough to ruin her mood.

The doorbell rang again.

"I'm coming!" she piped, trying and failing to raise her voice over the noisy whir of the air purifiers. They were boxy, ugly monstrosities hanging from the tobacco-stained popcorn ceiling, but they were a necessary evil when one lived in the smog-choked stratosphere of New York City.

The scooter stuttered, the tiller wobbling precariously. She cursed as the viscoelastic seat began to buck like a wild roan stallion. Once again, she'd forgotten to charge the battery.

Somehow the scooter, with considerably stilted ardor, made it to the front door.

She sighed and pulled out her pitted and paint-chipped cane. Her arthritic bones clicked loudly as she grudgingly removed herself from the scooter and its promise of sedentary relief.

With a groan she pressed the pad and with a pneumatic hiss, the door swished open.

Two burly men stood at the threshold, flanking an oblong metal crate. The crate was smooth and polished to high shine, looking for the entire world like some sort of futuristic sarcophagus.

"Are you Mrs. Rigby?" one asked, he glanced at a clipboard. He wore a tag with the name 'Dickon' embroidered in crimson thread.

"I am." She licked her lips, eyeing the crate with undisguised lust.

They brought the package inside on a hover cart, and deposited it unceremoniously on her living room floor.

Dickon held out a pad. "Sign here, please."

She grabbed the stylus and scrawled her signature on the capture pad.

"Thank you," Dickon said.

They left. Mrs. Rigby was alone with the crate. She circled around it on her scooter, running her hand over the smooth metal. A sticker had been placed across the lid, bearing the word 'Fragile' in stenciled vermillion letters.

She pressed her thumb against the conductor plate. The biometric scanner hummed and a blue capacitance light scanned the valleys and ridges of her thumbprint. It beeped, and the lid popped open with a solemn displacement of air.

With trepidation, she peered into the box. The contents were occluded by a sheet of polyethylene foam. Her liver-spotted hand grasped the foam sheet, and with annoyance she swept it onto the carpet. No need for tidiness, now. That's what he was for.

She leaned over and looked into the crate. Nestled into the fitted-foam was her man. Lying atop his chest was a thick instruction manual with a cheerful visage.

She picked up the manual, grunting at its weight, her eyes possessively tracing the compact contours of her android's body. His eyes were closed, his hands at his side. His skin was ashen and cold to the touch. Mrs. Rigby shuddered at her new purchase's cadaverous mien. She could almost see the network of circuits and servos beneath the transparent skin.

Soon she would raise the machine to life, like a mother giving birth to a son. Something she'd never known in all the long years of her life. It would become hers, finally, something of her own. She'd hoarded her retirement and social security checks for years for this golden opportunity.

She sighed and leaned back in her scooter. No need to rush, she told herself. Enjoy this moment, savor it. She covetously clutched the manual to her chest, its pressure bearing mute testimony to the tangibility of the experience.

At last she placed the heavy book onto her lap.

She opened the cover, reveling in the resistance of a freshly minted book, the barely audible squeak. She skimmed through the thick pages; it was filled with diagrams and incomprehensible techno-babble, despite the user-friendly disclaimer on the front cover.

Operating instructions. This was what she was after. For the most part, the android was self-functional and required a minimal amount of maintenance. The pneumatic controlled actuator basically neutralized the hydraulic noise. It contained a rechargeable attenuator battery and state-of-the-art neural and sensory processors.

Overall, it was the best money could buy, or at least the best she could afford on her limited income.

She slapped the manual down on her chipped and stained coffee table and maneuvered her scooter as close as she could get it to the sleek casket.

It was time.

She reached her hand into the android's mouth, felt around for the switch. The tongue was soft and pliant, so human to the touch. She found the switch--a tiny nub that would power the machine to life.

No longer would she be alone.

She turned on her machine.

He opened his eyes. His processors ran a quick check for anomalies—none were found.

A face was peering at him, curiosity burning in its rheumy eyes.

He did a quick calculation. Based on the degradation in skin-tone and the plethora of wrinkles, he estimated the human female to be anywhere from 65 to 72 years old. Her hair was gray and patchy, the pate liver-spotted. Her teeth were yellow-tinged and straight, probably prosthetic, made of the same acrylic resin as his own.

He sat up.

The old woman smiled. "Hello," she said.

He smiled, his Septom-constructed facial actuators easily processing the expression. "What may I call you?"

"I'm Mrs. Rigby. You may call me Mother."

"Mother Rigby..."

"Just Mother, please."

"Of course. What do you require of me, Mother?"

She backed up on her scooter, and patted the flower-patterned couch. "Why don't you come out of your box and sit down."

Deftly, he climbed out of his housing unit. He used the opportunity to survey his surroundings.

The air was acrid and burdened with must. He recognized the scent as tobacco—physiologically damaging to the human infrastructure. He would have to confront Mother. The ceiling was low, fissured and damp-stained, probably faulty piping. Luckily he was programmed with a remodeling subroutine.

He sat down on the couch, taking in the décor. The walls were sparsely adorned, a generic fruit-basket portrait and a couple of faded framed photographs. One showed a much younger Mother Rigby standing in a field of Indian corn, puffing on a pipe. The red kernels and green sheaths of the corn glowed spectrally in the sepia-print, reflecting some long ago sun. Another photograph—in age-dulled black and white, showed an adolescent Mother Rigby romping with an exuberant sheep dog.

The coffee table, some relic of pre-fab engineering, was cluttered with stacks of spine-creased romance paperbacks and an overflowing ashtray, surrounded by linoleum-blistering burn marks.

Mother Rigby pulled out a rumpled pack of cigarettes and shook one out, placing it between her chapped lips with a shaky hand.

He extrapolated the best course of action. His database on human-maladies was replete with the side effects of cigarette consumption. "There are over twenty-known diseases directly linked to tobacco use," he said. "The most prevalent being cardiovascular disease."

She lit her cigarette and eyed him warily. "I'm sure the world would mourn if I kicked the bucket, eh?"

Kicked the bucket? Ah, an archaic euphemism for death. "I would, Mother."

"How sweet. You're programmed to commiserate with your owners, aren't you?"

"Yes. Empathy comes pre-installed in all Adjunct models, it's standard."

She puffed in a wisp of smoke and coughed into her gnarled hand; though it could've been a laugh. "Your honesty becomes you, son."

Son? "Is 'Son' to be my designation, Mother?"

Her face twisted in consideration, and she took a couple more long draws on her cigarette before answering. "I think not. Though on occasion I'll address you as such. I am your mother, after all."

He should pose an alternative. "My factory designation was Arlo-X-three."

She waved away his suggestion. "That won't do at all, so bland and clinical sounding." She stared up at the ceiling. "Hmm..."

He waited patiently, keeping his expression friendly and receptive. Sometimes, humans had difficulty acclimating to life with a synthetic. His programming included numerous methods for easing the sometimes arduous transition.

"How about Feathertop?" she said, after several moments of deliberation.

"Feathertop?"

"Yes. We had a family dog by that name, when I was girl. I think it suits you." She gestured towards the wall behind him.

He turned and once more examined the black and white photo of Mother Rigby playing with the young canine. His namesake looked happy, with extended tongue and blurred tail, captured in the midst of wagging.

Feathertop looked back at his mother and smiled.

***

Mrs. Rigby sighed contentedly as Feathertop dusted the photos on her side-table. Over the past several days he'd been resilient in getting the house in order. He did the laundry, mopped the floors, and even worked out the knots in her neck with clever hands.

He was a dream come true. She could hardly believe her luck.

"Who's the gentleman in this picture?" he asked.

She glanced to where his feather duster hovered. It was a photograph of her husband. "That was your father," she answered. "The late Mr. Rigby."

"Where is he now?"

"Scattered across the verdant knells of Central Park." She remembered the day well. His ashes interred in an unadorned faux-bronze urn, the wind carrying the scattered offering back over the blacktop lanes, the bitter taste of soot on her tongue.

"How did Father die, Mother?"

She jolted at the memory and cast a jaundiced eye at her son. He was staring back at her politely, his lips curved into an easy—albeit preprogrammed—smile.

"You're the curious sort, aren't you?" It was really an admonishment, but Feathertop's friendly nod told her that it hadn't registered. She sighed at the dismal appreciation for sarcasm. "He committed suicide. Hung himself from that very chandelier." She gestured vaguely. Feathertop had recently polished the oxidized bronze to a renewed luster.

Feathertop walked over and examined the chandelier.

"Do you understand the concept of suicide?" she asked.

He nodded. "Self-termination. Such an act is forbidden within the parameters of our programming."

"Really?" She leaned forward. "What if you were sunk to the bottom of the sea? Covered with barnacles, the salt-water leeching into your system and corroding the machinery?"

"That's a highly unlikely scenario, Mother."

"Not everything can be determined through computation, Feathertop. Let's see...what if I were to pass away and you were thrown into a malaise."

His expression turned quizzical, and she could almost picture his inner turbines—or whatever, parsing out a solution. "I would still be restricted from self-termination. Unless the subroutines governing said mandate, were somehow damaged. Though the prospect of your death grieves me greatly."

Grief? What did he know of grief? She glanced one last time at the opulent chandelier, which she still hadn't the courage to replace. "Go about your tasks," she said.

Feathertop nodded and moved back to his efficient dusting. Taking to it as though every mote were an enemy to be eliminated.

She eyed her son appreciatively. He'd been fabricated with impeccable features and a handsome physique. And though he was programmed for sexual activities, she would never partake. There was something so licentious about people who engaged in such affairs with their droids. Not to mention that it was strictly regulated by the Synthetic-Human Relations Bureau.

She wasn't about to wade through the red tape to get off.

Feathertop hummed melodically while he worked, an affectation she'd encouraged. She found his pitch-perfect synthesized voice to be soothing.

He wore the finest clothing. She would not be serviced by a vagrant. Some of the new-agers actually let their droids walk around naked, which she found abhorrent. Though not protected under the constitution, they certainly deserved a modicum of decency.

She'd bought him a handsome waistcoat with the finest embroidery, second-hand, though, so it was a bit threadbare about the elbows. Still, he looked smart and proper—real gentry.

A clanging sounded from below.

"Damn that beatnik," she muttered. The girl was at it again, with renewed vigor. She stomped her feet on the floor in irritation, but the remonstrance was lost in the sound of clashing cymbals and what sounded like the screeching refrain of a piccolo.

"Feathertop," she hollered.

He promptly presented himself. "Yes, Mother?"

"Go tell that damn fool in Seventy-One-F, to stop that infernal racket. I can't hear myself think with all that discordant blaring."

He nodded. "At once, mother." He made for the door as though his rear end were on fire.

"One last thing," she said. He paused and turned. "Don't tell her you're my android. No need for her to nose into my affairs. Tell her you're my son."

He smiled. "Yes, Mother."

He scurried through the door, and though he'd only been gone a few seconds, Mrs. Rigby began to feel lonely and to wish for his speedy return.

***

He knocked on the door three times. His etiquette supplements, told him that two knocks was too indecisive, while four could be misconstrued as abrasive. Three was the perfect number.

The door was opened and a woman stood before him. She was slight of build, with long, coppery hair and soft features. Her eyes were of the deepest brown, almost black and matched the color of her smooth skin.

"Who do I have the honor of addressing?" he asked.

The woman gave him a dissecting onceover. "Who wants to know?"

"I'm Feathertop. Son of Mrs. Rigby, your upstairs neighbor." It was not in his programming to lie, but above all things he had to follow his mistress's instructions.

The woman continued to stare at him. His facial recognition software placed her in her early twenties. Her eyes were narrowed, suspicious. He took a step back and nonchalantly placed his hands in the pockets of the neatly-pressed trousers his mother had supplied.

"What does that old bat want?" she asked.

"Old bat?" Mrs. Rigby was decidedly not. And though he had several complex algorithms for discerning sarcasm, this one went beyond his scope.

"You're not a droid, are you?" Her voice hardened, her lips curling in disgust, though it could have been fear, he wasn't sure. "No synthetics allowed." She pointed at a small placard hanging beside the door jamb bearing the caveat 'No Synthetics!'

Mother Rigby's instructions had been explicit. "No."

"Well, come on in." She stepped back and waved him in. "Sorry for the mess."

A quick calculation told him that it was the same dimensions as Mrs. Rigby's apartment. But while Mrs. Rigby's apartment was rigidly organized, the woman's was cluttered. An easel had been set in the middle of the floor with a half-finished canvas. Instruments sat in the corner. Amongst them an aged piano—paint-chipped, the keys dulled and yellow.

"So, Miss..."

"Polly. Polly Gookin."

"Ms. Gookin..."

She smiled. "Polly's fine."

"My mother requests that you refrain from playing your music so loud. She finds it quite disruptive."

"Does she?"

Now the sarcasm was obvious. "I'm afraid so. Can you accommodate her?"

She rolled her eyes and walked over to the piano, she ran a hand over the lacquered wood. "Do you play?"

He smiled. "A little." It was part of his entertainment package. Not standard with his model, but customized per Mother Rigby's request. She wished to be serenaded on a semi-regular basis. Whistling was her preferred method of compliance.

"Play for me, please."

Something in her tone made him comply. He sat down, the torn leather seat creaking under his weight. He tested the pedals and gently rested his fingers across the keys. He followed a preinstalled pattern, a pleasing concerto in D-minor.

"Rather melancholy," she commented when he'd finished.

"Was it?" That hadn't been his intention. He'd have to run a full diagnostic when he returned home. It was probably just a glitch, no more than a code fragment, an aberration.

"What's your name?"

"Feathertop."

"That's a strange name."

He pictured the old sheep dog in the black and white photo upstairs. "It's a family name."

"Tell me..." She sat down beside him, her dark brown eyes tracing the planes of his face. She had a pleasant odor, or so his olfactory receptors suggested: cardamom with a hint of lavender. A unique combination. "Are you happy?"

"Happy?" An irrelevant question. Impossible to answer under the parameters supplied by Mother Rigby. He'd have to improvise. Possible answers were posed by his neural processor. "No," he finally answered, though it wasn't one of the supplied options.

She smiled for the first time, a gentle upward curving of her lips. She had high-cheekbones, a rather patrician appearance. The smile eased the sharp edges, softened her almond-shaped eyes. "Why not?"

Again, impossible to answer. Why had he said no? Happiness was an abstraction. A distinctly human state of being. "I don't know," he said.

The smile vanished. "A lie?"

"I am incapable of lying."

"Incapable?"

Had he exceeded his mandate? He couldn't disobey his mistress. She'd be most unhappy. What if she called the company that had created him? Had him returned as defective? He'd be decommissioned. Melted down. Used for scrap, maybe.

"My mother raised me better."

She shook her head in exasperation. She stared down at the age-tarnished keys. "I'll try to keep it down," she said.

He stood and walked to the door.

"One last thing..."

He paused and turned.

She didn't look up at him as she spoke. "Do come and

visit me again, will you?"

He nodded.

***

Where was he? "Blasted piece of plastic junk!" Mrs. Rigby said aloud, to no one in particular. "Damn rude. Damn rude."

She had a suspicion.

Well, that little harlot wasn't going to steal her property.

She revved the scooter and headed towards the door, just as it opened.

Feathertop walked in, wearing a smile.

"Where were you?" she demanded.

"I went to see Ms. Gookin."

"Again? That's the third time this week!" She'd been putting up with this nonsense for the past two months. It was growing wearisome.

"I'm sorry, Mother. I..." He paused.

"What?" Nervousness had begun to poke at her chest. She couldn't lose him too.

"I think I'm in love with her." He lowered his head.

She blinked in confusion. "Love?" Her face twisted into a scowl. "How can you possibly know what love is? You're a wretched machine. No more than plastic and metal with some fancy wiring." She was enraged, bouncing up and down on the scooter as she spoke.

He raised his hands in supplication. "Please, Mother, don't be angry with me."

"Angry." Beads of spittle flew from her mouth. "You're mine! Don't you understand? Mine!"

He knelt down beside the scooter and gently placed his hand on her arm. "I'm sorry. But I do love her."

She batted away his hand. Shakily she pulled out a pack of cigarettes and placed one between her lips. She breathed deep of the burning smoke, let it sooth her fraying nerves. Centered, she glanced down at her kneeling son. "You are never to see her again."

His mouth opened. "Never?"

"Never! I forbid it."

She motored away.

"Please, Mother Rigby. I beg of you!"

She didn't look back. "I forbid it!" she hollered.

She would not share him.

***

Polly turned over and placed her hand on Feathertop's bare chest. "You look troubled," she said.

He turned away from her and climbed off the bed, quickly redressing. "I can't see you again after today, my love."

She sat up, her eyes wide, the pupil's dilating. "Why not?" Her voice was thick, shaky.

"My mother forbids it."

She stood up and pulled on her robe. Her skin was luminescent, glowing under the sunlight pushing its way through the sheer curtains. "She can't forbid you to love," she said quietly. "You have free will."

If only she knew how wrong she was. "I'm sorry."

Little mollified by his apology, her face hardened. "Get out!"

He took a step towards her, raising his hands. "Please, Polly."

"No!"

He grabbed her softly by the shoulders, her skin was heated—the carbon nanotubes in his skin registered the spike. Tears had begun to track irregular courses down the dark wash of her cheeks. "I'm sorry."

Her hands balled into fists and she slapped them futilely

against his chest. "Just leave."

His programming was conflicted. He was required to obey his mother, but he couldn't do another human harm, and clearly she was upset.

Her energy depleted, she rested her head against his chest. "Please don't do this," she whispered. "I love you."

"I love you, too." If Mother Rigby knew the depth of his feelings for Polly, perhaps she'd reconsider. She'd have to!

***

Mrs. Rigby fumed. "With that whore again!"

She steered her scooter into the kitchen, pulling a long chef's knife from the block.

"She will see!"

She left her apartment for the first time in months, down the clinical white hallway and to the elevator.

She would make the thief see.

***

"I know you're in there!" The door vibrated under the heavy onslaught of his mother's fists. "Feathertop! Open this door!"

Polly grabbed his arm. "Don't open it, please."

He smiled and kissed her lightly on the forehead. "I have to. She's my mother. She'll understand."

He opened the door and his mother came zipping in, her face red, a bright blue vein asserting itself on her forehead.

"Whore!" she shouted at Polly.

"Mother, stop," he said.

"No. You disobeyed me, boy. I'm sending you in for maintenance."

No.

Polly's eyes widened in shock. "Maintenance?"

Mother Rigby gave her a cruel grin. "Oh, you didn't know."

Her eyes were bright with mischief as they settled on Feathertop. "Please don't, Mother. Please."

"He's a droid, you stupid girl. A droid! You've violated the Robotics Ethics Charter—a person's droid is sacrosanct, and not yours to meddle with. You'll be thrown in jail."

Polly took a step away. "You lie."

"Feathertop," Mother Rigby said. "Give me your hand."

He complied immediately.

She pulled out a knife; he recognized it from the kitchen at home. He often used it to prepare her meals.

She grabbed his hand and ran the blade across his open palm. The polyimide synthetic skin split easily, revealing blinking diodes and the hydraulic sensors which controlled the movement of his hand.

Polly blanched. "You...you lied to me?" Her voice was soft.

"I'm sorry," he said helplessly.

Mother Rigby snorted. "I'll leave you to it, then. I'll see you shortly, Feathertop." She left the apartment, a triumphant smile plastered to her wrinkled face.

"How could you lie to me?"

"At first I was following Mother's instructions, but later on I...didn't want to lose you." But he could see by her disgusted expression that he already had.

"Please leave," she said. "I never want to see you again."

She walked into her bedroom and slammed the door.

***

Mrs. Rigby smiled when she heard the door open. The air was crisp on the balcony, and she pulled the homespun shawl tight about her shoulders.

Feathertop didn't speak as he made his way over to her.

He didn't speak as he leaned over the railing.

He didn't speak as he flung himself over the side.

Speechless, she craned her neck over the decorative railing and watched as her son shrunk to the size of a tiny speck as he plummeted to the ground below.

***

The air rushed by him, his hard drive flashing a warning, a claxon sounding.

The ground rushed up to meet him.

Self-termination, it shouldn't have been possible, but it shouldn't have been possible for him to fall in love with someone other than his mistress.

Was he defective? He must be.

He would never know.

He struck the pavement and shattered into a hundred pieces.

***

Dumbfounded, Mrs. Rigby lit a cigarette with a shaking hand and listened to the blaring sirens, watched the spectral red flashes of emergency lights refracting off the smog.

What had she done?

She pictured her late husband swaying from the chandelier.

She pressed her hands against her reddening eyes, trying to blot the vision from existence, the vision of her son throwing himself to his death.

She hadn't understood. Was it possible for a machine to love?

Maybe he could be salvaged, repaired?

No! Never. He was too innocent for this world. It was for the best, really.

As the cigarette dwindled to a blackened nub, she tossed it after her son and lit another.

"Sleep now, my dear boy," she whispered.

She'd call tomorrow and order a replacement. This time, she'd keep it on a shorter leash.

Author Bio:

William Knight lives, writes, and attends college in Upstate New York. When he's not working, or ignoring homework, he enjoys spending time with his three nephews, Billy, Johnny, and Donovan, who treat his sage advice with derision. His work has appeared in Electric Velocipede, Space and Time, and Aoife's Kiss. He maintains an irregularly updated blog over at www.williamknight1.blogspot.com.

In Darkest Night
Sarah Penney-Flynn

As children, Jane and Sebastian were forbidden to collect fireflies by their mother. Upon walking into their room at night, she would frown at the faint, intermittent glow of jars on their bedside tables. The tiny, wild things belonged outside in the dark garden, she told them in her low, murmuring voice—imagine if they were taken from where they belonged and could never return. On those summer evenings that she drove them out into the garden, she told them explicitly not to bring back anything. It was not a rule they were meant to follow, the twins decided—very few of the rules their mother devised were such rules. It only meant they should regulate their collection, perhaps keep the jars hidden in closets or stashed away in drawers so that she would not find them. Of course, hiding things away in their house often meant never finding them again but, this was a risk they were willing to take. Jane devoutly believed that sleeping with a firefly jar beneath your bed would bring you sweet, dark dreams. And anything Jane believed, she knew Sebastien would believe too.

On those nights when they tramped through the long grasses in the back fields, Jane would recount for Sebastien the fairytales she'd read in their father's library. Father was an avid reader of such tales and had come from the mainland to attend the University and study folklore. He sometimes traveled the island to hear them from the mouths of storytellers sitting by wood stoves in coves and harbors, organizing them into tables and types so that they would not be lost. Their mother scoffed when he attempted to preach to them over dinner, about how the tales of a people were their beating heart. "Foolishness," she would mutter over the clatter of dishes, "Words. Nothin' more than words."

Sometimes Jane made up her own tales. Tales of a wondrous miniature circus in the basement that had tales of imps who beguiled babies from their cribs and beasts with fetid breath that would allow you to climb onto their backs and carry you away into the forest. A mime and midgets the size of a thumb who ate flies for dinner. Tales of things living beyond the boundaries of the house, things that would lead you into the fog, over the harbor, where you would lose your footing and be swallowed by the sea without a sound. If the tales made the twins shiver, they would stop to hold hands, eyes fixed on the stars that sparkled above them, gathering their courage. As they flew through the darkness with their jars held aloft, it became part of their naive magic—the tales, the fireflies themselves, the trampled mushroom circles and the lilies that only opened their pale petals under the light of the moon.

"Le's catch as many as we can," Sebastien would yell. "Jars and jars. We can let 'em go together, up high where we can see them fly away." They would hide them beneath their shirts, giggling hunchbacks, and ascend the stairs to the attic where they would climb out onto the roof. Sebastien first, since he was the more agile of the two. After Jane had passed out the jars one by one, he would give her a hand. "As fast as ye can," Sebastien would tell her. "Give 'er."

So Jane would unscrew the jars, holding them up to the breeze that came in off the cove. The fireflies would burst into the air in a flaming web while the twins sat, breathless, clutching each other's hand until the last had faded; their pulse in their palms, the steady *beat beat* of their hearts and the roof beneath holding them up close to the moon.

As they grew older, every time that Sebastien smiled at her, that was what Jane thought of...fireflies.

***

Jane knew somehow that she and Sebastien were different from other people, and that they should be ashamed of this. But what was shame to Jane when her entire world revolved around Sebastien—when she awoke to him leaning over her, fastidiously placing rose petals on her eyelids. What was shame to Sebastien when Jane said things he could not say, but felt—when he fell asleep with Jane's arms around him, her fingers slotted into the space between his ribs. When they were babies, their mother would always swaddle them together, binding them with blankets that smelled of rosewater. They shared her breast milk, passing it from mouth to mouth. Father would complain in his loud, logical voice that she was perverting them. Their mother would just smile—her queer, secretive smile—and pluck at their tiny fingers with her teeth. At night, she left their bedroom door open so that, at the slightest sound from the twins' room, she could slip from her husband's embrace to soothe them. As they grew older, their father's complaints became the glance from beneath his eyebrows, the mutter beneath his breath when they insisted upon holding hands beneath the table at suppertime. "Faggot," he would say when he came upon his son lying with his head in Jane's lap. "Sissy, mama's boy." The alternative—that he simply did not fit into the twin's world—was too terrible to be voiced.

***

Their mother was such a soft person, always reaching out to stroke their hair or pull them against her. Her laughter followed them as they passed through the house, leaving a long trail of mud and petals behind them. She never scolded them, and never seemed concerned when they disappeared for days on end into the various upper rooms and attics of the house, whispering through the vents. She joked endlessly about her 'darklings,' her 'li'l savages.' She too, seemed an outcast from the small village where they lived—wherever she went, the hiss...*witch, witch*. The fishermen at the wharf always watched her as she passed. Delivery boys left packages at the end of the driveway, refusing to come too close to the door.

Under her magic, their guileless sin was hidden from accusing eyes. When they slept curled together beneath a pile of blankets in the dusty darkness of the living room, Sebastien's fair head against Jane's dark one, Father could stand only inches from where they lay and never see them. Sometimes Mother would lie with them, making up her own stories about the house. They had always known that their house and garden were not like others'; it was easy to get lost in the tangles of rosebushes while playing childhood games and the wind that came in, faint, off the water held the musk of salt and fish but also brought a fog that crept in across the window sills. Their mother rarely cleaned all of the rooms, so often they found ancient dusty cupboards where they could barely fit or old moth-eaten costumes. Even after they outgrew hide-and-seek, becoming long-limbed teenagers, there were the vague memories of games played that involved fairies and trolls in those rooms, that garden, and the distinct feeling that it had not all been make-believe. But none of them ever said so.

Sometimes Jane caught Mother staring at them. "My wee tangly things," she would say, "I'll keep you close." And Jane told Sebastien, that sometimes Mother seemed as though she wanted desperately to belong to someone the way they belonged to each other.

When the policeman appeared at their door at 12:36 on a Tuesday morning to tell them that their mother had died, neither of them thought of why she might have been out driving without them. Why, with the blinding headlights of the oncoming car in her eyes, she might have turned to the lover sitting next to her and rested her lips against his as their bodies were crushed in a squeal of metal. Instead they thought of her laughter—what a bareness its loss would leave around them.

***

The gossiping came later, as it always does in a small town. "One of these days they'll come bearing torches" their mother used to say to Jane. They heard the stories at the funeral, as strangers came drifting in and out of the house—the Church Women's League bearing casseroles to put in the freezer and the fishermen who stood outside on the porch smoking hand-rolled cigarettes, tipping their heads whenever they caught sight of Jane or Sebastien through the screen door. A tragic affair; the car found upside down in a ditch with shards from the windshield sparkling in the blood-matted hair of two bodies, the children left behind to take care of the father, who had gone half-mad from grief and, besides, was well on his way to drinking himself into a grave alongside his pretty wife. No money to fend off the bank that was threatening to foreclose on the house.

Then there were the children: the daughter, a girl so beautiful that toads threw themselves at her feet, singing their throaty songs of love, wherever she walked. She could sometimes be seen playing childish games of war with the boy, her long black skirts tied up around her milky-white thighs. The boy spoke to himself, and was rumored to see things that were not there—a strange and rare illness. Him so pale, with bright blue eyes. As weird as his sister was wild, Jane heard them say.

The bank manager came after the funeral was over and the freezer was once again bare. Rapping on the doors and rubbing condensation away from the windows so that he could peer into the dusty rooms, he called their father's name repeatedly. The twins heard Father sigh where he was sitting amongst teetering towers of books in the library. The light that intruded through the dirt-covered windows carried luminescent motes of dust that settled on his shoulders and in his hair; he refused to eat, only emerging when the bottle in his hand was empty.

One afternoon, the bank manager caught sight of Jane as she was crossing the field from picking cloudberries in the forest. Sebastien watched from his hiding place beneath the porch lattice. When the bank manager held out the court's order for repayment, his meaty hand lingered for just a second over Jane's pale one. In the darkness, Sebastien growled. Some said the bank manager left town that summer, unwilling to face another harsh winter spent collecting debts from out-of-work fishermen. Some said he just disappeared. People looked sideways at Jane went she strode down to the corner store to buy more tea, but no one said a thing.

**

Three days after her mother's funeral, Jane awoke to the hum of voices. She rose from her place next to Sebastien, and went from bathroom to bathroom turning on all the taps, convinced that the water would drain counter clockwise—sure sign of magic coming. The chilled mid-dawn air creeping in through the half-open windows carried with it the scent of wet earth and lavender from the garden, but also something else— something that Jane couldn't distinguish. Moving out onto the porch, she saw that the rhododendron bushes that perpetually leaned against the siding of the house, long infertile, had burst into full, purple bloom. Something was changing. Jane felt as though if she pressed her hands against the cracked walls of the house, she would feel it breathing.

Someone had left a casserole on the porch steps; one of the Women's Church League—the only ones who seemed willing to walk down the long driveway. When Jane unwrapped it from the cloth meant to keep it warm, there was a tract hidden in the folds. She already had several of them neatly stacked in her bureau drawers. Some of them had been left on the porch steps with a tray of homemade molasses cookies and others she or Sebastien had found stuffed into their desks at school. She kept them for the Biblical stories they invariably paraphrased; sometimes, on those nights when Sebastien asked for a story to lull him into sleep after loving, she read to him by the light of the bedside lamp of resurrections and lush, fruit-laden gardens. Secretly, she also kept them because something in her admired the meddlesome women who dared to approach the front door, and suspected that her mother had as well. Her mother would smile, when she saw them, murmuring "'s another one, girly, come to cleanse our soot-black souls. There's all kinds of magic in the world."

Everything felt so much barer without Mother. Jane felt as though there had been too much she had never asked her; the ingredients for a tea that would make someone tell the truth, under which bushes the best blackberries grew, how exactly something as fragile as love could be kept from breaking.

Standing with her stomach pressed against the sink, singing to herself, Jane began to prepare a tray for her father's breakfast—the spoon, the bowl, the mug of chamomile tea with the shot of whisky. Even with the whisky, it was inevitable that one day Father would shake off his grief like an ogre woken from its sleep. Their love would be found out. Jane could not imagine leaving this house; to wander alone into the forest and find a gingerbread house that would take them in.

"Jane." She was startled from her trance by Sebastien, who stood in the kitchen doorway with his sleep-mussed hair and dreaming eyes. "We can't leave," he told her.

Jane began to cry. She buried her face in her hands, but the tears leaked through, staining the front of her nightdress. "Look," he said. A voice of wonder. So she looked.

Great salty tears pooled on the ceiling and fell to the floor where they puddled, seeping into the floorboards. "Look," as he reached across to take her hand. Small buds poked up, inch by inch, through the slatted wood. A rose vine there—by Sebastien's foot—and there, between Jane's toes—hot, heady roses that smelled like the rain. Vines that crept, crawled across the floor, twining around their legs, nudging thigh and hand and spine, up onto the walls. "It misses her," Sebastien said. "It's sad like us." When he placed his hands against Jane's body, she could feel rose petals pushing against her bare arms.

She began to laugh. "We can't leave." To leave all this, this savage garden of their childhood. To leave these rooms.

"We can't leave." Jane repeated, closing her eyes. There were fragrant smudges of red on her neck, a scratch where the thorns tore at her like an insistent lover. "We stay."

Seeing the marks when Jane carried him his breakfast meal on a tray, Father frowned and reached out with a firm hand to take her wrist. "How was that done?" he asked. She lowered her eyes and did not answer. "You two, you play too much," he said. "You could get hurt, in this house, in the garden...perhaps we should move from here."

As children, they had learned quickly that Father did not want them. Besides the evenings when he would gesture for them to join him in the library so that he could read aloud his newest find—a first edition, a rare written copy of a Finnish folktale—his disregard for them was impervious. It was Jane who persisted long after Sebastien gave up trying to win his father's attention, if not his affection. As a toddler, she would raise her grubby little hands to him even after he had already pushed Sebastien away from his knee, or turn her dimpled smile his way even after he had raised his voice. But it was not until, in the year she turned fourteen, that he began to really see her; one afternoon as she carried him a mug of tea, he reached out to grasp her chin in his hand. She stood patiently as he turned it this way and that. "You look like your mother," he said, not harshly. Jane held her breath for days afterwards, expecting the words to carry strange consequences in their queer, close world but he never said another thing about it. However, he began allowing her to read the tales in his library books. Although Sebastien was not given the same privilege, Jane carried the tales to him herself, divulging them in their own secret manner.

It was because of this that she could pity Father. She pulled her wrist from his grasp, set down the tray and slid quietly from the room.

***

The seam of light opening across the bed fell across Sebastien's face, sifting into his sleep. Snarled beneath and around the limbs of his sister, it took him several moments to ease up onto his elbows and, blinking, make out the shape of his father in the doorway. "Sebastien."

As Father approached, his eyes widened at the sight of his children entwined on the bed. "Sebastien?"

There were leaves and rose petals scattered across the rugs. The floor swelled slightly and he threw out his hands to grip the edge of the bed. What his hand touched was Jane's bare leg which made her mutter and raise her head. Her hair was a crow's nest. "Father," she said, raising her chin. He flinched.

The fermented stench of whisky was evident on Father's clothing, on his hands and on his breath as he shut and locked the door. Leaning against the doorframe, he turned his head away from them. His eyes fell on the framed photo of his dead wife resting against the bureau mirror opposite to the bed. Jane and Sebastien watched his watery reflection as he reached out to pick it up. He looked like a man who had awoken from a dream to find that he had been sleeping for a hundred years.

"Your mother loved this house," he murmured. "And it loved her. It was a witch's house—that's what the real estate agent told us—that's why we got it for so cheap. Rumors in the village, haunted rooms—your mother could barely resist. She was no match for a city boy like me." The kind of rueful smile that only ever crossed his face, appeared when he spoke of her. "So I bought it for her. For us." He turned towards the bed, his face crumpling in on itself. "And what did the bitch do? She went and left me. For some godforsaken fisherman. Left me with you."

Jane's hand snaked from beneath the blanket to find Sebastien's, finding the pulse of his heart through the palm of his hand. Sebastien buried his face in Jane's hair as Father sat on the edge of the bed and told them that they would be leaving the house. They wouldn't wait for it to sell, since it was unlikely that it would sell at all. He spoke calmly of his plans to separate them—strange, really, why he hadn't thought of it before. There was certainly a boarding school somewhere on the mainland that would be willing to take Jane for her last year of high school. Sebastien would be easy enough to home school. It made Jane shiver the way he refused to look at them—his eyes shifting across the floor, along the walls, towards the closet—anywhere but at their faces. But then again, he had never really seen them. They had just been shadows of their mother, darting specters that appeared suddenly in his peripheral vision in their hide and seek games through the rooms and disturbed him occasionally with the muffled sound of their laughter through the walls.

They would not be taking the books, the photographs, and the furniture. That would all stay in the house, he insisted. They would start afresh as much as possible. Sebastien and Jane were only to take what they absolutely needed.

"Nothing of your mother's," he said, massaging his temples; the slump of his shoulders and the dull gray pallor of his skin in the dimly lit room. The walls seemed to sag a little around them and Jane began to softly cry. "Nothing of Matilda's," he repeated again.

***

Black Hill Commons was not a place where fairytales belonged. The floors of the apartment were covered in pocked white linoleum; the sagging second-hand mattresses reeked of dust mites and sour milk. The landlord lingered in the doorway with a solicitous smile, as Father pulled back the curtains, sending light streaming into the corners of the bare rooms. "It'll do fine," Father told him with a nod. "How many bedrooms?"

"One," the landlord supplied. "With two beds. 'S down at the end of the hallway there."

Father nodded again, his eyes skimming past Jane and Sebastien where they stood, huddled in the kitchen. "That's fine. Sebastien can sleep on the couch," as he bent to test the springs. He pulled a wad of bills from his back pocket, counted them out carefully and held them out to the landlord.

Despite their father's protests that they bring only what they absolutely needed, Jane had insisted on drying flowers from the garden. She had hung them from the ceiling in the kitchen—a bunch of the black roses that their mother had grafted herself, a few hazel twigs which were meant to keep away interfering spirits. Sebastien unscrewed knobs from the bureau in the attic in which, as children, they had hidden away for hours, cramped against each other and dreaming that they were stowed away on a pirate ship set sail for foreign seas. Now, they were glad that they had managed to salvage some small part of their former life to bring here, to this place which seemed so unfriendly.

Father fiddled with the heat as they unpacked. They hung up clothes in closets and lined their shoes neatly in the corridor by the door. By the time they had supper and were ready for bed, the sound of trickling water had begun to emanate from the radiators. Jane tried to undress with as much modesty as she could muster, her back turned against her father's rustlings as he readied himself on the other side of the room. She burrowed beneath the blankets, stretching herself wide across the mattress so that she would not feel the empty space quite so keenly, and closed her eyes. As her father's snoring shuddered up from the darkness, seeming much too close, she dreamt of how, in the old house, the sea seemed to pour in over the window sills to cradle her into sleep.

It became Father's habit to sit at the kitchen table with deeds, papers and scribbled notes spread before him as he yelled into the phone, trying to balance the sale of the house and the search for an appropriate out-of-province private school for Jane. His position meant that he was able to keep a watchful eye on Jane and Sebastien as they sat on the couch reading or watching the small black and white television that the landlord had offered them for twenty dollars. Sometimes he would ask Jane to make tea, and watch her from his chair as she moved around the kitchen. She was made claustrophobic by his steady gaze; by the way he tilted his head as she leaned over him to set down the mug.

Sitting there on the couch, in the too-bright light streaming through the windows, everything in Jane felt strained and skewed. This place made them both sick. Jane could barely eat without retching. She did her best to make this apartment feel more intimate, but the small details that at home would have just been familiar—the cracked mirror in the bathroom, the tile in the kitchen corner that had obviously been torn up and replaced inadequately—here seemed ugly. She could not convince Sebastien to eat at all. With the dark sleepless bruises beneath his eyes and the vacant way he stared at the television, sometimes he looked like an entirely different person. She could no longer finish his sentences. When she reached out to rest her palm against the small of his spine, he would inevitably pull away, avoiding her eyes.

In Black Hill Commons, their love felt dirty.

Then, one day, Sebastien took the bureau knobs he had lined up lovingly along the window sill and chucked them all in the garbage, saying "They're just takin' up space."

***

There had been a night, when they were children, that Jane was woken from her sleep by the unbearable heat of Sebastien's body. He had been fighting a fever all week. Unable to wake him, she had run to fetch her mother. Mother had carried him into the bathroom where she knelt next to the tub trying to relieve his fever with cold presses, her hands fluttering over his pale face. She murmured words that neither child could hear; Sebastien in his feverish fugue and Jane staring at them both as though she were still asleep and dreaming. There had come a sound from the hallway, the creak of a foot on the floorboards, and peering, Jane had seen Father standing there, looking in at them grimly. Noticing her eyes on him, he had nodded, the way she had seen people do in churches, and stepped back into the darkness. At midnight, Mother had pulled Jane onto her lap and, stroking her hair, whispering wordless sounds of comfort. Jane had reached out to take her brother's icy-cold hand, his tremors passing up into her arm. It didn't seem possible to her that, if he died, she would live.

In Black Hill Commons, however, he did not belong to her; the separation between them felt like the severing of a limb. Trying to convince him to eat, she would cook him star-shaped pancakes only for him to tell her that he wanted cereal. She would bring him cereal, setting it on the table in front of him and he would just play with it, eyes darting towards where Father sat. He made desperate attempts to draw Father into conversation, to impress him with a scant knowledge of geography or art at the dinner table. He didn't seem to notice the tolerant tone of Father's voice, or the way that Father's eyes were always flickering to Jane. She felt as though he were slowly moving farther and farther away. All of her movements became uncertain, falling just short of him.

Eventually, tired of their constant quiet presence, Father told them to 'go outside and play for Christ's sake' as though they were only children. Without speaking they pulled on hats and coats and wandered out onto the road where Sebastien stood scuffing at the pavement. Jane crouched, watching. The afternoon was a cold, dull grey.

"School's gettin' out." His face was turned away from her. From across the road and down the embankment came the distant ringing of the school bell "We should skedaddle," Sebastien said. "They'll walk this way." He hated being around people. In elementary school, they had made games of hiding in the closets during recess where they would close their eyes and list off the names for the plants their Mother dried—fireweed, blue-eyed grass, starflower, cattails, and blood root.

"Do you wanna see what we can find back there," Jane twisted to point towards the trees that lined the apartment building's muddy parking lot, "in the woods?"

Sebastien shook his head.

Jane felt something in her chest tighten. She rose, brushing her hand across the front of her skirt and tossing her hair. "Sebastien, we are not *children* to be ordered about. Ye going to come or not?" But he avoided her eyes. "Fine then."

She deliberately brushed against him as she passed, scrambling down over the embankment towards the school. There were children skipping across the fields and flocks of boys loitering outside the doors, their collars turned up against the sea wind. Seeing her approach, they flicked away their cigarette stubs, nudging each other. Jane stopped just short of them. "Hey." One of them called, raising his chin in greeting. Turning, Jane saw Sebastien at the road, his hand raised to shield his eyes. He was frowning.

It became a habit, then, every afternoon for Jane to meet these boys outside of the school and, always with an eye towards the apartment building windows, lead them into the forest. She made them lie down in the swamp reeds and straddled so that with every movement water squelched up beneath the moss to wet her long strands of hair and creep into their lungs.

"Wild," they would say to her when they had finished, their hands territorial against her waist as they lit cigarettes, smirking. "You're wild, aren't you girly?" But wild was not what she felt with these boys whose names she could barely bring herself to remember. Wild was what she had felt when lying next to Sebastien, with the house pulling its dark starry skin over them.

Then, as they wandered back to join their friends, Jane would straighten her clothes and climb the stairs to the apartment. Her father would raise his eyes as she entered, squinting for a moment; as though, when he looked at her, he saw someone else entirely. "Get me some tea," he would mumble. As she set the mug in front of him, smiling nervously if he looked up, he would reach his hand to rest for a moment on her wrist. And without Sebastien to wash it all away with his soft words, the games he created to distract her—it felt like everything was leaving stains on her. Every touch felt like a bruise.

Even when she sat next to Sebastien on the couch, drawing her legs up beneath her, he would not turn his head to look at her. Her tears, in the flickering light of the television set, turned blue.

***

One afternoon, in the attempt to clean the glass panes Jane pried open the bedroom window to find a small heap of dried-up fireflies on the sill. She scooped them into her hand, their tiny bodies crackling beneath the touch and smiled. She remembered falling asleep to the light of a firefly. "Hey." she called in delight. Sebastien came from the living room, their father following along suspiciously. She pointed at the heap so that they would both see it. "Fireflies," she told them. "They must have been trying to get in." The suggestion sounded childish beneath the weight of Father's gaze. The phone rang and he left them.

"Don't ye see?" Jane held out a handful towards Sebastien. "They must have followed us."

"From where?" He shrugged.

Jane frowned, her excitement shrinking. She lowered her voice as if Father might overhear them. "From home. Maybe they tried to get in. But Father sleeps with the windows closed. 'Bastien, they came for us."

"For us?" he raised his eyes to hers, smirking. "Jane, fireflies do'n follow. They are not faithful bitch dogs that sniff out your scent and heel when you say." He stabbed a finger towards his forehead. "You're going feeble, you are."

Jane said nothing.

That night she went to bed early, feigning monthly cramps. She knew that she could lie with a thousand of these strange bay boys and Sebastien would never admit that things were different here. She could no longer hear his sentences unraveling in her head just by looking at him, or predict his moods before they changed.

It only took a few minutes for Father to fall asleep. His snoring swelled against the walls, drowning out the sound of the bed springs as she swung her legs over the edge of the bed and stole into the hallway. Sebastien was not yet asleep. He eased himself up onto his elbow as she came creeping up beside him, his face arranged into sleepy disarray. "Jane, what..."

"Ssshhh." She reached for his fingers. "There's something outside I wan' to show you." Tugging gently on his hand, she waited as he threw back the sheets. They were clumsy in the darkness, almost stumbling over the coffee table as they moved towards the door. He seemed to wake up as she jiggled the lock open, the night air hitting them through the screen door. "Jane, this is...Father..." but she was already outside on the stairs, the ghostly light of the moon turning her blue.

"What is it?"

"Look." She raised an arm. He looked, seeing the patterns of fireflies that hovered at the tip of her fingers. There were dozens of them, illuminated like small suspended bonfires—impossible. The summer insects would have died by now, unable to withstand the winter temperatures. Yet, here they were. Something flared inside of her.

He pulled his hand from hers. "Jane, we can't." His voice caught. "The house...it's closed up...Mother's gone...this is only a dream."

She slipped closer, resting a hand against his chest. "Is not. It's not a dream.' She pressed her lips to the space over his heart. "Wake up. Wake up now."

He let her lead him to the end of the driveway where she stood, waiting for him to move on his own. He glanced back. Following his gaze, she saw that he was looking back towards the room where Father slept, oblivious. And then he stepped forward and began walking down the street with a steady stride.

Black Hill Commons was sleeping, shop windows darkened and porch lights blurred with frost. Jane removed her own sweater as they walked and coaxed him to wear it, but still they were shivering. Several times he looked behind them, as if expecting to see Father jogging down the road towards them. "Do we even know where we're going?" he asked his sister, not recognizing the fields that slowly began to replace the houses or the fishing shacks that eventually gave way to uninterrupted shorelines. The murmur of the sea sounded like something much too vast and threatening in the blackness.

"Home," she whispered, turning a glowing face towards him. "Going home. Besides, look," she nodded towards the trails of fireflies that they were following. "They know the way."

***

The house was exactly as they had left it. Even in the early morning twilight, they could see it rising up out of the brambles like an apparition. They spent the last few hours of the night sitting with their backs against the shingles, below the parlor window, curled into each other's heat and hidden from the road by briars. Once the sun rose, they wandered around the house until they found a window ajar. Walking through the still rooms, they both felt tired, at this returning and, entwined together on a rug in front of the hearth, they slept.

It was evening when they stirred again, rising lazily to greet the rooms. As though displaying its pleasure, the house shifted its walls, showing them hallways filled with beautifully etched mirrors and rooms bursting with lavish roses. Upon entering the upstairs bathroom, they found the sink filled with water lilies, a toad gazing at them calmly from atop the faucet. "Do ye think anyone will come lookin' for us?" Jane asked. "Father will."

She looked up into his face. "I hadn't thought. I mean, I knew, but...how could I not have thought of that?"

He stroked her hair away from her cheek. "Don't. We'll keep the curtains drawn for now. That should keep the neighbors out."

The twins went from room to room, running their fingers along the dusty bureaus. Standing in front of Mother's old bureau, Jane draped strand after strand of glass pearls around her neck. They flashed as she posed in front of the mirror. "Do ye think she loved him?"

Sebastien turned towards her, holding a bottle of Mother's lotion in his hands. It smelled of violets. Mother used to tell them that, to secure the devotion of their most beloved, they should wash with water that had been colored with violets;

the scent aroused love in the most cold-hearted. "Who, Father? Could be. Once upon a time. Maybe she was in love with how he loved her." He smiled at this fanciful thought, then shrugged. "If ye ask me, if she loved him so much she wouldn't have left. Not how she did."

"Are you mad at her?" Jane asked. A question they had not asked each other before.

"Sometimes."

She nodded. She, too, was angry sometimes with Mother. It was eerie to think that, if she had not been killed, Mother still would have left them. She had been on her way to another house with her lover, and would have left them alone. "Do you think she loved him more?"

"Who, Father? More than us? No."

"No." She fingered the pearls. In the mirror, her mouth was a red petal. "The man. In the car with her."

Sebastien looked at her for a long moment. Her hair was loose around her shoulders like the etchings in Father's books of princesses in faraway towers whose faces were arranged into expressions of perpetual loss. She felt his sadness, coiled, too, in her stomach.

"I don't know," he said, and then, "Sometimes I think she was goin' somewhere else. Somewhere like this, but without Father and other people to come and bother us. And then she would'a sent for us. We could have lived like kings and queens together. 'S what I tell myself."

"I know."

They found the good linen—embroidered with tiny leaves and gold vines—in one of the hallway closets, which they carried up to the attic along with several patchwork quilts. There, they constructed a fort as though they were still children, draping sheets over chairs and layering pillows into nests. As they fell into sleep, the house gathered itself protectively around them.

Father came while they were dreaming.

Awoken by the shattering of glass—the front windows—they became immediately aware of the thick scent of saltwater and grief that filled the darkness. The house was awake, already grieving at this new presence. There came the crashing of bookshelves from the library and Father's distant voice. Jane could feel the house hurting at this intrusion—they could not let it lie.

Kneeling to sweep his hands across the boards in the general area of the attic trapdoor, Sebastien hissed, "It's gone. The house has closed it."

Scuttling towards him, Jane pounded her fist against the floor. Around them, fireflies were blinking into being. They illuminated the small room, the folds and billows of the fort. The house was trying to soothe them, to keep them to itself. "No, open." she demanded. The floor creaked slightly. The opening appeared as though it had never been gone.

The darkened lights in the second floor hallway flickered on as they passed—*blink, blink.* Father's voice was very close and yet, standing at the top of the stairs and peering down into the welling black, they could not sense any movement. Perhaps the house was moving the rooms, making it harder for Father to find them. "Jane, what..."

But Jane had paused at the open doorway to Mother's bedroom. There was an eerie hush to the untouched bed, the walls, as though they had interrupted a whispered conversation.

"Sebastien," she murmured. "Father loved her."

"As did we."

"Yes." Setting her mouth in a narrow line, Jane gestured towards the smooth quilt on the bed, at the photographs that Mother tore out of magazines to hang on her walls with thumbtacks. They were photographs of faraway places, of the endless gold of Asian deserts and the moist, black foliage of South American jungles. "And he hates us. He'd take me away if he could. But here, maybe…"

So, in the end, Sebastien stood where he could not be seen as Father came rushing up the stairs. Seeing Jane at the end of the hallway, Father stopped, his mouth agape.

"Matilda." His voice full of both love and fear.

"Jack." Jane felt uncanny. For a moment she was Mother, with Mother's mischievous way of tilting her head and flirting with her wide, dark eyes. "Come here to me." The house cast shadows across her face, hollowing her cheeks, changing the colors of her hair. Her skin, in the darkness, glowed.

Taking her outstretched hand, Father allowed her to lead him into the tense quiet of the bedroom. The window over the bed shattered, startling him momentarily but Jane was able to soothe him with a low hum as rose vines began to swell in through the broken panes. The vines scrolled across the walls and along the bedposts towards where Father sat on the bed, staring dumbly up at her. When she made to move away, Father grasped her nightdress in his fist, mewling. "Ssshhh." She reached out to stroke his cheek with trembling fingers. "You're fine here."

Sitting next to Father, Jane began to speak, "Once upon a time." Rosebuds unfurled around them, releasing the sharp scent of sea-mist. The lines on the wallpaper began to bleed into curious scenes of castle ruins and overgrown briars, knights in battle and thick, gnarled trees. Beginning beneath Jane's feet and rippling across the floorboard towards the doorway, the floor gave way to black, rich earth. Snarled within it all were the thorny boundaries of Jane and Sebastien's world, deftly revealed within the tales she told; tales of trolls burdened with the guilt of love, of spellbound witches and forsaken gingerbread houses. She did not finish until the last vine had coiled around Father's thigh, pulling him back down amongst the roses.

"I love you," came his voice as Jane rose. In the hallway, the twins turned to watch the light narrow across Father's face as the door closed. The last thing they saw was the sweet expression on his face as the thickets covered him over. Jane rested her cheek against Sebastien's chest, her quivering passing into him before becoming still. Fireflies began to settle tenderly on their bodies, alighting their peculiar love.

As their mother always suspected they would, they became something of a local tale told to naughty children at bedtime to scare them into going to sleep without an extra glass of water or another folk song sung by weary parents. Eventually driven by necessity, a real estate agent drove up the lane—as far as the overgrown thickets would allow—and, standing for a moment with his eyes shaded from the sun to stare at the front porch, drove a For Sale sign into the swampy dirt. The house never sold, even though it was in excellent shape, considering that no one bothered to keep an eye on the gutters when it rained or shovel the snow from the roof in the winter. Every now and then a newly married couple would come vacationing from the mainland and fall in love with the sight of the property. Sometimes even with the story itself; the peculiar family, the mother that had died in a spectacular car accident, the father and children that had disappeared. The house that seemed to be waiting for all of them.

Author Bio:

Sarah Penney-Flynn was raised in Newfoundland, Canada, where she became soaked in the folklore and rich heritage of the culture. Her love of fairytales, inherited from her parents, led her to complete her thesis at Concordia University - a collection of short stories based on the original dark fairytales of the Grimm's. She has been published in *Page One Digest*, a collection of Newfoundland writers and *Images and Words*, a

SWGC publication. Although she follows her own twisted and winding path, Sarah is currently living once again on the island where she pursues her writing.

The Tower
Jaidis Shaw

The hot sun caressed my face in warmth as I sat upon my favorite swing. The birds danced and sang around me, sharing in my childish delight. I loved playing in the garden with my animal friends. Day dreaming of the many adventures that the world was holding for me, I barely noticed the soft footsteps of mother coming outside.

"Rapunzel, you worry me with all of your day dreaming. I think it is time for a change," she said as she grabbed my hand and lead me from the garden.

"Do I get to leave the garden and explore now," I asked excitedly. We traveled along a forest road that opened up into a large clearing. A tall, stone tower stood coldly in the clearings center. There was no door and the only way to enter the tower was by a rope that hung from the window above. At a slow pace, I made my way up the rope and into the tower.

"Rapunzel, disconnect the rope from that post and toss it to me," mother yelled up from the ground below. Obediently doing as she instructed, I tossed down the rope.

"But how will you get up mother?" I questioned.

"Dear Rapunzel, I'm not coming up there. I cannot risk you leaving the safety of my watchful eye. You will remain here in this tower where you are safe and protected. I will visit you each day to bring you food." Mother turned and headed back off in the direction we had came, growing smaller on the horizon.

The years drifted by, as the memories of my childhood faded from existence. Watching the fluffy, white clouds drifting by helped me to pass the time. I do not remember much about my life before coming to this tower. It seems as though I have been trapped in this tower forever. Often creating stories to help keep my sanity intact, I imagined that my mother wasn't really my mother at all. Instead she was an evil enchantress who was jealous of my long locks so she kept me hidden away. Each day I waited, hoping for the day when someone would rescue me from this lonely tower.

"Someone always comes to rescue the princess," I said to the little blue bird that landed next to me. "You see little blue bird; the day will come when a handsome prince will emerge from those trees, riding a noble stallion. In most of the storybooks I've read, the horse is always white, but the color of the horse does not really matter to me. This prince will charge up and rescue me from this tower and take me back to his castle where we will live happily ever after," I sighed with a smile.

The blue bird eyed me as I continued to daydream. Just then, a flicker of hope sparked inside of me as a dark figure became visible against the darkened wood line. Just as quickly as the spark ignited, it was extinguished when the figure revealed itself to be the evil enchantress. The dark figure that appeared each day was always the enchantress who had the nerve to call herself my mother. She did not even know the true meaning of being a mother. There was no connection between us. I shared no resemblance to the imposter who was making her way to the tower. Taking flight, the blue bird left me to face the enchantress alone as she called to me from the ground below.

"Rapunzel, Rapunzel, let down your hair." I had no other choice then to be obedient to her will, always doing as she asked of me. I yearned for human interaction, and although I despised the woman calling my name, at least I could stare upon another human face. Climbing up my golden hair and entering the tower, the enchantress gazed down upon me dumbfounded.

"Why must you always look at me that way?" the enchantress asked.

"Please let me down from this tower mother. Take me with you. I want to see the world. I want to meet people. I want to feel the plush green grass beneath my feet."

"You know it's impossible for you to come down from this tower. How can I make sure that you are safe if you are out exploring the world?"

"Please can you just try to be reasonable for a moment? You cannot keep me locked up forever. Don't you want me to be happy?" I pleaded with her in desperation.

"Every day you ask the same question Rapunzel. Why must you keep persisting when you know the answer already?"

"Well maybe I will just cut off my precious hair! What will you climb then mother?" I threatened.

"You cannot cut your hair you foolish girl," she grumbled, "If you were to cut your hair, then you would be truly alone, without even me to keep you company. You would be completely cut off from any human contact." *She does have a point, I would be all alone without my hair,* I thought in misery.

"Since everything is alright here I will return home. I will be back tomorrow. Now, let down your hair so that I may go," she boasted confidently.

Having strong, beautiful hair that was long enough to climb should have been a precious gift, meant to be cherished. Instead my hair had become my personal curse. Years passed painfully by and each day always held the same scenario. With the passing of each day I became more restless and a part of me died inside, piece by painful piece, until I was just a numb shell. The sun no longer caressed me with its comforting rays. The songs that once danced upon my voice were drowned in silence and misery. There had to be a way that I could escape this torture that held me captive. If only I had a ladder, or even a rope, then I could climb down and run far away from this dreaded tower. I could disappear into the forest and be miles away before the enchantress would even know I was missing. *Maybe I could braid a rope from the bed sheets. Yes, that just may work,* I thought optimistically. Starting with the under sheets so that mother would not notice on her daily visits, I carefully tore the sheets into long strips that allowed for easy braiding. Each day the rope grew longer but after all of the under sheets were gone, the rope was nowhere near long enough to allow for my escape. I would have to use my blanket as well which was bound to be noticed.

"Rapunzel, Rapunzel, let down your hair," the enchantress called. Startled by her voice, I scurried to replace the rope into its normal hiding spot and rushed over to lower my hair for her to climb.

"What took you so long? You're not doing something that I would disapprove of are you?" She sent a suspicious look in my direction.

"Of course not mother, I was just reading."

"Very well then, here is your dinner. I cannot stay long today but I will return tomorrow. Now let down your hair for me so I can climb down." Mother disappeared just as the sun started to disappear below the horizon. Going to retrieve the rope, I heard a faint clinking near the window. I crept to the window and peered out.

"Rapunzel, Rapunzel, let down your hair," a deep unrecognizable voice said.

"Is someone actually here?" I breathed into the silence. Lowering my hair in eager anticipation, I awaited the arrival of this curious stranger. Within seconds a young man climbed through the open window.

"Why isn't there a door to this place?" the stranger replied as he looked around the dark room.

"Who are you?" I asked with a trembling voice.

"Oh, how rude of me, my name is Philip. It is a pleasure to meet you," he said.

"But how is this possible? I don't understand. In all the days that I have spent here, there hasn't been a single person to find me. How did you find me?" I sobbed as tears began to collect in my eyes.

"Please don't cry," Philip said as he took a step towards me. "I was riding out in the forest and stumbled upon this tower and noticed you staring out of the window. You looked so lonely and depressed. I tried to find a door to enter but could not find one. There was not even a ladder that I could climb, so I went back to hide among the trees and tried to figure out a way up. Sometime later a woman appeared and I heard her call to you for your hair. I waited until she was gone before I called to you."

"I'm sorry," I replied in shock, "I have been locked in this tower for several years with only my mother to visit me. I kept hoping that someone would arrive but nobody ever did, until you of course."

"Why does your mother keep you locked up here," Philip asked.

"I want to travel and see all of the amazing things that this world has to offer. She is very protective and does not want me to leave her so on my twelfth birthday she brought me here, where I have remained since."

"How old are you now?"

"I stopped counting long ago. There really is no use since I will be in this tower forever."

"Why haven't you tried to escape and just run away?" Philip asked inquisitively.

"I have thought long and hard about it. I've actually started to braid a rope that I can use to climb down. See?" I said as I went and retrieved the rope that I had spent so much time preparing.

"Well then what are you waiting for? Let's go, we can leave here together," Philip said as he grabbed my cold hand and dragged me towards the window.

"No! It's impossible," I yelled as I ripped my hand from his.

"I thought you wanted to run away?" Philip asked,

confused at my unwillingness to leave.

"No, you don't understand. I want to leave, really I do but it is impossible for me to leave. The rope isn't anywhere near long enough and I have already used everything that I can without my mother noticing the difference. The only thing that remains is my last blanket and mother checks on me daily. She will notice if it goes missing." I let the rope slip through my hands in disgust. There was no way I would be able to finish it.

"I have an idea," Philip said in confidence as he retrieved the rope from the floor. "All you need is more fabric right?"

"Yes. I would need a lot more fabric. Only then would it be possible for me to ever leave this tower that has kept me hidden from the outside world."

"Then it is solved. I will return home and collect fabric for you. I can visit each day and bring more fabric that you can use to make the rope the needed length. Once long enough, you can climb down to me and I will take you away from this awful tower."

Philip smiled at me and my stomach was filled with a nauseating wave of butterflies. Never before had a man stared at me, or any other human for that matter. I did not know what the future held in store for me but I could feel the flicker of hope return to my core, trying to spread its warmth in desperation. A cold rain started to fall to the thirsty ground below.

"You would do that for me?" I asked in shock.

"Of course I would! I'd take you away from here right now if only the rope was ready. The rain is starting to pick up so I must be going, but I promise to return tomorrow," Philip said as he headed towards the window. I reached out and grabbed his arm gently.

"You must promise to be careful. Mother visits during the day, every day. It is of grave importance that you do not let her see you. There is no telling what she would do if she ever found out you have found me," I pleaded with Philip in earnest.

"Don't worry, I will be careful," Philip said as he reached up to caress my face gently, "I will be back tomorrow." I let my hair cascade down the side of the tower and Philip disappeared into the wet darkness. Crumbling to the floor in disbelief, I tried to make sense of the rush of confusing emotions that hit me. Gasping for air I tried to catch my breath while painful sobs tore from my chest. I had always dreamed of the day when I would meet someone and had worked out the exact emotions that I would feel and the exact way that I would handle the experience, but nothing was what I expected it to be. So many emotions were running through me that I could barely focus. Anticipation and excitement began to make their way to the surface and a smile appeared on my lips. Reaching up to touch my face, the memory of what it felt like to smile became brighter and more vivid. I felt rejuvenated and could barely contain myself until I would see Philip again. I leaned against the towers cold stonewall and let myself be swept away with visions of the future.

Sunlight crept through the window and I cracked my eyes to the brightness. I stretched my body that had grown stiff from sleeping on the stone floor and began to rise to my feet. Twitching with excitement, I began straightening up the tower, preparing for Philip's visit tonight. On a normal day I wouldn't even bother with such frivolous tasks but the anticipation was going to drive me insane if I did not find something to occupy my time. Before long I heard a nagging voice from below.

"Rapunzel, Rapunzel, let down your hair." The familiar old routine took hold and I lowered my hair for mother to climb. Bound and determined to not let her spoil my mood, I greeted her with a smile.

"Good morning mother," I said cheerfully.

"Well someone is chipper this morning. Are you feeling alright, Rapunzel?" She asked.

"Yes mother, I feel fine. It is just a beautiful day out today."

"Well I am glad you are feeling better. You have been

giving me such attitude in recent years," she replied.

"I'm sorry mother. I just feel so alone up here in this tower," I began.

"Rapunzel stop! You already know that you cannot leave the safety of this tower. I am not going to have this conversation with you again. Here is your dinner. Now lower your hair for me," she replied as she went to the window in haste.

Doing as she asked, she climbed down the tower and began her journey back home. I waited at the window in eager anticipation, hoping that Philip would keep his promise to me. Hours passed without any sign of Philip and I began to question my sanity, trying to decide if my mind had been playing tricks on me. Just when I was about to give up hope, Philip appeared out of nowhere.

"I was beginning to think you weren't going to return," I said cheerfully.

"I told you I would return and look," Philip said as he pulled out a stack of sheets from his satchel.

"Oh Philip, thank you so much! This will help enormously," I said as I threw my arms around Philip, causing him to drop the sheets.

"You're welcome," Philip whispered in my ear, grazing my cheek with his lips as he pulled his face away. An unexpected twinge surged through me as I stared into his captivating eyes. I wanted to be wrapped up in his arms forever.

"The sooner we get started on the rope, the sooner I can take you away from here," Philip said as he released me.

I worked in silence on the rope while Philip told me stories of all the adventures he had embarked on. His stories were so enticing, which only made me want to leave this dreaded tower as soon as possible.

Each day Philip returned as promised and mother never suspected anything out of the ordinary.

"The rope is finally ready," I told Philip with cheer.

"Then I shall return later after your mother leaves, and you will be able to leave this tower at last and we can be together forever," Philip said. He kissed my soft lips and then began his gentle descent down my hair. "Until later my love," he yelled from the ground below.

After waving goodbye, Philip returned to the safety of the forest to wait for mother to leave from her visit. The sun would soon rise above the horizon and nerves danced within my soul making it impossible for me to sleep. In just a matter of a few hours, I would be rid of this tower and mother for good. The hours drifted by as I sat upon the windowsill, staring at the clouds floating by. A movement out of the corner of my eye caught my attention. Focusing on the trees, I watched as mother emerged from the trees embrace.

"Rapunzel, Rapunzel, let down your hair." Obeying her orders, I let my hair fall to the ground below and mother began her ascent on my golden hair. Finally, she reached the top and climbed in through the window. I pulled my hair back up and glanced at mother, hoping that she would be staying for only a short while.

"Rapunzel, something has changed in your demeanor. What is different?" She asked as she gave me a hardened stare.

"What do you mean mother? Nothing has changed." I could tell from her stare that she didn't believe me and I twitched nervously.

"Very well then, have it your way. I won't be staying long today; I have some matters to attend to."

Grateful for her quick departure, I lowered my hair for her. It seemed as though she couldn't move fast enough. I could taste freedom on the breeze that caressed my skin. Mother soon became one with the trees and I awaited Philip's arrival. Within moments, he appeared on the ground below. I rushed in the tower and retrieved the rope in excitement.

"Rapunzel, Rapunzel, let down your hair." Running back

to the window, I tossed one end of the rope over the edge. I glanced down over the edge at Philip in delight but was hit with a surge of dread instead.

"Philip! Look out, behind you!" I screamed in horror as the rope slipped from my frightened hands into a pile on the soft grass below. Mother was standing behind Philip with eyes full of rage. I watched in terror as the smooth steel cut through Philip's flesh like tissue paper. Even from far above, I could hear Philip gasping for air as he smothered in the gurgling blood that flowed freely from his pale neck.

"How could you betray me Rapunzel? After all I have done for you! You are nothing but a selfish little whore," she screeched from the ground. "Now you can rot in the tower that you despise so much," she said as she gathered the rope in her arms. My world came crashing down on me and my heart shattered into pieces. My only chance at escape was lying still in a puddle of blood. The urge to live retreated to the dark corners within my soul. I would never be free from this torture. With numb, trembling fingers, I tied my cursed hair around the pole near the window. Embracing my fragile neck with the golden hair that had decided my fate, I perched upon the windowsill, staring at Philip's lifeless body.

"You will never harm me again mother," I said smiling as I stepped off the window's edge, finding the bittersweet freedom that I had always longed for.

Author Bio:
Jaidis Shaw currently resides in a small town located in South Carolina with her husband and her beautiful daughter. With a passion for reading, Jaidis can always be found surrounded by books and dreaming of new stories. She enjoys challenging herself by writing in different genres and currently has a fantasy novel in the works. When not reading or writing, Jaidis is the

Assistant Book Tour Coordinator for Nurture Your Books, and enjoys encouraging her daughter to let her imagination run wild. She can be found at http://junipergrove.wordpress.com

Song of the Midshipmen
Alison J. Littlewood

On days when the wind blew from the north and made the salt tang of the sea ever-present, my father would not speak to me. He would only sit on the doorstep, looking out at the sea, his eyes as grey and clouded as the waves. He never told me what he waited for and I knew better than to ask.

It was easier to leave him there and escape over the dunes to the rock pools. I sometimes found fish that had been stranded by the retreating tide and sure enough, today, silver scales blinked and flashed in the sun. I rubbed my eyes. The water was also full of hair; it floated in the pool, clumped together like bladder wrack.

Then I saw a pale face, the eyes clamped shut, mouth open. There was a girl beneath the water.

I splashed into the pool, ignoring the cold shock of it. For a moment, the girl was light in my arms, then she thrashed like a fish that didn't want to be landed. She kicked my legs from under me and the pool closed over my head. I opened my eyes under the water and saw her. Eyes looked back at me. They were the deep green of seaweed.

Her lips moved and a moment later I heard her voice. It was soft, melodic: music become words. "Help me," she said. She gestured towards the sea. I expected slender fingers, but her hands were broad and fleshy. Her eyes were wide set, her nose a narrow slit. Pale blue veins threaded beneath her skin. Then I saw something silvery and lithe, scales shining in the sunlight.

I knew, then, what she was. Even under the water, I shook my head. I knew that merfolk were a legend only; something told of in ancient tales and late night barrooms, when the ale had been flowing too freely. Yet I could still feel the girl's cool skin on my fingertips.

I had to surface. Cold air rasped my throat. I glanced towards the cottage where my father sat and watched, but it was hidden behind the rocks. I took a deep breath and sank down once more.

"I need the sea," she said. "I'll die here. It's not enough."

I surfaced, droplets pouring off me, and pulled myself onto the rocks. The sea wasn't far. I could carry her there and watch her swim away, if I chose.

I could also carry her home. If I did not, no one would believe me. And I thought of my father, staring out to sea with those clouds in his eyes. How they would widen in astonishment.

I looked back at her. She wasn't looking at me. Her eyes were unfocused, staring at something further, something beyond; just like father's. I sighed, waded in and reached for her.

She was heavy, out of the water, and her hair felt like rough, hempen rope. I carried her across the sand, wet clothes clinging to my legs. The first wave foamed across my feet and she struggled. "Wait," I said, trying to go deeper, but I fell and she slithered over me. Her tail slapped my head down. When I fought my way clear of the waves, coughing and spluttering, she was gone.

I stared after her, waiting for some sign; a gesture of thanks, maybe. But only the grey waves looked back, giving their constant answer.

***

I thought father would like to hear of the maid, but when I told of her, his eyes grew hard and distant.

"Don't dwell on such things," he said. "Your feet are on the ground. Make sure your head isn't out to sea, or you'll drown." He clattered pots in the sink.

I tried to speak and he shrugged, smashing down with a skillet and shattering the mug my mother had always used. He stood quietly with his head down, looking at it.

I didn't say anything. I thought of the way he sat sometimes, his gaze fixed on the grey moving line that lay beyond the window.

"Have you ever seen such a thing, father?"

He picked pieces of broken china from the sink, laying them out carefully, one by one.

"I don't believe anyone has seen such a thing."

"I have," I said. "I saw it." After a moment I added, "She was beautiful."

He turned and fixed me with his gaze. "Was she, son? Was she, really?"

I paused. I thought of her pale, veined skin, the clumped hair, the flat nose. Her wide hands, the oily-grey sheen of her tail.

Father waited and I found I didn't know what to say. I only nodded.

"Well, not all that's beautiful is good for you. Remember that."

I stared out of the window.

"To save someone's life might make you love them," he said. "But it won't necessarily make them love you."

***

It was as though I had become my father. I sat by the rock pools, doing nothing, staring out to sea. I knew the look in my eyes was just like his. My skin was gooseflesh where the northerly wind breathed upon it, but I did not move.

The tide was drawing in and the waves were almost washing against my feet when, at last, I saw her. Just a glimpse of her pale face.

After a while, she resurfaced, closer to the shore this time. She raised a hand and waved, and in another moment, she smiled at me. Then dived, flipping her tail in the air. It caught the sunlight, a sudden flash of aquamarine.

She rose, slicked back her hair, and once more gave that strangely flat smile. Then she beckoned. Her face was expressionless and I realized she was holding her breath, out of the water. I stood and waded into the sea. The maid swam backwards, always beckoning, leading me further in. The waves pulled at my thighs, as though they, too, wanted me to go deeper.

She gestured for me to put my head under the water and, after a pause, I did. I forced my eyes open and they stung. She reached out, running her hands over my throat, wrapping them around my head. The pressure of holding my breath built inside my skull. Then she leaned in and I felt the touch of a cold tongue.

When she spoke, her voice was lower than before. "You may breathe," she said, and I found that the pressure had gone.

She took my hand and drew me onward. I do not know how far we went; I did not look back. Then we headed downward, deeper and deeper, until I saw the seabed, studded with black anemones and outcrops of coral. I glanced back at the pale pads of my feet. They looked broad, fleshy, no doubt distorted by the water.

"Listen," she said. "The first creature to sing was not a bird. It was a fish."

There was a curious thrumming on the edges of my hearing, deep and low. Another note joined it, and another, throbbing into a rhythm that spoke to my blood.

"It's the midshipmen," she said.

Golden arcs appeared through the water, like tiny, sunken slivers of the moon. As they came closer the shapes resolved into fish. The midshipmen were in reality squat and ugly, a little like frogs, but with shining lights like buttons along their bellies. They hummed, releasing jets of water that spiraled behind them with each sound. Some of the notes were higher, some lower. Some were constant, like waves on a beach. For a moment, they came together, all of the notes blending into one. Then they fell silent.

"They sing for our sister," the mermaid said. I turned to her.

"She loved one such as you. She chose to walk upon the land on those stumps you call legs. She gave her voice to the sea witch to learn the trick of it. But her chosen one did not love her, and when he gave himself to another she leapt into the sea, though she could no longer breathe its waters. Her body came back to us, falling to our garden in her ruin."

I didn't know what to say. And in another moment, such wonders were revealed that made me forget her words.

There were towers built from living coral, whose fronds waved this way and that, as though steeples bent and twisted in the breeze. Fish flashed by, iridescent blue sparking from their sides, while dark eels lurked beneath rocky outcrops. Everywhere, outlines were softened by anemones in pink and lavender and yellow, and here and there, vicious spikes of black. Tentacles withdrew beneath the ramparts of a palace, its walls faced entirely in pale pink shells. Giant fans waved in the motion of the tides, sending cooling draughts towards me. I closed my eyes. When I opened them, her eyes were staring into mine.

"You can stay," she said, "if you choose."

"Do you ask me to?"

She smiled and tilted her head. Her eyes were deep green and pearlescent grey, light and dark all at once. Her hair bloomed.

She rose, and I followed. I was light as air, heavy as water. Something tapped on my shoulder and I saw a fish, yellow backed, white bellied, marked by five black stripes.

"The sergeant," she said. "He says you should stay, too." And she turned, flipping her tail into my face. I chased her, then, ruffling the sea fans, dispelling peaceably grazing fish. I laughed as we went, water eddying past my face, faster and faster, in this wondrous blue world.

After a time the waves grew rough and I saw pale sunlight through the ocean. My heart thudded in my chest. Everything around seemed cold, but it felt good, like a breeze on a summer's day.

"I saw your father once." The maid pointed. I saw rocks rising, a dark shape through the grey water.

"You look like him," she said. "I beckoned to him too, a long time ago, but he would not follow."

My eyes widened. Then I remembered the way he watched the ocean, as though waiting for something that never returned.

I looked at the maid. I could see her clearly, every blue vein that hid beneath the skin. I remembered the way I had watched for her, day after day, hoping she would come back.

"I'll stay," I said, and she smiled her welcome.

***

The maid scooped an oyster into her mouth. She swallowed, her blunt lips glistening before the water washed them clean. Then she tore into a crimson sea fan, so that tendrils hung from her mouth like blood. I ate, too. Since I had chosen to stay, I hungered. I bit into a tuna fish, feeling its life wash over my lips.

The maid had not told me her name and had not asked for mine. I wondered what it would be like to kiss her. I did not know if I wanted it or not.

Others ate with us, cracking shells between their teeth. The maid had many sisters. Their hair shone silver and yellow and black. They did not speak to me.

My legs had bonded together. The maid had helped me from my clothes, and I didn't know if her expression conveyed lust or something else.

I thought of my father, his face blank, staring out to sea. I shivered, and let the tuna fall from my hands.

"You are finished?" I found her at my side.

I nodded.

"Then go," she said.

I stared at her, but she just looked back at me, her eyes a bright gleam.

"Go?" I asked, and she nodded. She raised a hand and pointed, away from the coral houses, away from the palace, to where the ocean lay deep and black.

"What do you mean?"

"You have seen our kind. Tasted our food. Now you will go, and wander forever knowing what you have lost."

I gawped.

"Our sister knew the ways of the land, before she was cast out."

I began to understand. "But I did not cast her out. I never knew her."

The maid's eyes narrowed. I could read her meaning plain enough.

"Go as you will," she said. "Live as you will. Go home, if you will."

"Home?" Suddenly I wanted nothing better than the old hearth, the glowing embers of the fire, and a seat by my father's side.

She let out a bubbling laugh, and I knew then what she meant.

I stared into the dark.

"I helped you," I said. "I meant you only good."

"Our sister had a good heart," she replied. "It was no use to her, in the end."

I looked around at the ring of faces, the others of her kind. They were closer now, and had paused in their eating, morsels suspended between their mouth and hands.

"Please," I said. The ocean looked quiet, a heavy, crushing silence. "Please."

The maid did not speak again. She only pointed the way, into the dark.

Outside the circle, the seabed was pale and featureless, the ocean deep and silent. I saw the occasional flash of fish, and once, a heavy, cumbersome turtle. I spoke but it did not answer; only stared after me with mournful eyes.

After a time I began to speak to myself. I turned towards the shore where my father waited, far away, and shouted to him. I wondered whether his face was turned towards the sea. I wondered if he heard.

I swam until my flesh ached. Still I went on, looking for another of her kind, someone with whom I could converse, who might lay a hand upon mine. Once I saw a pale figure circling below. My heart thudded, but it was only a shark, meandering through the deep. I was not afraid.

Her words sounded in my ears over and over. *My sister loved one such as you.*

I wondered what her sister had been like: whether she was beautiful, whether she was kind. I thought about the way she had chosen to return home, her body sinking into the deep, returning to her sisters. Leaving behind everything that was rich and lovely and alien and strange, to see her own land once more; even though she knew she could no longer breathe its air.

I looked around into the inky dark. Then I turned and began to swim, steadily and strong, back the way that I had come.

I wanted to look into my father's eyes. Just once more, to see if the grey blank would light up with recognition. He would be in his place on the step, his eyes fixed on the grey line of the sea. Maybe, before the end, we would be able to speak to each other.

Maybe that would be enough.

For a long time I swam, back towards my home, until I saw the pale light of dawn coming through the waves. Back towards the beach, where my father waited.

Author Bio:

Alison J. Littlewood has been obsessed with fairy tales ever since she first began to read. She lives in a dark, twisted forest in deepest Yorkshire, England, with a white knight, a secret library and several ancient mirrors that refuse to be dusted. Her work has appeared in Black Static, Aoife's Kiss, Dark Horizons and Midnight Lullabies, among others. Visit her at www.alisonlittlewood.co.uk.

The Red Flower
Justin A. Williams

Joringel put his hands behind his head, leaned back against a large tree and breathed the warm night air. He sighed contentedly as he listened to Jorinda's sweet voice, enriched by the afterglow of their lovemaking. His love's singing drove away all cares and sorrows. Here in this moment he wasn't worried about finding a Road to walk to guide his magic and make him a true mage. Here, now, he was content, though he knew it couldn't last.

Jorinda ended her song and laid her head against his shoulder, drawing him close. "What are you thinking about, my love?"

He smiled and kissed her forehead. "How beautiful your voice is, dear one."

Jorinda laughed, a sweet sound like water. "No thoughts at all about your search for the true color of your magic?"

He shook his head, smiling. "How could I think of any other magic when I'm entranced by the magic of your voice?"

She jabbed him in the ribs and he laughed. "Be serious, Joringel. I want to know what you're thinking."

"Yorale says that some mages find their Road right away, but some never do, or perhaps they tap into one but never see it. Perhaps that'll be my fate as well."

Jorinda squeezed his arm so tightly he gasped with pain. "Don't ever say that, Joringel! I believe in you. You've set out to become a wizard and I know in my heart that you will. You will find your Road, I've no doubt of it."

He kissed her and held her tight. What would he ever do without her? His lessons with the village witch went slowly. Her words during their last session had not been encouraging. But

Jorinda always believed in him, always kept him going.

"I hope you're right, Jorinda. I don't think your father will allow his beautiful daughter to wed a man forever trapped as an apprentice hedge-mage."

"I am not concerned." She began gathering her clothes. "We should get back, though."

"Of course." They dressed quickly and walked toward the village, hand in hand. But as each moment passed, Joringel felt they were going deeper into the forest rather than moving out of it. Jorinda must have felt it as well; she drew closer to him with each step.

"Joringel, where are we? We don't want to wander too near the castle."

He nodded. He wasn't sure he believed the rumors of a witch inhabiting the castle deep within the forest, but he'd no desire to find out. His abilities as a Roadless hedge-mage would be of little use against a seasoned sorceress with the power of one of the Nine Roads behind her. "Don't be afraid. We've just gotten turned around."

"The trees are so thick. I can't see the moon or the stars." Jorinda was holding him tight now. He could feel her trembling. "I'm afraid. I don't know why but I'm suddenly terrified."

Joringel felt it as well, a dread that brought sweat to his palms and a hot tingling to his shoulders. He tried to ignore it. "Don't worry, I'll work a finding-charm and have us out of here before you know it." He smiled at her. "But, you'll have to release your vice-grip on my arm, dearest."

"Oh, I'm sorry." She released his arm and moved back just enough to let him cast the spell. With hand and voice, he wove the charm, but it shattered and lashed back at him in a knot of sparks and strands of power.

"What happened?"

"I don't know." He looked around them, searching for the presence he felt. To his shock, less than a hundred paces from them through a gap in the trees stood the high grey walls of a vast castle.

He made to turn, to speak to Jorinda, but a powerful force held him in place. He could lift neither hand nor foot. "Jorinda, run now!"

"I can't move. Joringel, what's happening?"

There was a soft, thick fluttering. From high atop an old oak, a grey screech owl swooped down and landed behind a bush. A moment later, a withered bony old woman swathed in grey robes hobbled out from behind the shrubbery. To Joringel's eyes, she radiated power. He struggled to move, but his body ignored him.

The witch sneered. "How impotent you must feel, my boy. Your body won't listen, your unfocused, un-sourced magic useless against my binding spell." Her voice matched that of her owl form creaking and shrill.

"Let us go!" Joringel shouted.

Jorinda's eyes filled with tears as she struggled to move. "Please, Madam, we meant you no harm. We came here by accident."

The old woman laughed. "Very little that happens in this forest is by accident. I heard your lovely voice, girl, and decided I must add you to my collection. You will join all the other voices in my castle, to sing to me forever."

"Don't you touch her!" Joringel cried.

The witched smiled a graying smile. "Oh I shan't touch her, my boy."

The witch's old claws knotted through the air as she spoke shifting, sussurating words. Jorinda turned to Joringel with love in her eyes that changed to bald terror as her body became grey mist, shifting and changing, shrinking, compressing. He cried out, he tried to incant a spell but the same force that bound his limbs befuddled his mind.

Then Jorinda's voice rang out in a sweet note that rose

into the twilight tones of the nightingale she had become.

Joringel struggled, tried to leap at the witch, but to no avail. Tears ran down his face, the only thing moving, as vengeful thoughts of what he'd do to the witch filled his mind.

The witch raised her hand, a small golden cage in her grasp. The mist that still clung to Jorinda's new form pulsed and rippled, bearing her slowly into the cage. The witch shut the cage door with a snap.

She turned her eyes and her tombstone grin upon him. His mind burned with rage, with fear for Jorinda and hatred for the witch.

"Now she is mine, boy. At dawn the binding spell will vanish and you will be free. Don't entertain any ideas of being a hero. If you come here again, what I transform you into will be far less beautiful than a nightingale."

With that, she turned and hobbled toward the castle, her grey-cloaked form disappearing into the evening mist.

Joringel fought against the restraining magic, trying to go after them, but it was no use. He stood, alternately shouting in frustrated rage and weeping in cold fear for the safety of his love.

After what seemed like an endless alternation of screaming and weeping, Joringel's world went grey then suddenly black. In his exhausted standing sleep, he dreamed that small cracks formed in a patch of ground near his feet. Slowly clods of earth fell away as something rose from beneath the dirt. A small shoot emerged, growing and unfolding before his eyes. In moments, it grew into a beautiful red flower with many petals. In the center of it lay a drop of liquid; whether blood or water stained red by the flower he couldn't tell.

He knelt down before the flower and stared deep into that sphere of red liquid at its heart. He felt as if he was falling, flowing and then he was in a great field of the red flowers that stretched on as far as his eyes could see.

From across this crimson expanse he heard Jorinda's

sweet voice singing to him, calling out for help.

"Jorinda!" He cried. He started forward, but all around him the flowers seemed to wilt. No, they were melting, merging into a flowing red river, like rushing blood. It rose all around him, warm and fragrant. It pulled him along, faster and faster.

He awoke with a start, lying on the mould-covered floor of the forest.

The castle was gone. The witch was gone. There was no red flower, but more importantly, there was no Jorinda.

He screamed, scrabbling at grass and weeds, tearing them between his fingers as he clawed at the dew-moistened soil.

He ran through the woods, crying out Jorinda's name again and again.

Finally, when he had wept all his tears and his voice was hoarse he went to the edge of the forest and, after a longing look back through the trees, turned his gaze toward the village. He wanted to storm the castle, destroy the witch and bring Jorinda home. But he'd need help. And Jorinda's family should know what had befallen her.

***

Joringel stood at the door of the house adjoining the blacksmith shop, steeling himself for what was to come. The pain of watching Jorinda transformed and taken away still burned in his chest. Speaking to her father would only add anguish and shame, but he had to do it.

He knocked on the door, the wood darkened by years of wind-blown smoke. He waited. As he was about to knock again the door opened and Jorinda's younger brother, Kothen, stuck his round face around its edge.

"Where's 'Rinda? She never came home last night and Papa's furious! He thinks you took her off somewhere. But I know you'd never hurt her. What happened?"

"Kothen, I don't know—" Joringel saw the boy's eyes widen in fear and turned just in time to see Otheis towering over him, hammer raised.

"What have you done with my daughter, you worthless sack of manure?"

Joringel stepped back and pulled the hammer from the startled blacksmith's hand with a word and a gesture. "I did nothing. Jorinda and I were walking in the woods. Some kind of misleading-spell led us to the old castle. Jorinda was taken by the witch. She's a Grey Road mage, I think; she changed Jorinda into a nightingale and took her into the castle."

Otheis bent down and retrieved his hammer. He grinned a painful, crooked grin at Joringel. "Walking in the woods? Is that what you call it?" As he spoke, other men from the village began to gather. Most hefted clubs or tools of some kind.

"Otheis, stop this. I know you do not approve of me, but we have to save Jorinda."

"Save her? You speak of saving her, yet you steal her virtue, soil her again and again, then lead her into the woods to her doom!"

As he spoke, the other men circled around, slowly, quietly, until they surrounded Joringel. Aric the Tanner, Nothos the Chandler and Fayali the potter who made only rough, nearly formless vessels.

At a quick sign from the burly smith, they attacked. Joringel fought back with his hands and with what few spells he knew, but it was no good. They were too many and too strong. Kicks and blows from hammer and flail and weighted fist rained down on him. Red flowers of pain exploded behind his eyes, reminding him of the red flower of his dream. He reached out to it in his mind, but it was so far away.

Kothen's voice, filled with tears and terror rose above the grunts of exertion, the thuds of impact. "No, no!" he screamed. "Please, Papa, make them stop!"

There was a barked command and the beating stopped, just as Joringel's mind fell into blankness.

The next he knew, Joringel was being flung roughly to the ground amidst trees and cool shadows. He was back in the forest.

"If you ever set foot in the village again," Otheis' voice rasped from above him, "I will finish what we started here today." With a final kick to Joringel's bruised ribs, he left.

Moaning, Joringel curled on the soft leaf-strewn ground, weak with pain, shaking with rage and wept out his longing for Jorinda. Once he came back to himself, taking care not to exacerbate his injuries, he sat up and worked a few simple healing charms on his wounds. The pain lessened, and he found he could move again.

Joringel got to his feet. He turned and stared into the forest. He longed to destroy the witch, to free his beloved Jorinda, but he knew he could not. Not now. Not as he was.

Moving was still painful but, fashioning a prop from a fallen tree branch, Joringel walked out of the forest, and away from the village. He had to find the red flower of his dream.

***

For nine days he searched, walking far and wide seeking the flower. Each day his rage and sadness grew, but each night it was his love and passion for Jorinda he felt burning within him.

He dreamed of her and of the flower again and again. It was always the same dream and always ended with him falling into the river of red flowers that flowed into blood. Each night he prayed it would carry him to Jorinda, but each night he awoke cold and alone. Sometimes he felt as if he were closer, closer to her, but something was missing.

On the ninth night, he came to a vast, dark forest. For hours, he walked through it, searching for signs of the red flower. Deeper inside, something began to loom in the distance, and after a time he saw it was a castle.

The witch's castle. He had wandered in a circle all those days and made his way back to the place he started from, empty handed. Jorinda was there, waiting in a cage, somewhere inside. But he was still powerless to save her.

Power.

Power started within but came also from the Nine Roads. True wizards took their strength from combining their inner magic with the power of a Road.

The dreams. The red flower. The flowing river of blood.

The Red Road. It was calling to him. He had to answer.

Joringel fell to his knees and pulled out his knife. If he was wrong and the Red Road had not called him, then he would die here, as close to Jorinda as possible. If he was right...

He had to be right.

Focusing both rage and passion, calling out with mind and heart, Joringel slashed four times, forming a bloody cross upon the pale flesh of each wrist.

He held them up and his blood trickled, then flowed and finally rained down upon the ground. The soil drank thirstily of his passionate offering of both body and soul.

The blood flowed until he grew lightheaded, then dizzy and still the earth drank. He released a sigh that changed to a whimper. He'd been wrong and now he would die here, his life spilled upon the witch's very doorstep.

As consciousness slipped away from him there was the slightest stirring in the ground beneath him. Joringel fought with all his strength to stay awake and aware. Before him, just as in his dreams, the packed soil slowly broke and fell away, revealing a strong green shoot. Upward it unfolded; growing at speed until finally, at long last, the red flower of his dream blossomed before his eyes. At its heart shone a single crimson pearl of blood.

Joringel grabbed the flower, plucked it from the ground

and held it to his face. He flowed into that pearl of blood, carried away in the rushing torrent of a river of love and rage, of passion and resolve.

There was a moment of burning, pain and ecstasy together. Then he was back on the forest floor. The wounds on his wrists had crusted over with dried blood. The red flower was gone. No, not gone, but changed. Upon his left palm he bore the mark of an open scarlet blossom with a red pearl at its center. Flickers of crimson lightning played over the mark.

Power coursed through his spirit and body and a shining river flowed before his mind's eye—one moment it was wine, the next coppery blood and then a stream of raging flames.

The Red Road.

He got to his feet, staggered. The power flowing through him was tremendous. He knew no spells of the Red Road. The simple hedge-charms he'd learned had not prepared him for such an enormous force.

Desire.

The Red Road was about desire and passion. His need for Jorinda, for her voice, her face, her flesh. His rage at the witch for what she had done. These would be his focus, a channel for the limitless power of the Road.

Fixing his mind on those things, Joringel strode toward the castle. The magic of the binding-spell licked at his skin and mind. His left hand tingled, arcs of red light played across his body. He continued unhindered.

The castle gate stood before him. His newly awakened magical senses perceived that its metal lattice had been transmuted to a substance far harder and stronger than iron, glinting grey in the moonlight. There were enchantments upon its locks and gears as well.

Emboldened by passion and longing, Joringel decided to take a very direct approach. Stretching out his left hand he called upon the love and rage within him. Through them he linked his mind and heart with the flow of the burning river before him.

Joringel raised his left hand, the flower-mark on his palm pulsing with a scarlet glow. A word of power flowed along the Road into his mind. Crying out the mystic syllable, he unleashed a bolt of sizzling red lightning. It struck the gate, warping the heavy latticework and melting a small hole through its center.

Again, Joringel raised his left hand and cried out Jorinda's name. The floodgates within him opened and he saw only the Road. This time both lightning and fire rushed forth in a massive torrent. The blast ripped the bespelled gate from its hinges. It fell to the ground in a smoking, molten heap.

Joringel passed through the ruins of the gate into a courtyard of withered trees and brown grass. At the far end of this miniature wasteland were set two great oaken doors leading, he assumed, into the castle proper.

He was surprised to find these doors unlocked and unwarded. Of course, with the binding-spell on the outer grounds and the enchanted mage-iron gate, the witch likely saw no need to bar the inner doors.

Beyond them, Joringel found himself in a great hall. The few torches along its walls left its upper reaches cloaked in darkness. Two dark archways yawned to either side of him. Another before him flickered with greyish light. He heard birdsong from within and caught a glimpse of many gilded cages, but as he moved forward the hunched form of the witch shuffled into view.

"I'm surprised to see you here, boy." The harridan's rusty, shrill voice grated on Joringel's nerves. "I thought you would have forgotten all about your lady-love and already found someone new, as all the others did before you."

"How many have you taken, witch? How many lives have you stolen and how many loves have you destroyed?"

"Oh, many thousands over the years. The birds of my chorus sing until they die, and then I must replace them. Your

Jorinda will last me many years before she is exhausted."

Fury rose in Joringel's heart. Before his inner eye the Red Road became a river of boiling blood. "I will never let that happen! Jorinda will be free and you will be destroyed, you moldering old hag!" He lashed out with the flower mark, hurling a bolt of flame and anger at the smirking sorceress, her hands and lips already moving in a spell. Her form grew misty and indistinct. His attack passed through her, scorching the wall behind her. Still he heard a hiss of pain as the flames vaporized some of the mist.

"Hot enough to damage me even in mist-form," the witch said as she became solid again. "You have great strength, boy, but little skill I'm afraid."

She was right of course. He'd never fought another mage before, had never learned spells of attack or defense. He was acting entirely on instinct, rage and desire. Jorinda's freedom and their life together depended on him. He was not about to let her, or himself, down.

"Life is change, manling. It would be best for you to accept the loss of your lady love as just another of those changes." She clawed the air and spoke fluttering words.

Joringel found himself at the apex of the hall's vaulted ceiling, the floor rushing toward him rapidly. Without thinking, he wrapped himself in resolve; let his determination infuse his being. Manifesting his will, Joringel's body momentarily became like a thing of iron, cracking the floor as he landed. He stood and faced the witch.

"I refuse. I have decided to spend my life with Jorinda and nothing, *nothing* will ever change that!" He realized more blasts would be of little use against her mist-form spell. But it took time to cast. Perhaps he could try another approach.

Joringel imagined the flashing speed of lightning, the quickness of a wildfire and merged it with his urgent need to free the one he loved. He took this burning celerity and infused it into every fiber of his body and mind.

He took a step and found he could move at incredible speed. He began to run about the hall, over the floor and up the walls, everything around him a blur. He could barely tell where he was going, but the witch's aura was clear in his mind's eye.

Still moving, he hurled bursts of flame and lightning at the witch, aiming mentally. She deflected the attacks or became mist to avoid the slower ones, but the more he tested his new speed, the faster Joringel attacked. The blasts and bursts came too quickly for the hag to perform her mist-form spell, leaving her to deflect them with charms and the heavy ash wood staff she carried.

Joringel, his confidence growing, was gaining greater and greater understanding of his new power and managed to simultaneously unleash a streak of lightning, a spray of acid and a hurtling ball of flame. The harridan dodged the acid and deflected the lightning, but the ball of flame burst upon the right side of her face.

The witch screamed and held a hand to her face. Joringel stopped. His heart leapt inside him. He'd never hurt another person before. But thoughts of all this woman had done to Jorinda and himself replaced that feeling of sympathy immediately. He had to take this opportunity to defeat her.

As he raised his hand to strike, the witch gestured with her staff, wrapping him in cloying grey mist-webs. She lowered her hand from her face, revealing angry red and black burns. "You will pay for that, you stupid boy. I will send you to wander the grey between for all of time!" She raised both arms and began incanting, whispering words, slipping in and out of hearing.

Joringel strained against the webbing. It pulled and stretched but never gave way. Growling and moaning in frustration, Joringel fixed his gaze on the doorway behind the chanting old woman. His Jorinda lay just inside. Would he give up so easily, allow himself to be defeated when he was this close?

His mind and heart cried out at the thought. The mark on

his palm burned and throbbed with power. The strands on his left side began to relent with each struggle, and a wet burning smell reached his nostrils. He was breaking through!

The witch completed her spell, firing a shimmering stream of grey light from her staff just as Joringel freed his left hand and raised it to attack. The blast struck the glowing flower on his palm and rebounded. The triumphant look on her face melted into fear as the beam hit her squarely in the chest. She let out a high, wavering cry. Slowly the witch's shape grew hazy and indistinct as all color drained from her form. In moments all that remained of her in this world was a faint, grey outline.

Relief flooded Joringel's heart, along with a fierce, fiery triumph. He rushed forward to find Jorinda but, forgetting that the webs still bound his feet, fell to his knees. He burned away the clinging fetters and went into the next room.

Shelves lined every inch of the circular room's walls, all of them covered with cages. More cages hung from hooks set in the roof. Most were full. Larks, sparrows, nightingales, songbirds of all shapes and colors sat within, now silent.

How would he tell which Nightingale was Jorinda? They all looked alike.

No sooner had he thought it than he heard Jorinda's voice, singing the same song she'd sung that night. He followed the sound to one of the cages hanging from the ceiling.

"Jorinda! My love, can you understand me? Are you all right?"

He opened the door of the cage and the nightingale fluttered onto a nearby table.

He raised his left palm toward the bird, the mark glowing vermillion. "Don't worry, Jorinda. I'll change you back. I have found my Road at last! May its power and the power within me set you free from this evil transformation!" He felt the Red Road flow through him, joining with his hearts strength. It washed all around him in waves of scarlet light that swept past him and over Jorinda's tiny, feathered form. He nearly burst with joy and desire as the scarlet force destroyed the witch's spell, returning Jorinda to her true, beautiful shape. His head swam with exhaustion and he thought he might faint but the sound of his love's voice pulled him back.

"Joringel, dearest, I'm so very proud of you!" She flung herself into his arms and he clung to her, swearing to himself that he'd never let her go again.

She pulled back and looked into his eyes. "You must free the others. All of these birds, they are women just like me. All must have people who love them waiting somewhere for them."

Joringel smiled. "I know. I will try. I'm not sure I have the strength now, but I will try."

She stroked his hair and kissed him long and deep. "Know that another such kiss awaits you when the deed is done."

Joringel laughed for the first time since they had been parted. "Then I will certainly succeed. Open the cages while I prepare."

As Jorinda moved around the room Joringel closed his eyes, searching for the Red Road within him. He found it, and once again joined its power with the rage he felt on behalf of those the witch had imprisoned. It built within him until finally he raised his hand and cried out a single word. A massive pulse of red light burst from his flower-mark. When he opened his eyes, he stood in a room full of astonished young women.

***

Jorinda finished her song, enriched once more by the glow of love. She turned to Joringel and he held her close.

"What will we do now, my love? Can you forgive my father for what he did?"

For a moment, rage swelled in Joringel's heart at the memory of his beating. Then he saw fear flutter through Jorinda's eyes as she looked at him, and all anger vanished. He smiled. "Haven't I proven that I will do anything for you?"

"Of course you have, dear one."

He put his hands behind his head and breathed deeply for a moment. "We will return to the village. But, now that I have found my Road, I wish to seek instruction in its ways. Will you come with me to the city? As my wife? Even your father cannot object now that I am a true wizard."

She smiled up at him. "Yes, of course I will. And once you have learned the Red Way?"

"Perhaps then we shall return here, and make this castle our home. We can make it a refuge for all those who seek freedom, who follow their hearts first. My heart's love for you revealed my true Road. So it shall be for others." He kissed her forehead. "Will you help me in this, my love?"

"Whatever Road you walk, I will be by your side, Joringel."

He kissed her lips and let himself fall blissfully into the burning river of passion that lay before him, flowing always from the Red Flower within his heart.

Author Bio:

Justin A. Williams drinks a lot of tea and watches a lot of anime. He's been writing strange stories for several years now. Major influences include Tolkien, Ursula K. LeGuin, Lovecraft, Stephen King, Ray Bradbury and Simon Logan. He lives in Northwest Georgia with the menagerie of characters and creatures inside his head and a plush representation of Great Cthulhu. You can read his stories in places like Necrotic Tissue, the "Unspeakable" anthology from Blood Bound Books and Electric Spec Magazine.

CPSIA information can be obtained at www.ICGtesting.com
Printed in the USA
LVOW102103101211

258803LV00002B/79/P